ENEMIES
LIKE
YOU

Joanna Chambers
&
Annika Martin

A note about the spellings:

This story was written in two points of view—Kit's and Will's.

Kit was raised in the United Kingdom; Will was raised in the United States.

We decided to use UK phrases and spellings (recognise, rumour) when we were writing in Kit's point of view, and to use US phrases and spellings (recognize, rumor) when writing Will's point of view.

CHAPTER ONE

WILL
New York

I stand in my hotel room, hair dripping from the shower, blinded by the white of the dress shirt my CIA handlers sent over with the rented tux I'm supposed to wear tonight.

I don't go in for parties. Definitely not fancy ones. And I told them black.

Instead they sent me *this.*

They don't expect me to complain. They don't expect me to live long enough for that.

Their big hope for me is that I'll get lucky enough to slide a knife through Polzin's ribs before I get killed by whoever does his killing. I'm cannon fodder. A stupid tough guy with a grudge.

Yeah, they're right about all that. But I don't wear white—at least not tonight.

You'd think I wouldn't care what I wore to kill Polzin. But the black is a decision I made after I came out of Special Forces, out of respect to my men. I wear black as I avenge their deaths.

I yank one of my regular shirts out of the closet and button it up quick, then I throw on the monkey suit. No holster. No weapons.

There'll be plenty of security on the door of the club where the party is. No sense in bringing a piece just to give it up. I stuff a rolled-up garrote in my right sock, shifting it so that it rests neatly in the arch of my foot like a friendly rattler. There's a slim blade in each shoe. I'll use my bare hands if I have to.

Polzin dies tonight.

The desk calls up to say the limo's here. Limos. Five-star hotels. They *really* don't want me backing out.

The last five men to go after Polzin died, and those men were professionals—hitters going after the bounty they set on his head. The kind of guys the CIA works with when the CIA needs to keep its hands clean.

Five of the world's top killers, killed.

I'm what you'd call Plan B.

The CIA probably has the press release all ready to go for when I die. Maybe two—one for if I fail to kill Polzin and one for if I succeed. Both of them will frame me as an ex-soldier looking to settle old scores. Probably with a quote from a shrink about my mental state. *He was never right after the horrific firebombing of his men in Afghanistan. He blames the Russian for leaking their plans.* They'll deny helping me.

I head out to the elevator.

The agent I'm coordinating with, Agent Taryn Wagner, seemed surprised that I found out about the five guys before me. Even more surprised that I wanted to go forward with the whole thing anyway. She blinked. Said nothing. Like I'm stupid.

I don't mind.

Rain. The doorman holds an umbrella for me, walking me from the hotel canopy to the car. I don't like it, but I don't argue. Everyone's got a job, I guess.

So he guides me to the back of the limo, shielding me from the rain like I'm a fragile flower. Shuts me in. Young guy. Nice hands.

The driver starts talking as we pull out. "Polzin arrived twenty minutes ago with his girlfriend," he says. "No other people of his we recognize." The driver's CIA, of course.

I nod.

He doesn't look at me, not even in the rearview.

No other people we recognize is the important part of what he said there. Polzin's attack dog is in there somewhere, and the CIA has no idea what he looks like.

Meaning they don't know who I need to protect myself from.

I read this article about black holes in outer space once. Scientists can't see them, and there's not even a test for them. But they know the black holes are there because all the shit around them keeps disappearing.

That's Polzin's bodyguard for you. A man you can't see. A man who makes people disappear.

Two of the hitters were trying for Polzin from a distance, as snipers, and even they were taken out. Like a black hole of death, this guy of Polzin's. The CIA thinks it's maybe a team, but my gut says it's one man. One very dangerous fucking operator. That kind of excellence tends to be a solo thing. Well, hell, I'll kill him too if I have to.

We head down Broadway at a snail's crawl. The hotels stretch up into the dark sky, lights flashing and blazing. I look at the men and women hunched under their umbrellas and coats, going about their business.

Agent Wagner waves from under her hotel's canopy. The driver gets out with his umbrella and ushers her over. She's in a green dress with a glittering shawl. Her hair is in some complicated arrangement on the top of her head—all coils and curls.

She gets in beside me. "Evening, Will." She arranges her skirt. As the car pulls away, she looks at me, expressionless. "Ready for this?"

"Been ready for two years, Agent Wagner."

A cool smile. "Tonight it's Ava." Meaning her name.

"Ava," I say.

She looks me right in the eye. I like that she does me the courtesy of not avoiding my eyes. I know she'll do what she can to make sure I don't die, and I'll do the same for her, if it comes to it.

Wagner's an analyst of some sort. She mentioned yesterday that she was rarely in the field. Made me wonder whether they're using her because nobody's ever seen her face, or whether she's a little bit of cannon fodder, too. She seemed surprised when I put the question to her. Just shook her head. No to both.

We keep going, deep into the Upper East Side. Big money.

The limo turns a few times, and then it slows behind a row of other limos, edging up the rain-slicked street. Lights blear in the rain-spattered window as we near a palace of a place on Central Park. The Hayley Street Club.

The place is all gray stone steps and pillars with a red carpet clear out to the sidewalk, even in the rain. They walked me through the inside of it twice this week. Ballroom on the first floor, rooms on the three stories above.

The limo inches up, little by little. "Fancy people taking their fancy fucking time," I say to Wagner.

She smiles tightly.

We finally get up to bat. Our driver pulls out the umbrella and ushers us up the carpeted path. We reach the red canopy. Showtime.

I put out my arms and let the door jockeys do their thing, then I take Wagner's arm and we walk in.

The place is a lot of lights and flash and ceilings up high. People in their best. The thing is billed as a charity ball, ten grand a pop.

Nobody lives in the Hayley Street Club; it's the holding of some international conglomerate with its fingers in logistics and weapons and chemicals. A logo I remember seeing on battlefield gear has been carved into an ice sculpture in the middle of the room.

They've set me up to play the part of a military contractor. They know I can talk that talk. Less room for error.

Wagner says there's other backup around I don't get to know about. They think I'll give them away if they tell me.

I wouldn't, but I don't need to know either way.

I swipe champagne off a tray and grab something triangular off a napkin from another tray. Guy gives me the napkin, too, like I should've known.

Wagner gets sparkling water in a fancy glass. Once we're loaded up, we move around the room, talking about nothing. Easy, relaxed. Won't do to look for Polzin yet. I may not have gone to spycraft school, but I know how to hunt a man.

Polzin's protector is here somewhere, too, a dark presence in a glitter of stars.

Halfway around the room, I stop. It's a pretty good position. Backs to the wall. Good sightlines.

I catch Wagner eyeing my black shirt. I raise a brow at her. "Got something to say?"

She shrugs. "Going your own way, I see."

I return her shrug. I'm not the only one without a white shirt, but close. Makes me more memorable. Too bad.

"Isn't this lovely? And such a good cause." She's in character, partly for the benefit of the people around who might overhear. And partly for my benefit. She talks about the little bites the waiters are bringing around on their trays, telling me which ones she thinks I'll like, then she's on to the champagne—French, she thinks. What she's really up to is giving me a chance to get a better look at the room. I don't have to talk while she's going on. It's helpful.

I sweep my gaze lightly around, taking in all the furs and jewels.

And then I see him.

Polzin's a thick man with jet black hair on top and pure silver sideburns. He stands at one of the bars. Bored-looking blonde on his right arm. Serious-looking conversation with a group of three men to his left.

He looks tired, even from here. More businessman than wanted man. The woman on his arm is long and lean. Very blonde. I heard his taste ran to young, dumb, and stacked, but this one's classy. Beautiful. Model, maybe. Not at all my type.

I love beautiful women, don't get me wrong. But the women I'm attracted to tend to be strong, serious, down-to-earth types. No frills, no fashion plates.

Same with men—if I'm going to fuck a man, give me a fighter who can hold his own, not a clothes horse.

Still, I can appreciate a beautiful face.

Wagner's watching my eyes. I wonder whether she's worried. I glance at the blonde. "What do we know about her?"

She follows the line of my gaze. "Calls herself Kate Nelson. On-off girlfriend. He's got her all set up—nice apartment, nice car. *Very* nice credit card. She likes to shop."

"She doesn't do anything else?"

Wagner shrugs. "Doesn't seem to."

"What's her history?"

Another shrug. "Failed British model. Fitz says she checks out."

Another man walks up. Dark hair, muscular neck—a martial artist. Ice blue eyes, nice lips. I know trouble when I see it. "Is he somebody I should know about?"

"Low-level bodyguard, we think."

We think. So they have no idea.

Suddenly the blonde returns my gaze.

More than returns it—she gives me a look that goes to my gut. Brown eyes, feathered with lush lashes, but this one, there's nothing of the songbird in her. She's pure bird of prey.

"Garrett," Wagner says, voice tight. Garrett's my cover name.

I tear my gaze from the woman and look at Wagner. Her mouth is a little tight, her gaze a little bleak. She thinks I'm staring too long. She doesn't want to fail, doesn't want me to die. And I might, but even if I do, Polzin will be dead at the end of it.

Because when I say I'm going to do something, it gets done.

CHAPTER TWO

Kit

The man in black holds his champagne flute in a lazy, three-fingered way—like a beer bottle. It's raw and thuggish and bloody magnificent.

He doesn't belong in this crowd, but he's no professional. A pro would be able to blend, and that means not coupling a high-street shirt with a Dior tuxedo, for fuck's sake. Maybe he's a bit of rough for the woman beside him—she looks the refined type. Maybe it amused her to bring him along. To see how he'd react to the sheer vulgar spectacle of all this wealth. Whatever he is, he's no hitter.

I force my gaze away and scan the crowd. I need to be on my game tonight. Rumour has it they're sending somebody new this time—Nero, they're calling him. He's unkillable, apparently.

Or so I've heard.

I've heard that before, of course, about others who've tried to take out Polzin. And no one is unkillable. This is a fact I've proved—more than once.

I'm looking for somebody who knows how to blend, though chances are good that I'll feel him before I see him. It'll be somebody with the discreet polish of a diamond over a dark, twisted heart. Somebody at once evil and bland—that's how the real professionals come off. The strongest hitmen are nothing but shells. Often you can't even tell their country of origin.

The man in black, he's so very American it's laughable, just a hulking mass of an American male with the look of a fucking rugby prop forward—or whatever it is they call a chap like that over there. Massive shoulders, strong neck, very short dark hair, sleekly black against his well-shaped head. Brutishly beautiful.

I examine the girl with him again. She looks comfortable. Comes from money, I'm sure—she fits right in here. But I could see her being CIA too. She has that bright, competent look. Watchful. Not the man, though. He's too big, too obvious, too memorable. More than memorable—he has presence. A certain charisma.

And really, a black shirt? With a tux? It's a little Johnny Cash, isn't it? I find myself wondering whether there's the faintest chance he might've shot a man in Reno just to see him die.

Christ. I need to look for Nero, but I can't take my eyes off of this one. The one person who couldn't possibly be Nero.

Which, of course, makes me think—*could this be Nero?* My lips twitch at the audacity of that idea, but my head tells me no, it couldn't be.

Use your head, Kit. Never your gut. Work with the facts.

One of Archie's lessons.

"Who are you looking at, Katerina?" Polzin asks in his thick accent. *Katerina*, that's what he calls me when I'm playing the girlfriend.

I look at him. All this time in his delightful company and I still experience that inward shudder when I meet his gaze. There's something about Sergei Polzin that chills me in a very deep, very primal way, and that's coming from someone who spends ninety percent of their time with psychopaths and murderers.

Polzin has the flat, black gaze of a great white shark and a tenth of the natural charm. He's scanning the room. Does he *truly* not see the most memorable, most riveting man in the room?

"Do you see something?" he presses.

I sniff. "Yes, *bublik*," I say. "A lot of last year's gowns. They're burning my fucking retinas."

Polzin's smile is almost worse than his flat, dead gaze. He loves feeling like he's the most intelligent man in the room, the man with the most secrets.

I'm part of that, of course, but what's a girl to do?

It's a grim mission, protecting Polzin: killer, arms trader, blackmailer extraordinaire. He thinks I'm the best body-guard money can buy. Well, I *am* the best. I'll continue to be the best till I retrieve the Roc file.

Nobody gets to kill Polzin until I have that file in my hands.

On that glorious day, I'll end the slimy bastard myself.

I'm not sure how I'll do it; I go back and forth on it, depending on my mood.

Sometimes I think I'll make it painful and slow. Other times I think it would be best to do it offhandedly, as though he's nothing more than an unpleasant annoyance one needs to dispatch before one gets on with the day. That would be the most insulting. There would be a certain satisfaction in that.

Then there's choking him to death. A nice, visceral kill, as he stares into the eyes of his most trusted guard and pretend girlfriend. That would be fitting, I think.

His secret weapon, he likes to call me. He loves to have me on his arm. Loves to imagine his real girlfriends are jealous. That he's fooling the world. He smiles, chatting away with one of his henchmen in Russian, a language he thinks I only passably understand.

Never before have I actually looked forward to a kill. No good operative enjoys that part of the game—not even an irredeemable one like me. But Polzin is different. He's beyond the sort of evil I've come across before.

Most people do bad things because they hunger for something.

With Polzin, there is no *something*. He enjoys his vicious work for its own sake.

I'm not surprised by how many of the world's top hitters have tried for the bounty the CIA put on Polzin—it's good money.

The CIA won't send its own agents to kill Polzin because of the international stir it would cause—what with him being a high-profile Russian national. But at this point, the CIA probably wouldn't send its own even if it could be certain nobody would know. Because if the top freelance hitters are going down, the CIA payroll hitters wouldn't stand a chance. The top killers always go freelance.

A prickle runs up the back of my neck, and when I glance around, I catch the man in black just looking away. He was watching me. Or maybe he was watching Polzin.

Again the question pops into my head—*could he be Nero?*—and again I decide no. He's no hitter, no way. Not even a baby hitter. There would be no black shirt for a man with Nero's reputation.

Well, if Nero's out there, I'll handle him.

It should be a depressing thought—knowing that tonight I may have to kill again, but the truth is, it's become a humdrum task over these past two years, and it's increasingly difficult to summon up the energy to care. That, more than anything, tells me how profoundly changed I am.

I turn to bat my eyelashes at Polzin, telling him I'm going to powder my nose. He nods. He knows that means I'm going to walk the route, check that it's clear, while he stays with his other guards. I head toward the ladies', then slip off through a service door, taking the stairs to the third floor.

Once there, I make my way down the ornate hallway with its lush Axminster carpeting, senses on high alert.

It's quiet and still. No one around. I pause outside the room where the meet is to happen, listening, then go inside and do a quick sweep.

This is the staging area for an unimportant but nasty scam, one of the hundreds Polzin runs. He always starts them off personally.

I wonder whether there's any chance the CIA could have caught wind of this meet. My head tells me everything's clear—we've checked and triple-checked—but there's still a niggle in my gut. I examine the sightlines again, the terrain outside.

Dima, one of the other bodyguards, arrives. I ask him what he thought about the man in black.

He turns his ice blue gaze to me. "Man in black?" As though he didn't even notice him.

"We will still do? Yes?" asks Mikhail, another guard. He's heard the Nero rumours, too.

"Yes," I say. "We will still do. We will be ready."

Dima waves his hand at one corner of the room, then another, and then he pulls out his phone and looks to ensure the motion was captured. There's recording equipment in the flowers. This meet doesn't need to be documented, but that's irrelevant. Polzin gets clips of everything. There's always a chance he'll trap a man doing something he shouldn't.

I don't pay much attention to Polzin's minor operations. They're not important. Nothing is important except the Roc file, then killing Polzin—in that order. This is how I've stayed in the game unscathed—by staying faithful to the mission at all times. When you go deep undercover like this, there are a thousand ways to get distracted. Especially with Polzin.

You stick to the mission. That's how you survive.

There's a balcony off the room overlooking the street below. The balcony is mainly decorative, a place to wave from but not to sit on. The two stories below are sheer stone face—very difficult to scale. And I can't imagine anybody getting through our gauntlet of security.

I make sure the concealed rope ladder isn't tangled and then coil it back up. It's one of two emergency escape routes.

I go back inside and open the side door that leads into the adjoining room. It only opens from our side. That's the other escape, and besides that, everything's wired. Alarms will sound if anyone opens a door they shouldn't.

All in all, this would be a terrible place to try to make a hit. A death trap. If I were the hitter, I'd turn around, wait for a better chance.

Even so, I make myself consider what other options there are. I think of the man in black again, and my pulse races. Am I the one being played now?

Use your head, Kit. Never your gut.

My gut's uneasy, but my head's telling me he's not a hitter. I'm so certain of that, I'd stake my life on it.

"Maybe we call off?" Dima's watching my face.

"No," I say. "We draw this Nero out now. Let's see what he has for us."

Dima doesn't like it, but you can't defend against a danger you don't see.

"I'll handle it," I say. "If anyone gets in who isn't supposed to be in this room—" Here I switch to Russian. "—I will handle them." I use the Russian word for *handle* that we sometimes use to mean *kill*.

Dima nods and leaves, to speak to his opposite number. In ten, maybe fifteen minutes, the principals will get here, and the business will be transacted.

And we'll see whether Nero turns up.

CHAPTER THREE

Will

Polzin's girlfriend stalks out of the room like a tigress. The man gets antsy when she's out of his sight. He looks at the doors a whole lot, dark eyes flitting. Is it her that's got him all bothered? Doesn't he like her off on her own? Or is it the upcoming meeting?

Now that we've got a bead on Polzin, we make the rounds. Agent Wagner introduces me to some of the movers and shakers in logistics. This contracting is a cover she's used before. Maybe the agency will even arrange to slide some business to these guys we're talking to.

I feel the moment Polzin's blonde gets back. I feel her on my skin. I feel her in the air, in the crackle of it. The light feels brighter.

I feel her move behind me, moving gracefully across the room. I know when she's back on Polzin's arm, and the need to turn and see is something powerful.

I'm not one for games. If I want to look at a person, I look at a person. But I have a mission.

"She's somebody," I mutter to Wagner as we leave the group of guys behind us.

She draws her dark brows together. "Who?"

"Polzin's woman. Gotta be somebody. I'm telling you."

"The model?" Her gaze moves over my shoulder. "What are you thinking?"

"I have a gut feeling."

"A gut feeling." She doesn't exactly roll her eyes, but I hear the skepticism. After a pause, she gives a one-shouldered shrug and offers a compromise. "She's a gold digger. Could be a few layers there that Fitz didn't get." She might not be convinced, but she doesn't seem to think it's important.

"No," I say. I'm a dog with a bone when I get a gut feeling. "There's something more."

"We'd know if she was somebody," Wagner insists.

I shake my head. "Something there."

This time Wagner does roll her eyes. "Right. What is she, the *muscle*? Does she sic a little handbag-rat-dog on unsuspecting agents?" She laughs, making little claws with her hands. "Rarrarrrarr."

I grin, surprised. Wagner usually doesn't make jokes. "No, not that."

If she isn't muscle, she might be brains. To be honest, her looks are so distracting it's difficult to imagine what she might be. White blonde hair, white gown. Fierce beautiful features. I picture the sharp swoop of her cheek up to her cheekbone. Secrets in her eyes. Lashes like brown wings.

Kate.

There's that grace to her. It's no regular kind of grace, though; it's a predator's grace. I think about the raven tattoo that a Native American Army buddy of mine had. Fierce, swooping grace. The kind of grace that's got teeth and talons.

"We'd know if she was someone." The edge of impatience in Wagner's tone gets my back up a little. Mostly Wagner's okay with me, a little stiff, sure, but okay. But right about now, she's resenting getting stuck with me. Maybe she feels sidelined. Hell, maybe she is.

"I'm telling you," I say.

Wagner shrugs coolly. "Well, I hear she may be available after tonight. Her current meal ticket's on the way out."

We join another group, talk for a while, move on.

I make a point of not looking at Kate Nelson for a good long time after that. The blue-eyed bodyguard comes back around. He doesn't add up, either. Nobody here adds up.

Ten after ten is go time.

I head to the bathroom, leaving Wagner in the main room. I shove in my earpiece and climb out the high window of the bathroom and into the night.

The plan is simple. When I told it to Fitz and the other handlers, sitting all around their table in their swanky Washington DC office, well, you could tell *simple* wasn't the word that came to their minds. One of the top brass frowned so hard his eyebrows were like two worms frenching. "Your plan is basically one step up from hiding in a closet and jumping out when the time comes," he'd said.

"Take it or leave it," I told him.

One of the younger ones pointed out that my plan had no "exit strategy."

"I got an exit strategy." I pointed to my feet. "Two exit strategies right here."

I think they wrote me off as dead meat right about then. Suicide mission.

If there's one thing I learned in the war, though, it's that plans fall apart. Whatever can go wrong, will go wrong. Instincts are everything.

Being able to make the right call in a split second, that's what keeps you and your men alive.

So, my fucking simple idea is that I scale up to the balcony, then wait in the side room. Wagner's in communication with a few other agents in the back halls. They'll spook Polzin's guard, creating a threat in the hallway outside the door. That'll get Polzin's people to bundle him through the door, away from the threat.

And right to me, waiting in the side room.

And I kill him.

Anybody else gives me trouble, I take them, too.

"They're on the move," Wagner's voice tells me.

I sneak up on the guard standing at the service door on the ground floor and take his weapon before he can say *boo*. I knock him out, tie him up, and gag him.

Another guy is standing at the next door. He's not so easy to deal with. I take a hit to the side of my face before I can knock him out.

I start climbing, scaling up three stories without breaking a sweat. I've never been a rock climber, but after enough tours in mountainous areas, you learn to get by. I'm not even breathing hard when I finally slide open the door to the side room.

Silence.

The agency tech guys frayed out the alarms. Good. I pull my garrote from my shoe and wait in the dark. I have the gun I took off the first guy, but I prefer something up close and personal.

The minutes tick by.

Wagner narrates from below. "Small army followed him up," she says. "Fuck. You good?"

"Yup," I whisper.

The men in the hall are getting antsy—I can hear it. Locks click. Doors open.

"They're here," I whisper.

CHAPTER FOUR

Kit

The man Polzin's meeting with, Müller, said no muscle, but arm candy doesn't count with guys like this, so I'm there, standing around and acting bored. There are four of us—me and Polzin, Müller and Müller's girlfriend.

Polzin's just beginning to warm up when my wandering gaze snags on an ultraslim wire leading from the signal node to the balcony door. The wire is crooked. Just by a hair, but it's enough to set my heart pounding.

Polzin's tech guy, Vlastov, is too OCD ever to let a wire not run perfectly along the line of the skirting board. We've had to drag him out of places to stop his perfectionistic fussing.

This is not his work.

I should've noticed it earlier, when I did the final sweep—before Polzin was allowed to enter the room. I'm not on my game—too much obsessing over Nero. Fuck.

If the wire's been tampered with, they probably cut the alarm.

As soon as I have that thought, the whole plan comes together in my mind, and it's shocking in its simplicity. Nero is in that next room. Waiting. He'll hit Polzin, and then what? Wade out through gunfire?

That wouldn't be a normal hit, but I can't see how else he could do it. And whatever it lacks in cleverness, it makes up for in chutzpah, that's for sure.

Because it's fucking suicide.

Why? Why would a man do this? What's in it for him?

My senses tingle.

I haven't felt this...hell, I don't know—exhilarated? petrified?—in ages. I tell myself it's just the excitement of a new play in an old game, but I'm lying to myself. When I think about that door opening, it's the man in black I envision.

And Christ, but there's no way this is not suicide.

"Get them out of here," I demand, gesturing at Müller, my cut-glass voice sharp over Polzin's low, rumbling one. The German's eyes widen. I snatch his phone out of his hand. It's time to take charge. I do my best work when I'm in charge.

"I don't like the way you're looking at me." I throw the phone into the corner with enough force to smash it into several pieces.

The guards pile in. They begin to drag Müller out. The woman—who's screaming now—too.

Polzin frowns, but he doesn't argue with me. I nod my head at Dima, and he moves forward, smooth and strong, whisking an unresisting Polzin away.

I wrench out my Luger, which is strapped to my thigh. Sure enough, there's a loud thump on the door of the next room, and an instant later, the man in black bursts in, shoulder first, blade in hand.

Nero.

My advantage is fleeting. I see it in the widening of his eyes, in the telltale check of a powerful arm arcing towards me. He's too much of a gentleman to disarm a woman—even one who's pointing a gun at him.

I take full advantage of his hesitation. I get his arm in a lock, push his face to the wall, and shove the cold, hard barrel of the Luger up behind his ear. That's when I see the earpiece. I pull it out and crush it under my Jimmy Choo's.

"Drop the knife, darling," I murmur.

The blade clatters to the floor.

Adrenaline pumps through me. When he burst out of that door—bloody hell, I've never seen anyone that quick or that committed. He was about to take out my gun arm. He would have done it too.

Except...he didn't.

I'm honestly baffled. I know every kind of player in this sordid game, so many men and women with so many angles and facades and agendas, but this guy? He doesn't make sense.

I don't know what he *is*.

"Looking for somebody?" I ask, heart pounding, knowing that his hesitation is the only thing that saved me. Does he realise that?

Three other weapons join mine, all pointed at the man's head.

Dima spits on the carpet. He's such a pig.

"CIA imbeciles," Dima says. *Imbeciles.* He says that word in English a lot. He loves that word.

But this man's not an imbecile. He's...I breathe him in.

Good god, what am I *doing*?

I push up against Nero, pressing the weapon into his neck, my body against his hard bulk.

I can't stand it. I can't stand the thought of ending him. Or, worse, of these fuckwit psychos doing it. And in that instant, I do something very, very stupid.

"He's not CIA," I scoff in Russian. "He's my ex. This motherfucker's been stalking me."

The three guards, Dima especially, look suspicious. But I brazen the moment out. Because I just don't want this man's brains splattered all over the carpet. I can't allow it.

I try to prevent deaths when I can—I really do. But I've never risked my cover like this.

"He's a jealous asshole," I say in Russian, using the word *mudak*, which is tame as insults go, hoping Nero understands my play, but I quickly see that he doesn't understand Russian. Bloody hell, he doesn't even understand the language of his target! I move even closer to him, crooning in his ear in English, loud enough that they can all still hear, "I'm telling them about my jealous American ex. When are you going to stop this ridiculous behaviour, Cody?"

Cody, that sounds American. Too American?

The man stiffens. He keeps his hands on the wall above his head, twisting around just enough to glare at me. Soulful black-coffee eyes burn into mine, and his heat warms my skin. He smells of man—no perfumed products, no gels or lotions, just pure salty, sweaty man.

He says nothing, though. He's not stupid, thankfully.

I smile, feigning amusement, but I'm very fucking far from amused. Distantly I'm horrified at the risk I'm taking. And it's not just horror I'm feeling—I'm awash in emotions I can't name. The kind of emotions I should've left in a sealed box tucked safely away in a distant studio.

Suspicious or not, the guards don't question my story—they're used to obeying me. They glance at each other and laugh uneasily. They've always been uncomfortable with me, but they fear me too much to show it. They fear my influence over their boss, too.

A sheen of sweat covers my palms, greasing my Luger grip. *Fuck.*

"You want us to kill him?" one asks me in the simple Russian they use around me.

I shake my head dismissively. "I will deal with him," I reply in my own broken Russian, tone unconcerned. "Take the boss home. Dima goes ahead, two with Polzin. No mistakes, understand? Check every room."

We're talking about Polzin's West Side condo. It's relatively secure. This was too close.

They nod and stand down, holstering their guns and moving away. I feel the awareness of this in the body of the man I'm holding against the wall. The next part's going to be tricky. I hope my hostage is clever enough to realise that this would be the worst possible moment for an attack.

"Okay, Cody," I say. "You want to talk? Fine. I'll give you five minutes to convince me I was wrong about you being a cheating bastard."

Nero keeps his hands raised as he slowly turns. He eyes the goons for a long moment before he turns his gaze back to me. He looks almost tender.

Dima makes for the door. The others follow in his wake, like the butchest bridesmaids in history.

Softly, Nero says, "I wouldn't never cheat on you, baby."

Christ, his voice. It's deep and rumbly and warm. A shiver runs through me.

I smile affably to cover up my unaccountable reaction to him. "You do realise that if you fail to convince me I was wrong, I'm liable to shoot your fucking kneecaps off?

Dima and his goons are sniggering as they close the door behind them.

Cody—Nero?—returns my smile. He has a faint, almost imperceptible scar that bisects his upper lip. It's an inch long, just to the left of his deep, sexy philtrum. "What do I need to say to convince you, baby?"

We're alone now.

I look him directly in the eye, then shift my gaze very deliberately to one corner of the room, then the other, showing him where the cameras and microphones are. "I don't like airing my dirty laundry in public," I say.

Understanding flickers in his dark gaze. He's smarter than he looks. Which makes him dangerous.

Polzin's going to need to see something to convince him, though. I can't just let this guy walk out of here, scot free.

Plus I need to alert Nero to the thing he probably hasn't yet worked out before he says something that will make it patently obvious we've never met before.

I send him a nasty look—a Polzin look—and, heart pounding, lower my voice to its natural, deeper register. "Let's save the excuses for later. Why don't you *convince* me you're sorry by getting down on your knees and sucking my cock."

CHAPTER FIVE

Will

I stare at her for what feels like forever, but is probably only a second or two.

"What?" I say stupidly.

She—*he*—looks at me with those bird-of-prey eyes—so fucking fierce—and yanks up the fancy white dress.

Underneath, he's wearing white, silky panties with lacy bits, but they're covering a very male bulge.

And I can't breathe.

Oh, Christ.

I stare at that bulge. My mouth goes dry. My heart hammers. My cock is an iron bar in my pants. My head actually swims.

"You're going to have to be *very* convincing, Cody," he says, making my gaze snap back up to that beautiful face. He's smiling, lazily, holding his dress up, Luger still in his hand. He sounds like some kinda duke with his fancy English accent.

There's a grim warning in his eyes, and I get it. We're being recorded. I need to be playing this part if I want to get out of here alive.

I need to make this good.

Big fucking sacrifice, right? My mouth's already watering at the thought of what's hiding behind those scraps of silk and lace.

For some reason, this guy—Kate Nelson, gold digger, a.k.a. who the fuck knows—has decided to help me. It's a mad risk. I have no fucking clue why, but I'm taking the lifeline being offered me, because if there's one thing I'm sure of right now, it's that this is my only chance to survive tonight's spectacular clusterfuck. Me hesitating when I should've been full steam ahead.

I drop to my knees.

"Hands behind your head, my lovely," he says pleasantly. "And make sure you keep them there, won't you?"

It sounds like the politest of requests, but we both know it's a command, one I obey as I start moving toward him on my knees.

My savior watches me with an intent gaze.

I watch him right back, pulse racing. His butter-smooth legs go on for-fucking-ever. He's long and lean and sexy as all get out, and strong as fuck, too—I experienced that muscular, tensile strength firsthand while I was pressed up against the wall.

His white dress is high-necked and cleverly draped to disguise his flat chest and male package, but now, yanked up past his hips, it's not disguising anything.

When I reach him, I tip my head back to look up at him. Astonishingly, his expression gentles.

"Make it convincing," he whispers. "And then...we can go home and make up properly."

I realize that he thinks I'm straight, that this is going to be an ordeal for me. I almost laugh out loud. Then again, I have no idea what he is, what he prefers. Just because he makes a convincing woman, that doesn't mean shit.

For some reason, that thought makes me feel even more determined to make this BJ the best he's ever had.

Hey, there's nothing like a challenge, right?

I push my face right into his crotch and start rubbing my cheeks all over those silky panties. He makes a soft *ooof!* of surprise, squirming, but a moment later, he's steadied himself. He rests one hand gently on my head. The other, I know, still holds the Luger.

His scent is intoxicating. There's a clean-laundry smell coming off the underwear; behind that, a fainter, earthier smell. Unmistakably male. I groan and take an edge of the panties between my teeth, dragging downward.

He lets me struggle with that for half a minute before he finally helps me ease the fabric over his hips. A moment later, he's kicking the panties off and standing in front of me naked from the waist down, except for the fuck-me heels.

Christ almighty, he *pinned me* in those things?

My dick throbs. I swallow hard. I shouldn't be turned on by this—no way, no how. I like my men to be men. Macho with a side of testosterone and grit. I'm usually not the one kneeling, either.

I'm not the kind to take orders. I'm *definitely* not the kind to like it.

Except I'm liking it now.

But he's so gorgeous. His cock is lean and long, protruding from a scrupulously maintained nest of blond curls, darker than what's on his head. The rest of him is hairless and anatomically ideal, like one of those Greek statues, every muscle group perfect.

I stare at him for a long beat, dry-mouthed with admiration. My fingers are laced so tight behind my head, I'll probably have bruises tomorrow.

Then I lean forward again, driving my mouth down over his shaft, taking him in as deep as I can, relishing the brutality of that first thrust.

He grunts, surprised, and I grunt too, my voice muffled.

I use my tongue then, spiraling my way upwards, suckling and caressing, only to drive down again, as far as I can, until his blunt head is nudging the back of my throat. I do it over and over, suckling and licking, and there's no elegance to it. I drool, splutter even, once or twice. It's a fucking act of worship—the slurping sounds I make are testament to that.

Jesus, this isn't me.

Then his fingers tighten in my hair, forcing me into the rhythm he wants, and all I can think is that he's the hottest thing I've ever fucking seen.

Ever.

I remind myself that he's on Polzin's payroll, which means he's the worst of the worst. This should be strictly business. I shouldn't be getting any enjoyment out of sucking the cock of a stone-cold killer.

More, I think.

I'm loving his certainty, his hand directing my head, the sheer lethal beauty of him.

I stretch my mouth and do everything I can to spare him my teeth. He's moaning now, hand tightening, nearly ripping off a piece of my scalp, mercilessly fucking my mouth, battering into my throat. Using me.

I wish I could drop my hands, stuff one into my pants, and take hold of my steel-hard erection, but I've gotta keep 'em where they are.

I don't know this guy. I don't know what he does when you break his rules. I do know that he's got the gun. I know he's got muscle out in the hall. Part of staying alive is knowing what you can and can't get out of.

Not that I want to get out of this. Sherman tanks couldn't drag me away.

I let him feel my tongue, a hard, thick slide along the bottom of his magnificent shaft. I can't even breathe. Not that I give a fuck.

I take him even deeper, opening my throat right up to him, groaning long and loud enough for him to feel it, giving him everything. I tell myself the crazy feelings inside me are gratitude and relief. The man saved my skin.

I feel his dick swell a little bit more. I don't need him to tell me he's coming, but he does, in urgent whispers.

"Bloody hell," he whispers hoarsely, an instant before he shoots the warm pulses into my mouth.

He says *bloody hell* when he comes. *Bloody hell*, of all things. Even that's hot.

His fist still rests against my scalp; he's not yanking and pulling my hair anymore, just gripping. I feel the emotion through his fist. Hear him panting. His dick begins to soften, but I don't pull away.

I'm a dog at his feet, heart hammering, needing this to have been good. I shouldn't care, considering what kind of guy he probably is, but I do.

Sweat cools on my brow while he stands there, dick in my mouth. My own cock is hard and desperate, trapped behind layers of cotton and wool.

"Bloody hell," he says again, and his fist clasps and unclasps. His cock pulses weakly, and I know he'll be sensitive. I should let him go. It's over.

I begin to pull back.

"Wait!" he hisses, his grip tightening. Then, more softly, "Wait."

I wait. He gazes down at me, hand settled at the back of my head, watching me with those golden eyes that look a little sad now.

Is he as baffled as I am by what just happened?

Keeping the connection of his gaze, I remove my hands from behind my neck, the one thing he didn't want me to do. Yeah, I'm doing it now—I just am, and he doesn't stop me.

I watch him as I take hold of his hips with one hand, supporting his cock with the other as I pull off his shaft, gently as I can.

He sucks in a breath at the sensation, or maybe the separation.

I can't resist sliding my hands down, then, over his hips, over his ivory-smooth thighs. I tell myself I'm still just playing the part. The spurned lover who couldn't forget. Who couldn't let go.

His grip on my hair loosens. He strokes me with his open hand—gently, sweetly. Maybe he's telling himself the same thing, that he's playing a part. Part of me wants to kneel there forever, panting at his feet, ready to give him everything.

What the fuck?

I break his gaze to dip my head and wipe my mouth on the sleeve of my jacket. When I look back up, he's smiling in that amused way of his.

"That's an extremely expensive Dior jacket, you know," he says.

"Never gone in much for labels, sweetheart." I feel exhilarated. Half-crazy. "You know me."

Something flickers in his eyes at that, and wildly, I think, *He does know me*. Not on the outside, but on the inside, where it counts.

Afterglow, I tell myself grimly. Because—no way. I'm a loner. Always have been, always will be. I like my sex like I like my grenades: simple, fast, and furious. One-time use.

And with that thought, the game comes crashing back to me. Polzin's long gone. I tried to kill him, and I failed. Pathetically. Miserably.

There have been guards outside the door, listening—probably watching—while I'm blowing a guy who is, quite likely, the reason one of the world's vilest scumbags has never been brought to justice.

On my fucking knees for this guy.

Aside from missing the chance to get justice for my men, this *on my knees* bit is somehow the worst part.

Like a beggar on his fucking knees, waiting for this guy's next command. Hell, *lusting* for his next command, or just for him to say *bloody hell* again, dick hard in my pants.

Fuck that.

I get to my feet. I feel more like myself once I'm standing in front of him. I'm a little taller than he is and a lot broader. He might have the gun and the backup and the advantage, but he's got to raise his chin to look me in the eye, and that changes the dynamic between us in a small but important way, even if it's just in my head.

This is over—it has to be. This is not what I like. Not who I am.

I take a step toward him. "You think I came looking for you 'cause I'm jealous?" I slide a hand around the back of his neck. "That's what you think?"

"Of course," he says, arching one perfect, blond eyebrow. "Do you deny it?"

I open my mouth to do just that, but I can't make the words come out.

I just stare down at his maddeningly perfect face.

For a moment, it's as if I really am this Cody, the imaginary ex-boyfriend of the guy I've just blown. I've never been a jealous man, but right now, I can actually imagine how Cody would feel at the thought of this strange and beautiful man putting his hands on anyone else.

So I do what I figure Cody would do. I tug him toward me, ignoring the Luger he's holding between us, and crush my mouth over his, taking his lips in a bruising kiss.

CHAPTER SIX

Kit

My gun is pressed between us as Nero takes my mouth, invading me, exploring me, all heat and whiskers. He doesn't care about the Luger shoved up against his pec, my finger still poised on the trigger. It's like he's daring me to pull it—or maybe showing me he knows I won't.

Or maybe he really can survive hails of bullets. Maybe even one to the heart.

His tongue presses into my mouth, and I taste my spunk on him alongside hints of scotch. He has a salty, musky scent that's purely him. A scent that's new to me, one I'm sure I'll never forget.

He brings his strong hands up to my cheeks and forces my head to the side as if he needs me at a very specific angle for maximum devouring. I let him do it, even

41

though allowing someone else to take control really isn't my thing. I let him because somehow I know this is different. This is important to him. He's trying to regain something after what just happened. He's going to have to face the guards outside in a minute, after all.

So I let him devour my mouth with all that hungry desperation of his, and it's so good I start kissing him back just as desperately. His tongue probes and thrusts; it's as if he can't get inside me deep enough, hard enough. It's obscene. It's invasive.

It's fucking amazing. I feel like I could come again, just from this.

He pulls back for a second, and I assume he's done, but no, he tilts my head again and kisses me with fresh ardour, mauling my lips until he finally takes my upper lip between his teeth. I can feel his hot breath on my lip, in and out. In and out. I open my eyes to find his closed. Not just closed but shut tight with emotion, as if he can't quite bear it all.

And then he lets go of my lip and pushes me away. My hand, still holding the Luger, falls to my side.

"I'm not jealous," Nero scoffs. "You go right ahead. You enjoy your Russian sugar daddy."

He doesn't add *while you can*, but it's there, hanging between us, a threat. *I'm going to kill Polzin.* That's his message.

I give him a tight little smile. "I plan to." My cruel, clipped tone is a warning. I need him to hear my resolve, to understand that I won't be so kind again.

"You'll never do better than me, baby," he growls, playing his part.

I smile, playing mine. "Best you don't show your face near me again, Cody. As nice as that blow job was, I'm not up for a repeat performance."

His jaw tightens. "You think I take orders from you?"

I cant my head to the side, bat my lashes at him. "Yeah. I think sometimes you do."

And he goes red—actually blushes. And oh, yes, I *do* want a repeat performance, I *do*. I want him under me, I want him at my feet, under my spiked, five-inch heel. I want him every way I can get him. I don't want to have to kill him.

Somehow I just know this man's going to force me to kill him.

I sigh.

"I won't be so nice next time," I warn him.

In the silence that follows, images of *not being nice* to him come to my mind unbidden. None of them are about killing him, though. I recover my clutch from the floor, where I tossed it earlier, and tuck the Luger inside, then I wind my arm through his and draw him from the room.

A driver and two of the guards still linger out in the hall. Polzin left them behind for me—in the eyes of the world, I'm still the trophy girlfriend who needs his protection instead of the other way around. Appearances are so important to Polzin.

The guards watch, feigning boredom as I pull Nero to the lift at the end of the hall.

We stop at the sealed doors, and I press the call button. "It's over," I say, hoping he'll accept this. Deep down, I know he won't. Some men don't stop until they're dead. I'd expect nothing less of Nero.

He gives me that black gaze—really, it's a very dark brown; burnt umber mixed with a little lamp black—and his lip quirks. "You're breakin' my heart, baby."

"Don't push me," I say as the doors swish open. "I mean it."

He calmly backs into the lift, never tearing his eyes from mine. Without even looking, he pushes a button.

I force myself to turn away before the doors slide shut, switching my attention to my comrades.

They tell me Polzin's still downstairs. *Shit.* Of course, he would've refused to go back to the condo, when the guards informed him the interloper was known to me. I need to get him out.

I tell Vlastov to stay and start dismantling the equipment. Polzin will go through the recordings later—tonight probably. Sometimes he has somebody else do it, but something like this, he'll view personally.

Vlastov nods once, curtly. He doesn't like it, what I am. None of them do. They don't like that I'm twice the man they'll ever be and prettier than any woman they could ever get.

What can I say? I've always been an overachiever.

I glance at Dima and Dmitri. "Come on. Let's get the boss out."

We take the lift down, then they go off to collect the car while I look for Polzin.

He's at the bar. When he sees me approaching, he smiles widely, holding out his arm. "*Pchelka*," he says. He wants to introduce his girlfriend to more people.

Pchelka means "little bee," a Russian endearment related to honey. No doubt Polzin's thinking about the stinger, too. He does love his little secrets. Though he'd die to learn that the bodyguard he has posing as his girlfriend is a British government agent. That's not the type of little secret he would enjoy.

I slide in beside him and greet his new friends coolly, acting bored. They weary of my rudeness and make an excuse to leave. As soon as they toddle off, I put my arm through Polzin's and start moving him towards the door. "I'm tiring of New York," I say. "We need to leave."

He furrows his meaty brow and touches my chin. "Why, *pchelka*?"

"It's a bit of a bore."

He smiles widely. "I heard about your friend. Your lovers' quarrel." He clucks his tongue, as if I've been a naughty child.

I smile coolly, imagining how easily a blade would slide into his jugular. "It's not about that." I lower my voice. "You had too many enemies at this party tonight. Far too many. We need to get you out of here."

"We're leaving Wednesday, *pchelka*."

I scan the room. "We need to start packing up now. We go tonight. You're in danger here."

"And that's why I have you. You protect me." He pauses. Shrugs. "Nowhere is completely safe."

"Yes, but part of my skill is removing you from danger before it happens, isn't it? Knowing when to leave." I settle my hand onto his chest. "My *bublik* enjoys breathing, does he not?" I smile. *Bublik* means "bagel-type pastry", a Russian pet name that I rather delight in calling him.

"You distress me," he pouts. Pouting Polzin. Not an attractive sight.

"Do you want me to do my job? If you do, here's what I suggest—go back to your penthouse with Dima and pack up. We could be in the air before dawn."

He frowns. "I have...an assignation."

"Not any longer. You can sleep on the plane."

He laughs. "So bossy," he says. "My Katerina enjoys telling people what to do, I think."

"Your Katerina enjoys keeping you alive."

For now.

He sniffs, but he'll obey. Like anyone else, my *bublik* enjoys breathing.

"I'm going to head back up to check on Vlastov. You go now with Dima and Dmitri."

He grumbles his assent and I slip away, sending a signal Dima's way when I pass him to get Polzin into the limo.

Instead of heading upstairs, though, I go to the ladies' room. Once inside, I pull my second phone from the lining of my clutch and call Archie. Archie has connections to the CIA. He typically doesn't like using them, but this isn't the typical threat.

Archie answers straightaway.

"It's your loving niece," I say drily.

"Kitty, darling."

He says it like a greeting, but I can hear the faint question in his voice. It's nearly three in the morning in London. Is he drinking Glenlivet and playing Patience in the library? He has trouble sleeping sometimes.

Archie took me under his wing after the explosion in Sudan that killed my parents. It became a ritual, me doing my schoolwork at the big mahogany desk while Archie dealt and flipped, dealt and flipped. All night sometimes, and into the early hours. We never talked much. Archie is a man of few words. The ones he uses tend to stick.

It's an unspoken rule between us that, scheduled reports aside, I only call him *in extremis*.

"Quick question," I say briskly. "Have you heard of a chap called Nero?"

There's a pause.

"You *have*," I conclude.

"Ludlow's been saying he's actually three chaps," Archie says at last. "Typical CIA hyperbole. The Americans do so love their superhero nonsense."

"Well, I think he might be one chap. He showed up tonight. On the job."

"Tonight?"

"Tonight."

"On the job, you say." Archie sounds thoughtful.

"Yes, and he's good. He almost got at Polzin. He's not a pro, Archie. I don't know what he is, but I don't think he was working alone tonight. He was with a woman. I think she was agency. I think this is a change of tack. The agency putting someone unpredictable in. A wild card."

"Hmm." Silence. Then, "What do you think we should do?"

So typical. Archie's the kind of man who answers every question with another question.

"Can you find out where the agency is putting people up just now? Use your IT back door? It should be there," I say, meaning the credit card trail. Archie gets a great deal of intelligence from the credit and accounting arms of various multinationals and governmental organisations—including Interpol and the CIA. Amazing what a few compromised people in major financial networks will do.

Archie doesn't respond immediately. After a few long moments, he asks, "What are you going to do, if you find him?"

What indeed?

I clear my throat. "Warn him off."

There's a silence on the line. Then, "You say he's not predictable."

I know what Archie's thinking—if he's not predictable, then he's dangerous, so why not simply kill him? It's a good question.

"I don't know what he is," I say. "That's what I want to find out."

Knowledge is everything to Archie, and I'm offering it up as a bribe. A reason not to kill the American.

Why am I bargaining for his life?

"It's risky, Kit," Archie says. "Every second you spend engaging with a target increases his chances of survival and diminishes yours."

"On the other hand, there's no sense in leaving a trail of bodies where a warning would do. We don't want the CIA looking at this entire mess any harder than they already are."

"Yes, but if they sent somebody like this, I'd say they're looking rather hard now," Archie notes flatly. There's a silence, then he adds, "Nobody's better than you, Kit. No one's faster or cleaner." He pauses, then adds, "I'm surprised we're having this conversation, actually. It's not like you to leave a loose end trailing."

He doesn't understand why I didn't kill Nero earlier. Nero's just another hired gun, after all. I've taken care of more than one of those.

"It was the right call," I insist.

In truth, I know it wasn't. Or at least, it wasn't the right call for the mission.

"Kit—"

"Look, I'm on the ground—I know what's best. I'll keep the situation under control. If I have to take Nero out, then I'll take him out. You know that."

"If you *have* to?" Archie sighs. "Kit, you know as well as I do that if you let this man go, he will quite certainly return to finish the job. You're the best, but you're not bloody Zeus, casting lightning bolts down from the heavens."

"I take the utmost exception to that statement, darling."

"Kit." He sighs, impatient. "Your talent for all of this is your strength, but it's also your weakness—you need to stay cognisant of that, or it'll bring you down. You're far too used to things going your way, which means you don't see the possibility of failure. It's your blind spot."

"I see perfectly well. You need to trust—"

"I *need* to be sure," Archie says. "This situation is far too dangerous for us to be anything but sure. You understand? Find out what he knows, then *handle him.* I'll get you the address." He pauses. "Too much is at stake. You know this. I know that you do."

For several long moments, neither of us speak.

"The address will show up," Archie says. "Give me an hour."

It'll be an ad at the top corner of a website I sometimes visit. *News and views on designer shoes.* The name of the hotel will be there. It's a way we sometimes communicate.

"Call me after," Archie says. "So I know—everything's all right."

"I will," I promise. Then I hang up, reapply my lipstick, and head back upstairs.

CHAPTER SEVEN

Will

The first thing I do when I get back at the hotel is strip off the monkey suit, right down to my boxers. Second, I call in a report.

"Nero!" Fitz exclaims. "Shit, I didn't expect to hear from you!"

Nice to have your confidence, I think. But I don't need their confidence. What I need is justice for my men. So they can rest in peace.

What I need is Polzin dead.

"Wagner said the mission went south—that you were taken," he adds.

"That's a matter of opinion," I say. "I'd call it more...an interaction."

"How the hell'd you get out?"

I'd thought about how to deal with this question on my way back to the hotel, and I'd already decided to tell Fitz everything. What do I care? I'd let him know about Pol-

51

zin's bodyguard—the man who saved my life—and let Fitz decide what to do about him. Not my call. Above my pay grade. I'm here to ice Polzin. End of story.

When it comes to it, though, I pause.

"Lucky break," I say at last, voice curt. "Confusion about identities. Enough for me to get out of there."

Fitz greets my story with silence. He wants details, but he doesn't ask. "Okay," he says at last, wary. Maybe he thinks I'm lying. I suppose I am.

I say, "Here's the thing—I see how to get in now. Got a few things clarified in regards to his organization. I'll get him Tuesday." We have him at Cafe Boulud on Tuesday. A meeting with a local operator.

"Not now you won't—he's on the move, or about to be. Our spotters at Westchester County Airport saw his Airstream being serviced and fuelled."

"But he had plans for Tuesday...our sources said—"

"Seems his plans have changed. His people have filed a flight plan for Moscow. The whole crew is moving out."

"Moving out," I say. Maybe I should feel flattered. I only feel disappointed.

"Yeah, so..."

I don't like Fitz's tone. As if the mission is over. "So get me on a flight for Moscow, then. A commercial flight, cattle car, I don't care."

"Their flight plan is for Moscow. Doesn't mean that's where they're going. No, no, we're bringing you back to DC to regroup."

"When I start a thing, I finish it, Fitz. If I can just get one more shot. I just need—"

"We're bringing you back, Will. End of discussion."

"But I know how to work his people now."

"And that's all well and good," Fitz says. "It's good you have insight. We need that kind of insight. We'll use that. *You'll* use that. We'll send you out again once we have a sense of their plans."

"If I could go at him now—"

"It's not up for debate. We have a process."

"I want him, Fitz."

A huff of laughter at that. "Oh, don't worry. You'll get another crack at him—we don't exactly have agents lining up for this mission. First, we bring you back, then we do the intelligence, *then* we send you out again." He pauses, then adds, "It could be a while. For the next few weeks, he'll be operating on maximum security. Maybe you could even take a few weeks, cool your heels at home. Get back to your contracting business. Visit your dad."

Back in Nebraska, he means. I know he's right about the increased security. Still, it pisses me off. I had a chance tonight, and I fucked it up.

"We'll send a car in the morning," Fitz says. "Ten or so."

"Fine. I'll be ready."

I hang up feeling unsettled. I can barely wrap my head around the thought of having to wait weeks or even months before having another chance at killing Polzin. I'd gotten myself so worked up for this mission—it was do or die. And now I can't help but picture the faces of my men, those brave, loyal men, killed in an instant because of the secrets Polzin sold.

I flop back on the bed, staring at the ceiling.

Back to square one.

Waiting for the kill.

Waiting to serve up a cold dish of justice that's been waiting too long. Trying not to think about all the things I could've done differently back there in that dusty little village. If only I'd been a little more alert. A little more suspicious, they might still be alive. My brothers. My best friends. Guys who trusted me with their lives.

I don't know how long I lie there, brooding, but after a while, my stomach rumbles. Hungry. Of course. There were only fussy scraps of food at the party. Pretty little bits and bites on napkins and sticks. Such a bother, all that pretty.

My mind goes to that beautiful bodyguard again. God, the look of him as he lifted that dress. And the sheer hotness of his bulging cock, trapped behind silky girl panties. And then that fucking voice. Like the queen of motherfucking England—*Why don't you* convince *me you're sorry by getting down on your knees and sucking my cock.*

And the long, lean lines of him, all elegant and refined. He reminded me of a hound my uncle had when I was a kid—a saluki.

Salukis are desert hounds. They hunt gazelles, and they run like the wind. Beautiful dogs, but overbred if you ask me, so skittish and quivery and picky about their food.

Fucking lethal, though—they can run down a rabbit like you've never seen.

Caused my uncle no end of grief, that crazy dog. And he cried like a baby when the mutt died.

I push the memory aside and pick up the phone to order room service: a steak dinner with sides of fries and onion rings and two beers.

The food shows up good and fast. I'm so happy to see it, I tip the waiter double. I flip on ESPN and settle into some heavy-duty eating. Afterwards, I dump the tray outside my room and do a quick check of the hallway before I lock up for the night and head for the shower.

The bathroom in this place is like a spa, huge and fancy. The towels are plentiful and plush, and the tub is big enough for three.

Also, the shower area doesn't even have a door—it's like a tiled cave, complete with recessed lighting and shower-heads the size of dinner plates. As if that wasn't weird enough, there's no soap to be found. Guess that would be too simple for a place like this.

Instead there's a basket of little bottles next to the sink. I paid no attention to them earlier, but now I pick them up and examine the labels one by one. Lime and coconut shampoo. Mango and dragonfruit conditioner. Body washes in exotic fruit flavors. They're so tiny, I feel like it would take the entire bunch of them to wash a person as big as me, so I just dump the whole damn basket out on a shelf in the shower-cave. I toss the empty basket out of there and crank the hot water.

The shower has extra sprayers at each side that I can direct how I want. Like the overhead fucker isn't gonna get me wet enough.

I wash my hair and body quickly. Just two little bottles make lots of suds, as it turns out. Then I turn the temperature up as high as I can bear and stand there in the fancy shower-cave with its fussy mood lighting, letting the overhead spray pound down on my neck and shoulders. They're tight with tension. I turn the side jet on high, too. At least there's nothing fancy about the water pressure. Like a fucking fire hose on my back. Just how I like.

I close my eyes, head bowed, shifting occasionally, allowing the water to massage different spots of my body. The stiffness in my shoulders eases but doesn't disappear—instead it moves south, taking possession of my dick.

I wrap my paw around it and start rubbing one off, long, slow, firm strokes, up and down, tipping my head back to let the water soak my upturned face.

And then a voice says, "Well, isn't *this* awkward?"

My eyes spring open, and I nearly jump out of my skin, hand stilling on my rod.

I'm looking at Polzin's bodyguard, except this time he's dressed as a guy. Not just any guy, but the most beautiful guy you ever saw, and he's leaning on the sink with the business end of his Luger pointed right at me.

My hand's frozen right on my rod, which thickens even more, something I wouldn't have thought possible a minute back. I'm not loving that Luger, but my dick is pretty goddamn happy to see this guy.

His black clothes are skin tight. Good quality gear designed for climbing and running—and fighting. His bright blond hair is tied at the nape of his neck. The severe style shows off the mad perfection of that face. There are probably names for how he looks, the perfect ideal of masculine and feminine together: high cheekbones and a straight, perfect nose. Haughty brows over amber eyes that make me think of a bird of prey all over again.

"Please," he says in his fancy English accent. "Don't stop on my account."

"Never been much of an exhibitionist," I say. Yet I don't let go.

The silence stretches. The heat in the room rises. Builds.

"You should finish," he says finally.

I know then that he's come to kill me. I thought it before, of course, but now I know it for sure. One last orgasm, he's giving me, standing there like Death, Luger resting in his hand, somehow loose and intent at the same time.

My dick should be shrunk to nothing by now.

It's not.

How did I not hear him coming? Even with the shower running, I should've heard—should've been ready. It's because I'm still fucked up over what happened earlier. Over my rookie fucking mistake.

I'm so messed up over it, I made another one.

My mind races as I try to find some opportunity in this situation. It's not that I'm scared of dying. Hell, I'm good with dying—go ahead, bring it on.

As long as I take Polzin with me.

But now I'm trapped.

The bodyguard's gaze travels over me, following the path of the water droplets down my body.

His lips part, tongue darting out to moisten them in a telltale gesture that amazes me.

And it's right there I see my way out of this. Him.

He wants me.

Heart pounding, I slide my left hand over my balls, caressing the side of them just a bit, just because I can.

His gaze drops to where the action is. Just that gives me a thrill so intense, it feels like an electric shock.

I take a proper grip of my shaft again with my right hand. Slowly and firmly, I stroke up the whole length, my fingertips dragging slightly on the tender skin.

He watches.

Knowing I can command his attention like that blows my fucking mind. "You left me hanging before, baby," I tell him, forcing a smile in my voice.

He looks up again, and our gazes meet. He says nothing.

"That was a dick move."

His lips twitch. "I saved your fucking life."

"Yeah, but for how long?"

A muscle in his jaw tightens. We both know what this is.

"If your dick's bothering you that much," he says, "make yourself come. I can wait."

I raise one brow. James fuckin' Bond. "Why? You wanna watch?" My eyes are glued to his, waiting for his reaction.

He laughs, but it sounds hollow. "I have some questions for you—I'd prefer to ask them when there's some blood flow to your brain."

Yeah, sure. That's why his pupils are blown wide and black and his dick is straining against the tight fabric of those stretchy pants he's wearing.

I don't point that out, though. I just shrug. "Okay then."

I let go of myself and reach for one of the little bottles on the shelf beside me, keeping my movements exaggerated and slow. "I like a little something to work with," I explain, my eyes on him the whole time.

He nods. Licks his lips.

I flip open the lid with my thumb and squeeze some orange stuff onto my palm. It's thinner than I expected, and it spills over the sides of my hand, running into the water, swirling around my bare feet, filling the steamy room with a tropical fruit scent.

I manage to save some in my cupped hand, and I rub a bunch onto my belly, then farther down, onto my cock and balls. I massage my body slowly, trying to make it look good, trying not to feel self-conscious about putting on a big show.

This isn't my kind of thing—not usually, anyway. But right now, my cock feels hard enough to beat fence posts into the ground, and it's because *he's* watching me.

Those intent, hawkish eyes are riveted onto my slowly moving hands, following my every move. Yeah, he likes what he's seeing.

I like it too. I like his eyes on me, watching me touch myself. Owning me. I get a strange pang in my belly from that thought—the thought of him *owning* me.

What the fuck?

Now is not the time to be getting carried away with this. But human bodies—human minds—can be screwy, and for some reason, mine is really getting off on this.

I slide my fist up and down my slick, slippery shaft, nice and slow. Water still pounds over my head, and that fire-hose of a jet is starting to feel like it's boring a hole into my back.

Need to concentrate. Need to make the most of my chances, but it's hard to concentrate on anything other than my dick with those amber eyes watching me.

"It's nice in here," I say at last, arching an inviting brow at him. "Wanna join me?"

A slight smile. He looks amused. "Much as I'd love to, I think I'll decline on this occasion."

"Temperature's perfect, baby."

He smiles, rueful, but shakes his head. "Sorry. Do carry on."

I shrug, like it makes no difference to me. Playing for time, I reach for another of the little bottles, upending this one straight onto my pecs. A berry scent this time.

He watches the bright red liquid drip down my chest with fascination.

Turns out these fussy little bottles of goo are good for something.

His gaze is fucking intense; I swear I can feel it on my skin. I swallow hard, my mouth dry.

I remember so clearly how it felt to kneel at his feet earlier, his cock in my mouth. The memory makes my already painfully hard dick harden further. Shit, did I really think I could use this as a way of diverting him? Already I can't even think straight, I'm so turned on.

"What's your name?" I ask, trying to wrest some kind of control back. "I'm thinking it's not Kate."

"Kit," he says. He pronounces the word precisely, with a hard *K* and an even harder *T*, but his gaze is absolutely trained on my cock.

"*Kit?* What kind of name is that?"

One side of his mouth hitches. Apparently I really amuse this guy. I might be offended if it wasn't for his gaze eating me up like I'm the best dessert he's ever had.

"My kind."

I grunt. I'm not sure how long I can last, him watching me like that. Unlike *Kit*, I didn't get to come earlier. "Kit," I repeat, voice husky. I like it better when he says it, all crisp and fancy.

I slide my hand up my body, up over the scars on my belly, over my chest, and right up onto my nipple where I pause, stroking a lazy thumb over it. I let him see me shudder. I usually won't let a guy see that kind of thing.

"I like Kit, for you. It suits you." Not a lie.

I've run out of soap again, so I grab another bottle, then pause, holding it up to the light. "Something wrong with this one. Some dirt or some shit got in this soap."

He clears his throat before he speaks. "It's an exfoliant."

"Ex-what?"

"Exfoliant. Abrades off the old skin cells. Might not be quite the thing you want." He nods at my dick, words like cut diamonds. "Down there."

"Right. My dick likes to keep its skin cells right where they are." I grab a different bottle—green—watermelon?—and continue soaping myself, gliding my hands up over my long, thick shaft. "Who'd want to abrade their own skin?" I ask.

Kit's eyes follow the path of my wandering hands. He licks his lips before he answers me. "It makes it feel smooth. Like silk."

God help me, but I love the way he's looking at me. I feel like his prey. Like I'm in his sights, and he's closing in on me, like that saluki after the rabbit.

How fucked up is that? I should be thinking about how I make him *my* prey, but it's impossible to think in any kind of rational way under his watchful gaze with my dick so hard it's throbbing in time with my heartbeat.

"I bet you use stuff like that all the time," I say, remembering the feel of his pale thighs, so strong and tensely muscled—the legs of a man used to hard exercise, no question—but so smooth.

The second I think of his legs, I'm awash in the memory of dragging his lacy white panties down them with just my teeth, of having all that silky skin against my cheek. Just the thought of it sends a surge of lust barrelling through me so hard, I have to bite my lip.

It's not that I don't like him in men's clothes—he looks just as amazing in the skin-tight getup he's wearing now. The truth is, I like both. My mind keeps jetting back and forth between how he looks now and how he looked earlier, and I can't decide which I like more.

Kit doesn't bother to answer me. Instead he says, his voice low, "Touch your cock again."

Ah fuck, but this is gonna end me. If I don't lose my mind first.

Obediently, I take hold of my dick. The soap's all gone now, but I don't care. I almost relish the snag of my calluses as I take myself in hand and begin to slowly pump. I feel like—I don't know—a tuning fork or something. Like I'm resonating with him in some weird way. Like we're synced together and Kit's controlling the pleasure coursing through me, determining the pace and intensity of each pulse.

And I can't—I literally *cannot*—look away from him.

"You really want to come, don't you?" he says softly. It's more of an observation than a question.

Yeah, I want to come. Really bad. My dick's throbbing so hard, I could weep from the pain of all that unfulfilled desire that started building in me hours ago, back in that room, on my knees, with his cock in my mouth. And now this...

I give a faint humiliated moan, but I can't tear my hand from my dick or my eyes from his face.

His smile is slow and satisfied. He feels the shift between us too.

"Not yet, darling," he croons. After a pause, he adds dreamily, "I could watch you do that all night. I wonder how long you could last."

The noise that emerges from my throat is embarrassing. A whimper. At his chuckle of amusement, mingled shame and excitement ripple over me.

"Please," I choke out. The word startles me, even as it falls from my lips.

With a few words, a raised eyebrow, and that amused fucking voice of his, he's got me in the palm of his hand. He *owns* me.

And oh, but my dick likes that notion.

Distantly, I'm disgusted at myself. Demeaning myself like this when I only started this show in order to draw him in. But the truth is, it feels so good I don't want to stop.

"No coming until I say," he whispers. His eyes are intent on mine and bright with approval.

I manage a ghost of a nod, my hand moving in a steady rhythm now. My agreeing has nothing to do with the gun he's holding and everything to do with his golden gaze and the air of certainty coming off him.

"I think I'd prefer to see you doing this on your knees, though," he muses.

Jesus.

I don't think twice. I begin to lower myself down to the stone floor, but he stops me, just with a look.

"Not here," he says shaking his head. "Bedroom."

He steps aside, gesturing with his gun toward the door.

I nod and step out from under the water.

CHAPTER EIGHT

Kit

I have never met anyone like this man.

Everything he does, he does with single-minded devotion. There's something so pure about that. Something shining. It makes the blood in my veins sing, to watch him.

He's not faking this. He couldn't fake the glittering eyes, dilated pupils, flushed skin. And that cock. So hard and needy, leaking precum. His breath sawing in and out of him. The break in his voice as he begs me for release.

Please.

Fucking hell.

He walks into the bedroom. I see him take in the sheer drapes over the balcony doors gently billowing in the breeze—that's how I got in, and it's how I'll leave. He doesn't say anything, though, just turns to face me. Drops to his knees. Waits.

"I wish I could take my time with you," I hear myself say.

He hisses, vermilion-tipped cock bobbing in front of him.

We both know that won't happen. Too many risks—for both of us.

"Not tonight," I add.

His eyes widen a little. Perhaps mine do too.

It implies maybe some other night I might just take my time with him. Am I seriously thinking about walking out of here and leaving him alive?

It's not like you to leave a loose end trailing...

It really isn't.

That thought prompts me to be brisk. "All right then, make yourself come for me now," I say. "And make it good, darling. I want a show."

I see the movement of his throat as he swallows, then he reaches down, taking hold of himself again.

"Other hand behind your head," I say.

He obeys, wrapping the fingers of his left hand round the back of his neck.

"Spread your thighs more."

He does that too, bringing his body closer to the ground, abasing himself for me. I see how much he likes doing my bidding, a faint flush painting his cheekbones.

"So, tell me. How do you prefer me?" I ask conversation-ally, as he begins stroking himself again, getting into it. "As Kit or Kate?"

"I like both," he gasps, hand pumping.

"Bit hard to climb through hotel windows in a frock," I say.

He groans at that, a pained sound, and his hand begins moving faster, tugging hard on his leaking cock.

"I'm gonna come," he gasps.

"Not yet you aren't," I say. "I'm quite sure you can go a little longer."

He lets out something that sounds almost like a sob, his expression agonised. His skin still shines with water, and maybe sweat now. His belly is scarred, chest lightly furred, droplets gleaming in the low hotel lamplight, square jaw set, determined.

"You look bloody gorgeous," I say, genuine awe tinging my voice. "But put those shoulders back a little more— and get that chin up. Really display yourself to me. And spread those thighs more too. I want to see everything you've got."

The way he struggles to obey me is something to behold. He shifts that beautiful big body around on the floor, opening everything up to me. He makes an offering of himself, and all the time, his hand is working his hard, ruddy shaft, and I can see how close he is. How he's at the point of pain now as he simultaneously tries to climax and hold that climax off.

"Please," he begs. "I need to come. Let me come for you, Kit."

Kit.

Jesus. His words send a weird thrill through me, and I find myself whispering, "Tell me your name."

He doesn't hesitate. "It's Will."

It's just a name. Not much at all, but it feels like everything. Like a gift. His name, given up. His trust, his body, open and offered to me. Not because of the gun in my hand but because of his desire to give me those things. And because I have demanded them of him.

"You can come now, Will," I say, and with a half-sob, he does, curling in on himself a little as he begins to shoot, the first pulse going high enough to hit his shoulder. He comes in rhythmic spurts, groaning loudly, and cursing too, a senseless stream of profanity tumbling from his lips.

"Oh, fuck. Christ Jesus, so fuckin'—"

I palm the aching erection in my trousers as I watch him, cursing the fact that there's nothing I can do about it right now.

When he's done, he leans forward, one hand flat on the floor, as though to steady himself. He's a mess, covered in his own come, his chest still heaving from his efforts. He's fucking beautiful.

Will.

Will.

As I watch him recover, it occurs to me that, for the last few minutes, I've had this man completely in my power, and it was the best feeling in the world. God, the trust he gave me. Me—his enemy.

The feeling that comes over me as I consider this is pure awe.

But when Will finally looks up at me, his expression has changed. The naked need is gone. Now he looks wary.

Regretful. His gaze flickers to the Luger in my hand, and I wish I could throw the bloody thing away—throw it away and cross the room to him. Pull him to his feet and take his mouth with mine. But already that possibility is gone. Instead, I adjust my grip on the firearm and return his gaze with an expressionless one of my own.

"Well, that was quite a show, Will," I say. "All in all, most entertaining."

This time he flinches at my use of his name, closing his eyes briefly.

"Gonna kill me now?" he asks flatly. I can't bear the defeated expression on his face.

Still, I force myself to quirk a wry smile. "Not quite yet. I have a few questions first."

"Such as?"

"Such as, who are you?"

"Nobody important." He makes a move to rise up.

"Stay down, darling." My voice is a silky threat. "I prefer you on your knees."

He subsides, his gaze never wavering from mine. His flaccid cock curves gently against his thigh. Vulnerable.

"You're with the agency," I say.

"No."

"Who then?"

"Nobody," he says.

I laugh. "You're nobody, and you know nothing."

"I didn't say I know nothing," he replies evenly.

I sigh, feigning boredom. "Enlighten me, then. What do you know?"

He looks right at me, his dark gaze burning. "I know that Sergei Polzin needs to die." His voice trembles with conviction.

I don't disagree with him. Christ, I've fantasised about killing Polzin myself, but this is different. Will burns with the fiery conviction of a martyr. It's obvious to me this is personal. No doubt Polzin is responsible for the death of someone Will knew.

I sigh again. "This is rather awkward," I say. "You understand I can't allow you to kill my boss. You're not giving me many options here."

Underneath my veneer of world-weariness, my stomach's churning. Can he tell I'd do anything other than put a bullet in him? If only he'd cooperate, stand down.

Either he doesn't get it, or he refuses to play along, because he looks me right in the eye and says, "Polzin dies."

Shit.

We're at an impasse now.

It's not like you to leave a loose end trailing...

And right then—just as I'm readying myself to do what needs to be done, adjusting my grip on the Luger and bringing the muzzle up—there's a swift, determined rap at the door.

A woman's voice, soft but urgent. "Will, open up. Fitz wants us."

Will watches me.

This is one of those moments—now or never. For the past two years, my life has been built on these moments, on my ability to act in the midst of crisis. To step over the impossible line between inaction and action. Change the course of events.

All I need to do is squeeze the trigger—it's nothing I haven't done before. One shot, then out the balcony. By the time the woman comes in, I'll be long gone.

We stare at each other, Will and I. His eyes gleam in the low light of the hotel room.

I sense the moment that he makes his decision, before he moves even.

"Just a minute," he calls out. And then he's rising, slow, lifting himself to stand tall, naked before me, his dark gaze challenging me.

And still, I don't fire.

My weapon's on him, but the grip feels slippery in my hand. Unstable. A tremor goes through me.

I can't do this.

The things I've done over the past two years would turn most people's hair white. I've constantly amazed myself with my ability to perform the most loathsome of orders. Archie says it's what makes me a good agent.

Sometimes you have to disengage your personal conscience in order to achieve the greater good.

Taking out this man—Will—is very far from the worst thing I've ever been asked to do. For Christ's sake, he threatens my whole mission.

But—*I can't do it.*

Heart pounding, I drop my gun arm.

He doesn't move. I half-expect him to charge me, but he just stares at me, as I'm staring at him.

More rapping at the door. "Will, come on!"

"I'm coming, Wagner," he calls, his gaze unwavering. "Give me a sec."

"This isn't over," I say, walking backwards towards the balcony. My own voice sounds strange to me.

"Sure isn't," Will says.

My gaze is still on him as the filmy drapes close over me, as the darkness enshrouds me. Through the sheer fabric, I see him start towards me, but he's too late.

I vault the wrought-iron balustrade and head out into the night.

CHAPTER NINE

Will
London

Ten at night. I find the hair salon on a quiet side street in Camden Town, the last in a row of shabby retail units. The others offer tattoos, piercings, bongs, incense and the like. This one just has a couple of bald, naked mannequins draped with fairy lights and a huge black and white photo of a guy with an asymmetrical haircut and sparkly earrings.

The sign on the door says "closed." I knock twice and wait. The interior is lit weirdly by blue neon lights. I lean in close to peer through the darkened window. I can just make out the outline of more mannequins inside, ropes of lights twisted around their plastic arms and legs.

A shadowy figure shifts, then begins moving toward the door. I step back from the window. A moment later, the door opens. A woman with blue hair looks at me, one eyebrow raised in query.

"Greg sent me," I say.

The woman nods once and lets me into the place, which is chock full of crazy leather costumes and chains and things.

"I'm Andrea. I'll be styling you tonight."

I'm in London, but this woman's accent is as American as my own. Boston, maybe? She closes the door behind me and flicks the lock.

Her face is lit in blue. I suppose I'm lit in blue, too, and I have a feeling it'll only get worse, judging from the grin she shoots me. "Your friend is already here."

"Something funny?"

She looks me up and down, then she spins, leading me past rows of hair dryers. "Some of these assignments happen to be more amusing than others."

I groan and follow her.

"Don't worry. I have a vision for you. For your club persona. It'll be perfect, perfect, perfect. Nothing too bad."

Nothing too bad. That doesn't exactly fill me with faith. "If you could make it black..."

Andrea holds aside a curtain. I duck into a back room, and there's Wagner, perched on a high stool. She's in some manner of complicated catsuit—zips and snaps and hooks. An outfit no sane person would wear.

"What the hell..."

She slips off the stool and balances in front of me on heels so high I'm surprised she doesn't topple right over. "Hello, Will," she says, in her slightly formal way. "Glad you were able to make it. I was beginning to think you must've gotten lost."

"You get attacked by zippers, Wagner?"

She lowers her voice. "I feel like a dork."

I nod, appreciating her honesty. She's usually all business.

"Stop it. You look fucking hot," Andrea says with a wink. "Just make believe like you're a sexy little sub girl. It'll be easy."

"Whatever it takes." Her grim tone reminds me the CIA wants this guy dead, too. Maybe not as bad as I do, but they want it, and that makes us convenient allies. The CIA wants Polzin dead because his death triggers the release of some file. Me, I just need to settle the score.

I eye the many enclosures on the suit Wagner's wearing, all strategically situated to give a special friend, or friends—maybe even a few woodland animals—access to all the good parts. "Some folks sure do like their sex complicated."

"And dangerous," Andrea says. "You don't want to catch anything important in those zippers, trust me, dude." She winks. "Proceed with care."

I nod. I know what she sees—a big, clumsy lawman, all in black. Square jaw, square outlook. The type of guy who likes beer and football. Well, I do like those things.

"Go ahead and take a seat."

"I'll stand. I just flew for ten hours."

"Siddown!" She disappears behind a curtain.

"I'm fine," I growl.

Wagner pushes out a chair with her foot. Or more like a hoof, in those shoes. "Warning: If you fuss, she threatens to make you into a diaper-play person." She pulls out her phone and starts scrolling.

"Not gonna happen," I say.

Andrea reappears with an armful of—I don't even know. It looks like nets and leather and chains. "Hey, diaper-play getup is awesome for hiding firearms." She dumps the heap of stuff on an empty chair, then disappears through another curtained doorway.

"How about it, Will?" Wagner asks, eyes still on her phone. "How bad do you want Polzin?"

I pull off my jacket and throw it on a counter. "I get the feeling we're both willing to do whatever it takes." I nod at her shoes. "Can you walk in those things, or do I need to carry you in there?"

"No shit, right?" Sounds funny to hear her talk like that. She holds out a hoof. "I have toe tennies underneath. Still, takes a bit to get them off. No foot chases for me tonight."

Toe tennies. I don't know what they are. I don't think I need to know.

"Well, I got your back," I say, undoing my shirt cuffs. Because that's really what she's getting at with the foot chase business. That she'll be counting on me.

And she can count on me—I won't be falling down on the job again. Or kneeling down on the job.

Even now, I can't stand to think about how the guy had me on knees, panting for him, when I should've been walking through him and taking out Polzin.

He should've iced me when he had the chance—he had to know I'd come back. Well I'm back. Polzin dies tonight.

Best part: our intel says Kate won't be around. After last time, I let the Agency know Kate was . . . a problem. I didn't go into detail, just said it'd be easier to get to that scumbag without her around.

I didn't tell them the rest. They didn't need the details; they just need the kill. They don't need to know why it's hard to get at Polzin when Kate's around.

I pull my holster and shirt off. Then my pants. I leave my boxers. Wagner scrolls and scrolls.

Since that night, the agency's been chasing down intel on when Polzin and Kate can be found together—and when they can't. They found reports of just one place Polzin never takes his faithful girlfriend, and that's Cage, a select sex club and dungeon whose patrons come from the ranks of the uberwealthy.

Thirty-six hours ago, Polzin was headed for Vienna, but for some reason, he changed his flight plan to London. Twelve hours later, his PA booked a private suite at Cage for tonight.

Fitz called me to tell me the mission was on. One minute I was directing a crew working to restore the intricate original windows on a historic college library outside Omaha, and the next, I was on my way to the airport.

I had to cancel a dinner with my dad—he settled down in a farmhouse on the outskirts of town. I had to take a time off from running a building renovation contracting firm with a buddy. I like fixing up old buildings. It's something

I'm good at. A hundred years ago—that's when they knew how to build things right.

Well, my buddy'll handle the library project. I warned him it might happen. He knows I was in the service, that I still do some "consulting."

I'd cancel anything to get at Polzin without Kit there.

It's only smart, right? You always want to take the path of least resistance—it's an easier kill, that's what I tell myself. But there's another part, too—that I don't know how to feel about what I turn into when Kit's around.

I like my men like I like my firefights: hard, fast, and furious—with me winding up on top. You wanna call me a caveman, you go right ahead. I've been called worse. When I'm with a guy, I'm the one on top. And if there's any fucking going on, it's me doing it. End of story.

I pull off my ankle holster with my nine and set them on the counter.

Andrea wheels in a rack full of leather garments. Lots of chains and loops. She eyes me in my boxers. "No, no, no. No undies." She looks discreetly away as I take them off. I glance at Wagner—she's still transfixed by her phone. Not that I care if they watch. You get used to it in the military. Your body is every bit the tool your mind is.

"Have you ever been to a place like this?" Wagner asks.

"Nah. But I get the gist."

"Good," she says. "So, I'm the submissive. You're going to be the dom. Most of the weapons will be on me. They won't really see me so much, being all passive and tied up. We won't do anything fancy, though. We're honeymooners. Tourists here in London from Akron, Ohio, and new to the kink scene. We haven't found a kink place at home, but we knew we'd find something here in London, so we bought some clothes, and here we are. Our tastes are mild."

Andrea chuckles and throws me a pair of leather pants.

I start to put them on. They barely go up. "Too tight," I say.

Andrea raises an eyebrow. "Try a little harder, hon. The more they look at your package, the less they see your face, right?"

I pull them up, with some effort. There's a strip from front to back held on with snaps. It's pretty clear how it works, though. Tear that strip off and you got pants covering everything except what pants were designed to cover.

"Modular chaps," Andrea says. "Easy access for fucking or whatever else takes your fancy."

I sigh.

"Don't worry, soldier," Wagner says. "Nobody's going to be tearing that piece off."

"Easy access for the bathroom, too," Andrea points out. "But if you don't like it, we can still go with the diapers."

I give her a look.

Wagner's pulled up a map of Cage on her phone. She shows me the different rooms, points out the suite Polzin's staff hired on the fourth floor. "Polzin's tastes go to sadism," she says, "according to our intel, anyway."

We walk through the layout. Two different stairways at either end of the building, a bank of elevators in the middle. The Polzin suite's situated halfway between the elevators and the east staircase. There's a network of back hallways we'll use. She assures me nobody knows about them. The Cage owners keep them a secret.

"Put out your arms." Andrea slides on a beat-up leather vest and gives me fingerless leather gloves to wear, then she buckles a belt around me. It's got a holster for a whip and a crop. She steps back and nods. "I love it. Vest over man chest. Very barbarian. And with those scars of yours?" She makes a smacking sound.

For fuck's sake.

She heads back into the curtained area.

Wagner and I finish going over the plan she and Fitz worked up while I was in the air. "So, we're thinking we'll take this room here," she explains, expanding the picture on her screen with a slide of her thumb and forefinger. "It can't be prebooked, and none of these rooms tend to get busy till after midnight. There's an option here to have it open to viewers, but that's not our thing. We're just taking the room to use the equipment, got it?"

I nod. "Yeah."

"We'll make some sounds and crack the whip a little, just to make it sound real, but then we'll put on the sound recording and get to work. You'll break into his suite via the back hall system here." She expands the view, pointing with one polished purple nail. She goes on to cover every contingency—how we can cut power if we need to, several ideas for escape, where advance has stored weapons. "All subject to your veto, of course," she adds.

I study the map, kick the tires a little, but it's a decent plan. The only one that would make sense. "Looks pretty straightforward to me."

"Good."

Andrea's back with different gloves for me to try. These ones lace clear up to my elbows.

Wagner shows me the entry point they've identified for Polzin's suite. It seems they've used this place before. The owner's open to bribery or blackmail—I don't ask. It's not important. I just know that's why they hustled me across the Atlantic. This is the kink dungeon version of Polzin falling into their lap—without Kate. All systems go.

Andrea hands me a leather cap with a chain over the brim. "Try this."

"Seriously?"

"Oh, put it on."

I sigh, but I do it. And when I look up, they're both grinning. "Take a look in the mirror," Andrea says.

"I'm not looking in the mirror." I nod at Wagner. "Where do you see Polzin's security detail staking out?"

I'm thinking, of course, about Kit. He's not supposed to be there, but he's unpredictable.

She slides the view to a long hallway. "This is the only logical place. They won't know there's any other entry. There's no way Polzin's people could possibly know our agency uses the back tunnels or that there even are any."

We go over the plan a couple times.

Our inside person will alert us once Polzin is ensconced in his suite by knocking softly on the door. I'll sneak into the back tunnel and slip into his room and kill him. The challenge will be doing it quietly enough so as not to alert security, which will surely be waiting just outside his door. He'll have a woman with him, but she'll likely be a hired woman, unlikely to rise to his defense. Possibly even unable to rise to his defense—he likes them tied up and helpless, Wagner says. Big fucking surprise.

"You go streetside once the knock comes," I say.

"Are you crazy? I'm not leaving you."

"I get veto power over all plans—that's the deal. This is my show."

"I'm backup."

I shake my head. "I work alone. I'm willing to wear this dumbass outfit. I'm not willing to die in it. Any backup is somebody more I gotta worry about. You get me in— you're my cover, and then you go."

"You almost got clipped last time."

"But I didn't, did I?" I grab her phone. Of course she's right. It's safer for me to have backup. But I don't want it. It's not just about having somebody more to worry about. It's also because when I close my eyes, I still see all those bodies of my men, dead in that godforsaken truck. Fire-bombed to hell while I was out securing the area. Those men trusted me, and I would've done anything for them. Fuck, securing the area was supposed to be the dangerous part.

This time I handle it alone.

Nobody else dies but Polzin.

"Look." I swipe at her screen to get back to the earlier schematic. "Once you're out, I go in here, then move into the back way. I take out Polzin, I go back out the same way. Vehicles here and here. Done. Clean. Neat."

"I won't get involved in your plan, but my instructions are to hang back and monitor things." She yanks back her phone.

Suddenly I get it. "If I die, they want you to try and finish the job? Make it look like I succeeded?"

"If I can."

"That man surrounds himself with some pretty dangerous people."

She shrugs. "We need those files to be released. Anyway, dead is dead, right? You'll have your wish."

"What's in the files?"

"Let's just say, the release of them will provide solutions for some crimes the agency is very eager to solve," she says.

"A blackmail file," I guess.

The way she tips her head tells me I'm right. "I can't divulge any more than that." Wagner's expression is serious now. "We've never had such a good shot at him. Alone in a secure place. Hardly any civilians around." She pauses. Gives me a look. "And no obstructionist girlfriend." Her gaze asks a question. Not one I'm going to answer.

I get she's curious. They were all curious when I told them the girlfriend was a problem. I didn't tell them anything beyond that. It's not important why. Just that the kill will be easier without Polzin's girlfriend around. Understatement of the fuckin' year.

CHAPTER TEN

Kit

"You've got to be fucking kidding me." My voice drips with ice, but Polzin doesn't even flinch. His great white shark gaze is flat and black. Inhuman.

"Not in the least, Katerina," he says. "I want you with me tonight."

"Going with you isn't the problem," I reply. I point at the outfit lying across my bed. "*That's* the problem."

That is an ensemble made up of a few scraps of leather and a whole lot of straps and buckles.

"Is much more than most of my companions wear, Katerina."

This doesn't exactly reassure me. The worst part—the part my gaze keeps creeping back to—is the head section. There's a part that goes in the mouth, to keep it open, like a channel. If you wore that, your jaw would be kept in an obscenely wide position, your teeth too far apart to do any harm to whatever was fed into you. You would be voiceless too, unable to make your tongue connect to your palate or lips. The only sound you could make would be garbled, animal noises.

The thought of anyone having to wear that for Polzin makes me want to vomit. That kind of sex requires the utmost trust, and I can't even imagine how badly a monster like Polzin would enjoy betraying that.

I wonder how desperate the girls he usually takes to these places must be, how much they're paid, or whether they're paid at all.

Polzin chuckles. "Come, Katerina, you will look like pretty girl in it, just the way you like."

Hatred roils in my gut. I want to point out that he knows nothing about me. That I don't dress as a woman for any reason other than for professional advantage. That I have absolutely no ambition to look "pretty." As usual, I let Polzin think what he wants.

"It's entirely unsuitable," I say instead, my tone crisp. "Where do I put my weapons? How do I protect you with that thing over my mouth? It's ridiculous and far too revealing. The last thing we need is anyone discovering your supposed girlfriend is really your male bodyguard."

Polzin's flat gaze flickers with a series of microexpressions before defaulting back to the bland, creepy smile he wears most of the time. But I caught that flicker. It was disappointment. He'd wanted to wrong-foot me. Unsettle me. I wonder why.

"The safest look would be dominatrix," I say. "Neck to toe leather. Everything hidden."

Polzin doesn't bother to hide his disgust. "*Bladny.* No woman of mine holds the whip."

"Yes, but I'm not your woman," I point out.

"Everyone thinks you are," he says. "This means that, in the dungeon, you would be the one on your knees. You would be the one in a collar. There will be no doubt who is the master."

I can't quite suppress a shudder at that. Polzin's never shown any sexual interest in me—so far as I'm aware, he's one hundred percent straight—but weirdly, he's never seemed to mind that I'm male either. On the contrary, he often seems oddly titillated by it. I've always put it down to his love of secrets.

"Collar. Fine," I say, though my skin crawls at the thought of him buckling one round my throat. "But not that."

Polzin sighs heavily, displeased. "Fine," he says at last. "But I want you in a collar and the—" He frowns, searching for the word. He circles his left wrist with the thick fingers of his right hand, mime-fashion. "—the leather ones."

"Cuffs," I say shortly.

"Yes, cuffs." He looks me up and down. "Maybe it's not so bad. A corset, a collar, cuffs." He smiles thinly. "For my pampered and expensive little pet."

The only reaction I give him is a careless shrug.

"Good, then," he says. "It's settled."

Despite the thread of animosity that's always there between us, he has confidence in me. He believes in my ability to protect him, and why shouldn't he? I've proved my worth to him over and over.

In his mind, the astronomical amount of money he deposits in my Swiss account every month is enough to keep me loyal, even though it's just a minor business overhead to a billionaire like him.

"I'll have new outfit delivered," he says.

"No," I say. "I'll take care of it. Leave it to me."

As much as I hate Polzin, I know he's right about one thing—I should wear something submissive-looking at Cage.

In truth, Polzin's sexual taste runs to curvy women rather than the flat-chested thoroughbred variety, but he likes the prestige of having someone who looks like a supermodel on his arm, and I fit the bill perfectly.

Plus, it's the ideal way to divert attention from who I really am.

I act vacant, wear expensive clothes, and if anyone talks to me, I make sure only to talk about my Kate-self. Kate's pretty self-absorbed. No one hangs around her long enough to figure anything out. Polzin's girlfriend is a beautiful bore who just wants to look pretty and acquire beautiful things.

Kate's choice of outfit would be submissive-lite. Something that misses the point of a place like Cage but that won't look out of place. Catwalk BDSM. Once I've got that vision in my head, it doesn't take me long to figure something out.

Polzin sends a car to pick me up at seven. We always travel together when I accompany him places. My stipulation.

He's pacing the floor of the penthouse living room when I walk in, a glass of amber liquid in his hand. No fancy outfit for him. Just a plain black suit, white shirt, no tie—with the addition of leather gloves.

I stop in the middle of the room in my long black coat and wait for him to speak.

"Well? What are you wearing?" he snaps, and I realise he's nervous about this. I shouldn't be surprised—Polzin's biggest weakness is his ego. How people see him matters to him.

Unhurriedly, I unbutton the coat and open it up, though I don't take it off. "This do?" I ask, my tone bored.

He looks me over, and I see his tension subtly ease. "Your instincts are good, Katerina."

I've gone for Roman slave girl. A short white tunic covers me from shoulder to upper thigh, leaving plenty of long smooth leg on show while disguising my non-existent breasts. Gold clasps at the shoulders hold the tunic in place, and my collar and cuffs are tooled leather with gold buckles. The stuff is decorative rather than functional—nothing that would ever hold if anyone tried to restrain me.

The butter-soft leather straps of my gladiator sandals criss-cross my lower legs, almost to my knees, and I'm rather pleased with the twin blades I've managed to secret in each of the rear straps that stretch all the way from my heels up my calves. Two twelve-inch blades. Ingenious, if I do say so myself.

All in all, it's a perfect Kate outfit, giving an impression of feminine beauty that's unthreatening. Submissive.

That train of thought dredges up a visual memory I've unsuccessfully been trying to suppress for months now. The big American agent on his knees with my cock in his mouth. Then, later, pleasuring himself to my order.

"Please—I need to come. Let me come for you, Kit."

"Tell me your name."

"It's Will."

Will.

Like a fool, I let him back out into the world to fight another day, knowing that he wants Polzin dead. Knowing that he'll be back for him.

After that night, I stepped up Polzin's security detail another whole level. It's why I'm going to Cage with him tonight. Cage is an exclusive dungeon for rich fucks like Polzin to play in, so the security is incredibly tight.

In the past, I'd've been content just to do a walk-through before his arrival, then leave him with Dmitri while the rest of the team and I watch the outside. No one would try a hit in a place like Cage.

No one except the American.

Will.

"It's perfect," Polzin says, as I do up the buttons of my coat again. He sounds pleased now. "You'll be quite the little pet. We can tell everyone it's your first time and you're only observing for tonight."

Christ, the thought of watching him working some poor sub girl over—maybe in that fucking headpiece he showed me earlier—makes my gut roil, but I keep the bored expression in place. It's not as if I don't know what Polzin is.

I remind myself of Archie's oft-quoted words—*Sometimes you have to disengage your personal conscience in order to achieve the greater good.*

If I were a different sort of person, maybe I'd have those words tattooed down my arm, in Hindi perhaps, or Japanese. But I'm not the sort of person that believes that inking words on your skin makes a thing any more true or personal or meaningful. And besides, what sort of life mantra is that? It's hardly something to be proud of.

We go down to the garage in the internal lift. Dmitri's waiting at the doors with Gleb, a guy Polzin brought over from the old country recently. Dmitri's a big man, but Gleb's huge. Slower-moving than Dmitri, but still a good man to have at your back.

They shepherd us to the waiting limo. Gleb opens one of the rear doors for me, and Dmitri opens the other for Polzin. We slide in, and Dmitri follows us into the back. Gleb gets in the front, beside the driver. His heavily muscled frame fills his own side of the car and abuts the driver's space too. His big, square head is near enough brushing the car roof.

Fucking ox.

We stop at a Marriott hotel, and a shapely redhead in a long Prussian blue coat totters out, flashing a huge smile at the limo. Gleb gets out and opens the door for her, and she slides in. "Hello, sir," she says to Polzin. She glances at me without real curiosity.

"Eyes down, trash," he commands.

She casts her eyes downward, seeming unsurprised by his harsh tone.

I study her fingers clasped obediently in her lap, hoping he's paying her well. This night cannot be over quickly enough.

The journey doesn't take long. Cage is in Bloomsbury, just a short drive away. The driver circles the block twice before we stop. Gleb gets out first and strolls up and down the quiet street a little way in each direction before he returns to open the rear passenger door and lets the rest of us out. It's all of a ten-yard walk to the anonymous black door, which swings open as we approach.

A handsome Asian man stands in the doorway. His thick hair is tied at the nape of his neck in a short ponytail, and he wears a neat goatee. He's of a similar build to Dmitri. A tall, well-made black woman stands behind him, her expression impassive.

"Master Sergei," the man says, with a small respectful bow. "How good of you to visit us again." His accent is as anonymously upper-class as my own cut-glass vowels. His gaze moves to me and the redhead, then to each of the goons, assessing us before he stands aside and waves a welcoming arm. "Please come in."

Polzin—who has absolutely no manners whatsoever—doesn't say anything in response, just gives a curt nod and strides toward the inner door that the black woman is now holding open. She doesn't look at us as we pass through. The redhead and Dmitri and I follow in his wake. Gleb returns to the car.

I murmur a thank you to the Asian man as I pass and catch a glimmer of something in his eyes that I can't quite interpret. It's a speculative sort of look, but I fancy there's a distant echo of pity in there.

I follow Polzin through the inner doors to another larger room, aglow with soft, muted lighting; there are several plush couches and low tables and a small bar situated off to the side. Behind it, a beautiful young man stands waiting, hands behind his back.

A woman in a skin-tight carmine dress with absurdly high stiletto heels steps forward to greet us and take our coats. The redhead shrugs hers off to reveal an outfit composed almost entirely of straps and hooks. Her pussy and breasts are exposed for all to see. It makes my slave-girl ensemble look like a nun's habit.

Polzin grins at the hostess. "Sometimes one is not enough."

She doesn't blink an eye, just asks Polzin—she's careful to address him, not his underlings—whether we'd like some champagne.

"My suite is not yet ready?" Polzin asks irritably.

The woman murmurs that she's sure it must be, but she'll just verify it. And perhaps we'd like a glass of champagne while we wait? She signals to the barman, who springs into action, removing a bottle of really rather decent bubbly from a fridge. He starts peeling off the foil.

Something feels off.

Polzin looks at me and the sub girl, then points at a sofa. "Sit," he tells us, and we do, though I look at Dmitri and signal with my eyes where I want him. Obedient to my order, he retreats to the back wall, halfway between the door we entered through and the one that leads, I assume, to the play areas.

The barman unscrews the wire top and uncorks the champagne with a discreet pop. He fills two glasses, pouring slowly and carefully to retain the bubbles.

I keep my expression passive and bored, but my brain is ticking, ticking. Something's definitely wrong here.

It's not just the holdup—though that's strange, given how wealthy Polzin is and how professional this place looks. No, it's something more. I keep going back to the black woman who held open the door. The way she avoided our eyes. I glossed over it as we walked in, but it had registered with me. A flash of something, something hidden, something out of place. What?

The barman brings the champagne on a silver tray. Polzin takes one, and I get the other. Nothing for the redhead. I smile at the barman briefly when I lift my glass. He's very pretty indeed, and very young. "What's the holdup?" I ask.

I can tell from his expression that he doesn't know—I didn't expect him to, but I wondered whether he would find the delay unusual. Hard to tell. The hostess returns. Her smile is too easy.

Could this be a trap?

"You are pouting, Katerina," Polzin says.

Oblivious, as usual. Polzin is ex-KGB—a fact he loves to tout—but I'd bet anything he was never a field agent. He has no...*awareness.*

I bat my lashes, ignoring him. My senses are pinging, even if his aren't—something's definitely up. Dmitri and Gleb supposedly checked this place out, but they don't catch everything, especially when there's a hint of sex in the air; they may have been more interested in the club-goers than the club.

I stand and go to Dmitri with a flirty smile. I press a taunting finger on his chest. We're pretty much eye to eye, height-wise. I whisper, "How thoroughly did you go through this place?" I repeat it in broken Russian.

"Very thoroughly," he says.

"And your check on the owner? I assume you ran a full check."

"He has large reputation for kink," Dmitri says, switching to broken English. "Well known. Discreet. He runs this place for years."

No, then. "A large reputation for kink," I mutter. Had that been enough to satisfy them? "Cameras?"

"None in the suite. We swept it with the 471. We have today already. Is clean, this I promise."

"Mmm." I trust the 471, but I don't trust Dmitri and Gleb. Dmitri is lazy, Gleb stupid, and while that's helpful to me in my real mission, at times like this it's frustrating. "Floor plan?"

"On file."

I see Polzin coming toward us out of the corner of my eye. "Send it to me ASAP." I turn and smile.

"Our room is waiting, Katerina. Are you ready for our fun?"

I hand my glass to Dmitri and let Polzin guide us forward, his hand at my elbow. We walk side by side and the redhead follows in our wake, looking like a depraved bridesmaid, her hands already secured behind her back.

We're ushered into a posh room, something like a cross between a dungeon and a gothic living room with black leather seating and wrought-iron lamps that cast a cadmium red glow on the room. The colour puts me in a different time and place, calls up the mellow, slightly metallic smell of my favourite brand of paint, the deep, rich smudge of pigment on a palette, the bumpy feel of the paint tube.

I snap back to reality as the door shuts. Polzin wastes no time ordering his playmate to her knees in the corner.

I glance around the room, getting my bearings. There's equipment and accoutrements aplenty: crops and floggers are displayed in neat rows on the back wall next to a St. Andrew's Cross and another, simpler whipping post. Selections of dildoes, gags, weights, and clamps are laid out on red lacquer trays. I pick up a wide blindfold and hand it to Polzin. I don't want the sub girl seeing me—or, rather, seeing my absence.

"For our little friend," I say. He smirks as he ties it around her eyes.

I take out my phone. Dmitri's sent the floor plan. I pull it up, studying it for a couple of minutes, ignoring Polzin and the redhead who are already getting into their groove, Polzin muttering obscenities as he runs his hands over her trussed-up body.

I walk the perimeter of the room, inspecting the paint and the mouldings, the pattern on the rugs. My attention is drawn to a vertical display case with another selection of whips. It seems superfluous, given the wall display. I push on it gently.

It moves slightly. Too much to be a regular section of wall. I feel around behind the case and find the catch—very carefully hidden. A door—one that's not on the floor plan.

I turn back to Polzin, just in time to watch him deliver a vicious open-handed slap to the girl—so hard, it sends her to the floor. She lies there, panting, and it's all I can do to keep my game face in place.

No weakness. Not in front of Polzin. Any kind of empathy is a weakness to him.

"Darling," I say, to get his attention.

He glances at me. "My sweet?"

"I'm just going to sit here quietly and watch you do your magic." Even as I'm simpering the words, I'm miming my true intentions to him, showing him the secret door. I mime going in, and he nods.

"Of course," he says. "This time just watch, Katerina. I use this slut to teach you."

I turn back to the open door, pulling my Luger from under my tunic. I step through.

I'm in a tunnel. Muted floor lights, the type that illuminate airplane aisles at night, run in either direction, but they're few and far between, leaving plenty of shadows in which to hide. I put on my phone light and flash it all around until I'm satisfied that I'm alone. Then I pull the door shut and arrange myself in a shadowy nook. I slip the blade out of my left sandal strap—that will make for a quieter kill.

My heart pounds in the darkness.

I flash back to that New York hotel room. To the man who knelt before me in the dim glow of a bedside lamp, his name like a gift on his lips—Will. His body, open and offered to me.

I'm going to see him again.

I've known this moment would come, no matter how hard I've tried to prevent it.

Recently, I've been searching for clues to the Roc file's whereabouts more desperately than ever. I've combed up and down every one of Polzin's many residences. I've studied flight manifests, invoices, correspondence, anything I could think of to get that file so that I can kill Polzin myself.

Anything to avoid having to make a choice between Will and that fucking file.

Because I'll *have* to choose the file. I'll have to stop Will. And not like last time. This time, I'll have to stop him permanently. He's too much of a risk to leave out there, even though the thought of ending him guts me.

And what the fuck is that about? I don't *have* a conscience anymore. Not one that stops me from doing whatever's necessary, anyway.

The thing with Will is mere lust, I tell myself. That's all. Simple animal lust, a chemical in the brain. The Roc file is about so much more. Family and loyalty. Agents' lives. Blood.

It can never be released into the world.

I won't allow it.

CHAPTER ELEVEN

Will

The room is like a cheap stage set for a sexy Dracula movie. The wood floor is stained nearly black—with a coat of antibacterial business over it, no doubt—and the walls are padded in red pleather. There are tables around with complicated straps and buckles. A human-sized X on one wall, a human-sized T on the other, also with straps and buckles. Gas torches mounted up high on all four walls add flicker to the place.

A sign in the hall leading here read "explore your fantasies," but this feels like the opposite of exploration, at least to me. It feels as dumb as my hat. I really fucking hate the hat.

Agent Wagner stops in front of the X-shaped frame and gives a low whistle. "St. Andrew's Cross." She fingers a leather strap that looks like it's meant to secure a wrist—or hell, maybe an ankle, for all I know. Do people get tied up upside-down on these things?

"How would you like to be strapped to one of these while someone whales on you with a riding crop?" she asks.

"Not much," I grumble.

She laughs and wanders over to investigate a tall black cylinder that turns out to be a bushel of whips and crops. She yanks one out and swishes it through the air. The whistling sound makes the hair on the back of my neck stand on end. She smacks the crop experimentally against the red pleather wall. *Thwap.* She chuckles softly.

"Oh, master," she moans loudly. "Please may I have another?"

"Stop goofing around," I hiss.

"I'm not," she protests. "We're pretending to be customers. At least until I get the recording going."

"So get it going," I snap, sitting in front of another display of hardware—rings and ropes and rubber cocks—so I can get organized. I screw the silencer onto my Glock 9 mm and hide my garrote and my blades around my body.

"Trouble," Wagner says half a minute later. When I look up she's scrolling on her phone.

"What?"

She hesitates.

I stand. "What?"

"The girlfriend. Kate."

My heart pounds. "What?"

"She's in there with him."

A fist grabs my belly. It's not because my mission just got ten times more complicated. Scratch that—a hundred times more complicated. And it's not because the agency's intel got something so big so wrong.

No, it's more twisted than that.

It's me hating that fact that Kit's in a place like this with *him*.

I've wondered whether they were together. God knows I've spent enough time trying not to picture it.

And now Kit's here with Polzin? Playing these sorts of sex games with *him*? I imagine Kit gazing down at him from on high like a bird of prey, expression suffused with harsh affection. Pale skin. Pale hair. Clipped orders in that cut-glass voice: *Shoulders back. Get that chin up. Spread those thighs.*

Polzin wouldn't be able to resist it—how could he? The way Kit looks at you. His amber eyes. The way he stands.

Or does Polzin boss Kit?

Polzin's a known sadist.

I suck in a breath. My skin under the leather vest feels clammy. No, Kit wouldn't like that, would he?

"What are you thinking?" Wagner asks. "Do we call it off?"

I frown as I work my long blade into the vertical pocket at the side of my calf.

"It doesn't make sense," I whisper, just to say anything. "You had his pattern as him coming alone with a paid sub that he'd pick up on the way. That was the intel. Him and the sub alone in the room. A few bodyguards in the hall."

"The sub's there, but they're not alone. The girlfriend came along, too. I don't know, maybe she's got a jealous streak or something."

I nod.

Fuck.

She takes a few steps toward me. "What are you thinking, Will?"

Truth is, I'm barely thinking at all.

"Maybe he has them both tied up," she says unhelpfully. "They're sure to be distracted, in any case."

I shake my head. "Kate is very..."

Wagner waits patiently to see how I'll finish that sentence. I should tell her about Kate. Kit.

"She's very perceptive," I say finally.

"You need to call it off?"

I rub my forehead, picturing burnt, twisted bodies in a bombed-out truck. My men. They trusted me. It was me who should've been blown to bits. I made the twelve of them stay behind so I'd be the only one in danger, and it got them killed.

It was Polzin who sold us out to the other side, but there on the ground, it was my call that got them killed. "No," I say softly. "He needs to die. Today."

"Okay, then." She holds out a hand, and I take it. She pulls me up with a grin. "Well, you *look* badass. So there's that."

I smile. "Too badass for the likes of you, Agent Wagner."

She snorts and lets me go. At a table in the center of the room, she attaches her iPod to a cylindrical speaker and turns on a soundtrack of loud moans and mumbles. I slip a blade into the outer pocket of my fingerless gloves, then I check the chamber and shove my piece into a pocket inside my porno barbarian's vest. Not the kind of outfit a man wants to die in.

Such a ridiculous thing to be concerned about.

She shows me the schematics on her phone once more, speaking softly. "There's a waiting alcove here, a water dispenser here that our guys moved to create sightlines to the door of Polzin's suite. He has two of his Russians on the door here. I'll take them out if I see them unlocking it. Wait as long as you need for a good shot at Polzin. Our intel is his sessions are usually two hours. If you get done and clear, slip back to our room and text me. We'll go out the back way. Simple. Just how you like."

If.

"Sure. Simple." I pull off my hat and toss it aside. I can live with dying in the rest of this outfit but not the hat.

There's the sound of a whip and a squeal on the recording.

I force a smile. "I can see you guys had a lot of fun making that tape."

"It was pretty funny." She sticks out her hand. "Good luck, Will."

I take it and shake. "You too."

She puts on a robe and shoves a knit cap over her hair and slips out to play the waiting game in the alcove.

I take a deep breath and head for the far wall. I find the door easily between red cushioned panels, next to the St.

Andrew's Cross. I pop the catch, then slip into the low-lit corridor. I pull my flashlight from my holster and play it around the space, all shadows and musty undertones. Plumbing and electric run above, bare concrete below. According to the schematics, Polzin's suite is some twenty yards up. I flick off the light and move quiet as a mouse up the length of it and around a corner.

A tingle at the back of my neck. Is something wrong?

Or is it just the idea of Kit in there with him, doing lord knows what? And what do I care?

Kit's a killer, too. Maybe not so vile as Polzin—he's only killed other contract killers. That I know of. Anyway, he has to go now. We're all going down.

Still, something nags at me. I stop, unable to tell whether it's my battle instinct or something deeper and baser.

Get it over with, I tell myself, heading onward.

I reach the door to their suite. I shove in the earbuds and press the small plate to the door.

A man grunts. Heat steals up my neck as I hear female panting. Not Kit. Kit's tone is different. I'm glad Kit isn't making noise—maybe he's just watching.

Stupid. I should *want* Kit making noise—noise would give his position away. He's the one I need to worry about.

I grope around for the finger hold, planning to pull it out slowly, quietly.

That's when I feel the blade at the back of my neck.

"C4," comes a whisper. "Arguably the worst bone in the neck to sever. Though I say they're all bad."

Kit.

"Hands up on the wall."

I comply, heart thudding. He pats my vest, removes the earbuds, the blade, the nine. He kicks apart my legs and moves downward.

Lust and fear surge through me. He's got his blade at the main artery in my thigh as he pulls my blade from the pocket next to my calf. Assured death if I go for him. He pats his way back up. My cock goes hard as steel under his touch. He straightens and continues on up to my gloves and finds the last blade.

"These are nice," he whispers in my ear.

"I thought they were a bit much," I say.

"Of course you would." I can hear the sad smile in his voice. A rustle behind me. "Hands crossed behind your back."

I comply. I feel a tuff-tie close around them—tight. Naturally. Kit's a pro.

"Come on, then," he says. "Turn around. We'll leave the lovebirds alone." He nudges me, and I turn.

He's in some kind of outfit—a Roman slave or something. He has my Glock in his hand, and he's fucking beautiful. My stomach twists.

"Why couldn't you have left well enough alone?" he asks.

"You know why."

He sighs. "How many others are there?"

"Just me."

"Will." His obvious annoyance at the lie makes me feel stupid.

"Okay, I came in with one other, but that was just to get inside. I'm working alone."

He watches me for a few seconds, then he gestures with the gun at the closed panel. "Is she in there?"

I wonder why he assumes my partner is a woman, but then maybe it's no assumption. Maybe he saw us earlier. I think of Wagner loitering outside in the corridor. *Fuck.* I should have told her about Kit. She promised to get out. Will she? She didn't seem entirely on board with my plan.

I shake my head. "She's gone," I say firmly. "It's just me."

He gives me his silent attention for a few seconds, and it's like he's reading me. It's fucking unnerving.

"Do you know," he says at last, like he's sharing a secret with me, "I don't think I believe you. I think your partner is still here somewhere and you're playing the cowboy." He cants his head to one side and considers me again, like I'm a puzzle.

All the while he holds his piece on me, steady as the moon.

As the silence stretches, I become more and more convinced he's going to shoot me right here.

My heart pounds, waiting, ties biting into my wrists behind my back. I feel like some yawning chasm is opening up in my chest as I face the fact that this, *this*, might be my end. I die without taking out Polzin.

That's not how it's supposed to go.

He flicks his amber gaze up and down the length of my body.

"So let me get this right," he says at last in his very precise English voice. "You and this woman came in here posing as customers?"

I let my gaze travel over the slave-girl getup he's wearing. "Looks like we're not the only ones."

He unbends enough to smile at that, one corner of his mouth lifting in a self-mocking hitch. "Do you like my outfit, Will?" Without waiting for an answer, he adds, "Anyway, how do you know I'm just posing?"

Again I conjure up the image of him kneeling before Polzin in that thing. I swallow hard against my disgust.

Kit notices, naturally. His eyes go wide with surprise, and he lets out a short, humorless laugh. "What? You can't really think that I'd—" He breaks off, then adds in a dangerous, silky tone, "Have you forgotten already how our last encounter played out, Will?"

I swallow again, only this time it's not because I feel nauseated. It's because of the excitement that's started writhing in my guts. It's because of the way that amber gaze is fixed on me.

"And let's face it," he adds coolly, arching a single brow, gaze moving over my barbarian vest. "You're no dom. Leather or no."

My breathing's grown heavier, and despite the threat of fatal violence still hanging between us, my cock has started to fill.

Fuck.

It seems he remembers our last encounter as well as I do.

"You know, as enjoyable as this conversation is, I think we'd better take it elsewhere, don't you? How about we go to your room? I assume you and your partner have a room?" He offers a mocking smile. "Seeing as how you were posing as customers."

I frown, hoping he doesn't see the tic I can feel pulsing in my cheek.

Kit laughs softly. "There is only a handful of rooms on this stretch of tunnel, and I'm pretty sure I know which is yours. But why don't you lead the way?" He gestures with my piece, and I go.

I'm amazed he hasn't ended me yet. He warned me he'd kill me if I went after Polzin again, and the man is nothing if not a pro. The only reason I can think of—unbelievably—is that he can't, somehow.

This man who has coolly dispatched each and every hitter that's been sent after Polzin for the past two years can't—or won't—do me. My heart pounds.

"Is this the room, Will?" he asks softly.

I stall. Wagner better have left, dammit.

"Let's take a look inside, shall we?" Something about my reaction has confirmed his guess, and he's not wasting time asking more questions. "Not that I don't believe your story about your partner, but I always like to be sure."

"Fine," I say—or, rather, croak, my voice giving out on me as my mind races ahead, looking for a way to turn this clusterfuck around.

He stretches one arm and releases the small catch at the top of door with a snick, keeping the Glock pressed up close against my back. I feel the fabric of his tunic brush against my bound hands.

A whisper of touch. It's comforting.

"Push the door open with your body," he says. "Nice and slow. I'll be right behind you, so if there's anyone in there, you're going to be between me and them. Best to remember that."

I push the door open like he says. There's the sound of a woman moaning, the crack of a whip, then the duller sound of impact. I sense Kit stiffening behind me, and the Glock presses harder into the center of my back.

"You said—"

I lead him in. "It's a recording. See?"

He pushes me forward, into the room—just like I want. While he's looking for the source of the sound, I break away and lunge into one of the upper arms of the St. Andrew's Cross. My shoulder crunches painfully as I use every last bit of my body weight to dislodge the hulking thing from the wall. I spin-kick the fucker into Kit.

Kit yells. There's a thud as he hits the ground, then the sound of something—my Glock?—skittering across the dungeon floor.

I curl onto the floor, quickly pulling my arms under my legs and back in front of me, and then I spring back up.

My wrists are still bound, but they're in front of me now. Back in business.

Kit's dazed, but he's up—and he's going for my Glock.

I dive for it, sliding into it like it's the most important home base of my life. I grab it quick and hop to my feet, aiming for his head. "On the ground. Slow."

He raises his hands partway. Just enough to be dangerous.

"I don't think so," I rumble. "All the way."

He eyes me with that bird-of-prey look. Gorgeous. Lethal. He raises his hands all the way, lithe and fierce in that slave-girl outfit. Kit with his hands raised is nothing like a capitulation and everything like a taunt.

My mouth goes dry. "Knees."

"Me on my knees? You sure that's what you want, Will?"

"Knees. Now," I growl, pretending not to catch his meaning.

He lowers himself to his knees before me, cool and calm.

"On your belly, legs spread, fingers knit behind your head."

He just watches me.

I've been outnumbered in battle more times than I can count. I've disarmed dozens of enemy combatants at a time—groups that could overtake me by rising up with the right coordination. How does one man at the business end of my Glock feel so dangerous?

I circle around to the back of him. "Do it." I plant a foot at the center of his upper back and give him a light shove.

He falls over, catching himself on his hands.

"Legs spread. Fingers knit."

He complies, finally.

I focus on his sandals—strange strappy things with a leather strip up the back.

"Well, wouldya look at this." I kick his foot, forcing his legs apart some more. I lean down and slide the blade out the back of one of the sandals. My knuckles brush his smooth, muscular calf. The bloom of electricity shocks me. I ignore it.

"Thank you. Don't mind if I do," I say as I use the blade to cut my wrists loose. The tie pops off. I slide out a second blade from the other sandal and tuck both of them into one of the pockets of my ridiculous vest. Now that my arms are free, the circulation's coming back.

Kit's down on the floor. I tell myself this room is under control.

I slide my Glock into a pocket where I can get at it quick and pat him over, looking for his other weapons. I push up his skirt and find the holster, high on his thigh. The piece can only be pulled out from the front.

"Turn over. Slow. Hands nice and high."

He turns.

I feel his eyes on me as I push his skirt up from the front. He has some kind of white silk briefs on, except they're way tighter than normal tighty-whities. Looks like they're smashing his cock and balls into submission. His junk's all wrapped in that tight, tensile silk. The pressure must be intense.

All I can think about is ripping that silk away and taking him in my mouth. I remember the taste of him vividly from last time; being so near him like this again, it makes me dizzy.

It's with Herculean effort that I get back to business, forcing my gaze downwards to the white holster wrapped about his right thigh. The leather looks soft as butter.

Fuck.

Swallowing hard, I unsnap the flap, pull the nine, and quickly flip the skirt back down over him.

"Spoilsport," he pouts. "My Sig's the least interesting thing under there. Why not take another look, Will? I know you want to." His voice is taunting. Flirtatious.

"Your piece is plenty interesting to me." I examine it with pretend fascination. "Platinum, Kit? Really? Black not glamorous enough for you?"

"Platinum goes with my ankle bracelet," he says, a sly little smile teasing one corner of his beautiful mouth. His voice is like slivers of glass, just digging into me. "You like the outfit, Will?"

Goddamn, I want to kiss him.

I stand over him with that platinum nine, still warm from his thigh, in my sweaty paw and with my mouth gone dry. Feels like all my words have dried up too—I'm just standing in front of him like a dope, staring at him.

"Roman slave girl, huh?" I manage at last, just to say something.

He smiles, slow and wicked. "We could have some fun."

The platinum piece *does* go with the ankle bracelet.

"Sure thing," I say. "Once I've taken care of your boss, we'll get right to it, baby. Just turn over so daddy can get you all nice and secure before he goes to work."

I mean it to mock him, but he chuckles like I'm the idiot. Smarting, I nudge him roughly with my foot. I need him back on his face, hands knit behind his head. Standard protocol. He casually assumes the position like it would be dickish to make me say it.

Like it doesn't put him out at all.

Keeping my eyes on him, I go to the line of hooks on the wall and pull some heavy-duty cuffs from the large selection, plus a couple of thin, strong chains. "This place is full of shit till you gotta tie somebody up for real," I say. "Then it's actually pretty convenient."

"What do you mean, 'full of shit'?" Kit speaks in a friendly, almost humorous tone, like we're just shooting the breeze in some podunk bar. Like he doesn't even need to worry about me. Like he's amused by me. And fuck if his amusement doesn't turn me on. I stifle a groan at how stupid my head is. Both my heads.

He still has his fingers knit behind his head, but now he turns to watch me. His long white-blond hair is half in his face, his pure, sharp profile just peeking through the pale strands. He looks like a goddamn angel.

I've lingered here with him too long already. I need to secure him and move the fuck on. Kill Polzin.

"Alls I mean is, it's a lotta fuss for a simple fuck." I slap the first set of cuffs on his wrists. The cuffs are good quality and sturdy with a longish chain between them—he tests the length of it immediately.

Planning ahead already.

I take advantage of his brief inattention to slap the ankle cuffs on him. He jerks with surprise—he hadn't noticed those. I'm already hooking the two long chains into place, one hanging from each wrist cuff, as he turns his head to look at me, trying to meet my eyes. I keep mine turned away. Which isn't like me. Usually I like to watch my opponent's eyes. Most guys have ways of telegraphing when they're gonna try something. But I don't want to see how he looks as I do this to him.

"What the fuck, Will?" he snaps.

"Just wrapping you up nice and secure," I reply flatly. "Don't want you following me when I go to take out your boss."

"You think chains will stop me?" he sneers. "Really? You should try a bullet if that's what you're aiming for."

"I'm not like you," I say coldly. "I don't just go around killing anyone who happens to get in my way."

"Oh, fuck you," he spits. "You think you're so moral? Newsflash, Will: If you go crashing around like a bull in a china shop around a man like Polzin, there are consequences—maybe not for you, but for someone. If you go over there and end him, fine, but don't pretend you're the white knight in all of this."

I don't respond, just grab his bicep and haul him to his feet. The lengths of chain attached to his wrist cuffs dangle past his knees. Potential weapon. I wrap them up in my fist and use them to tug him toward a bench I've had my eye on. The Sig's secure in my other hand.

"What did he do to you anyway?" Kit demands, even as he allows me to drag him to a bench. "I'll go with something personal—that much is clear. Is it a family thing? Is that it?"

I give a harsh laugh.

"Is that a no? You have family you care about?"

I shove him down so he's sitting on the flat bench. "Not much."

"Not much? What does that mean, Will?"

"It means my mom died when I was six. I got no brothers or sisters."

"What about your dad?"

I shrug, examining the bench, trying to think how best to secure him. I don't like him faceup because of the way he looks at me—sometimes even through me—but facedown gives him too much opportunity for movement.

"Come on, tell me. You're in charge here. You're about to end my career at best. Just tell me. What's your dad like?"

"He worked a lot. We're not close."

Kit's eyes seem almost to sparkle. "Lawman?"

I suppress a smile. This guy is nothing if not perceptive. "Police sketch artist."

Kit raises a brow at me. "Are you kidding? A *police sketch artist*? Who does that?"

"My dad," I say tightly.

What the fuck am I doing? Revealing so much information about myself is idiotic. I examine the bench. It's about five feet long and three feet wide and upholstered in pleather. I test the strength of the frame. Solid.

"A police sketch artist, hmm?" he muses. "That's fitting actually. Straightforward, functional drawing. No artistic aspiration. Art that isn't quite art."

"Oh, you'd know," I scoff. "What with being a fuckin' merc." I point at him. "Lie down on your back. The chain between the bracelets should be long enough that you won't have to lie on your hands."

He looks at me for a moment, and his expression is weird. Then he glances away and lies down. Sure enough, the chain is just about long enough that he can have his hands on either side of his hips, though the chain's pulled taut behind his back and probably digging into him. Well, at least he's not lying on his arms.

The bench has straps built in that go round the waist and chest. They're secured with clips like the ones you get on a backpack, so they're easy to fasten with one hand, while I keep the gun trained on Kit. As I tighten the thick fabric straps over his torso with a couple of rough yanks, I can't help circling back to what he last said, even though I know it's just playing into his hands.

"What did you mean by that?"

"Mean by what?"

"When you said it was 'fitting' my dad's a police sketch artist?"

His eyes gleam. "The way you went after Polzin last month? Like a bull in a china shop? There was no art to it, no finesse. It was so…functional."

"And I almost got him," I say, annoyed.

He eyes me challengingly, the motherfucker. Lying there on his back, strapped to a table, immobile and helpless, and still looking down his goddamn nose at me. "Not even close, Will."

I scowl. "You know what your trouble is? You don't know when to stop pushing."

He laughs. "Oh, stop flirting and just suck my cock. You know you want to."

He's right, but what I want to do and what I will do are two different things. "What I know, *Kit*—" I say his name in the most condescending way I can. "—is that I got you all tied up like a Christmas ham and you still think you're running the show."

"Oh, Will, a Christmas ham?" This like I've disappointed him. Wounded him. "A *Christmas ham?*"

"And if you don't shut up, you'll find yourself wearing one of those red balls in your mouth. Is that what you want?"

He just laughs again. Laughs in my face, and now my banked-up anger is flaring, and I *know* I'm being a fucking idiot, letting him get to me.

Secure him and go.

I make myself look him over. He's flat on his back, arms tight to his sides, torso strapped firmly in place. His legs are still free—though not for long. I tuck the Glock into my vest. I feel his sudden, narrowed attention on me as he watches my hand, tracks my movement. I can practically hear the gears in his brain turning.

In one smooth, swift movement, I grab his lower left leg, bending and pushing it forward before he can react, hooking the chain hanging from his left wrist cuff to an eyelet on the ankle cuff. He strikes out at me with his right foot, but I anticipate the kick, jumping back, though he still manages to catch me a glancing blow in the chest that has me grunting in pain. Fuck, but that's gonna leave a helluva bruise tomorrow.

I go for the right leg then, same deal. He knows what's coming this time, but now he's more than eighty percent tied down, and the outcome's inevitable. He still doesn't give in, though, struggling for all he's worth, till I finally have the second chain in place and stand back to look at my work.

I nearly come, just from looking at him.

The length of the two chains keep his feet off the ground, forcing him to bend at the knees; his long legs are suspended and held wide open. The skirt of the tunic has ridden up over his hips, revealing those tight, silky briefs and his flat, lean stomach. He's quite the sight—helpless, yet fierce. Expression furious as hell.

I want to touch him bad, but I know better. Instead I reach out and slide a finger under the delicate chain of his ankle bracelet, which circles outside his sandal straps. "Guess it does go with the piece," I say.

He jerks his leg, but it just underscores who's in control here—me. The ankle bracelet's a pretty little thing with a silver charm attached, but it's really his smooth, pale shin I want my hand on.

I force myself to stay focused on the charm. There's a picture of a boat on it. I squint at the inscription below the boat. "Something...Island," I say. "Madeline Island. What is that?"

"You don't know? It's in America."

"I don't know every place in America." I release the little thing and watch it fall back over his ankle, wishing it was my fingertips grazing his skin instead of some cheap little piece of metal. "Is that a place you've been?"

"It won't work, you know," he says. His voice is as silken as ever, and just as sharp. I don't know why it makes me so hard. It's that Brit kind of sharpness—smooth, but cutting.

"Oh yeah?" I say, adopting a flat, uninterested tone. "What won't work?"

"This attempt to dominate me."

"I don't know. You look pretty goddamn dominated to me."

His eyes glitter. "That's not how it works, and you know it."

My gut twists at his words. Despite everything I've done to him—and his total physical helplessness in this moment—he's as formidable as ever.

More so even.

And as mortifying as it may be, I find I want—*need*—to hear just why he thinks my physical control of him means nothing. Why I can't dominate him, despite having all the hardware.

I suspect it's something to do with the fact that there's a part of me that would pretty much give anything to be in his place right now. To feel the bonds on my wrists and ankles.

I flash back to that first night, in my hotel room. The way he commanded me while I was in the shower. How fucking good his words felt, just the right kind of hard, just the right amount of fond contempt. The way it felt to be on my knees in front of him, obedient to his whims. A little debased, even.

Slowly, softly, he says, "You can't seriously think I'm going to allow you to leave me here, Will."

I swallow hard, knowing the bob of my Adam's apple in my throat betrays me. I can't seem to mask my reaction to him. "Somehow I don't think you'd be much help killing Polzin."

"No," he agrees. "Not just now anyway." A pause. "Does it really have to be now, Will?"

"It's already taken too long." My voice sounds hoarse.

He watches me for a moment, eyes sharp and knowing. "It's personal with you, isn't it?"

"You could say that."

"He killed someone important to you. But not family. Who, then?"

"How about you zip it?"

"A lover?" His eyes search mine, then he shakes his head. He tries again, throwing out ideas as he watches me. "A friend...someone you're close to..."

"For fuck's sake—"

"Oh, your *men*," he exclaims then, understanding blooming. "Of course. Men under your command, yes? You were some kind of military commander, and Polzin fucked your guys over—maybe got them killed..."

"I said *zip it*," I say, too quick, too loud.

"That's it, then." He sounds triumphant now. "Fucking *military*! I knew it! Marines? But no, that's not your style, is it? Army, maybe..."

That's when I snap, leaning over him and hissing in his face, "How do you sleep at night, huh? Working for a man like that?"

His smile right then is huge—like I just gave him exactly what he wanted. "We all have our motivations, William. Mine's cold, hard cash."

My pulse races. My face is so close to his, I can feel his breath like a warm feather on my lips.

Stand up, back off, get away, I tell myself.

I can't.

Maybe I just don't want to.

"Polzin's a fucking psychopath," I bite out. "And you're his attack dog. So what does that make you, Kit?"

His eyes glitter dangerously. "A very well paid puppy."

I need to get away from his orbit, but instead I draw closer—loathing him—loathing everything. "You disgust me."

"But you still want me to fuck you, don't you?"

I suck in a breath, hating how hot that gets me.

He bucks up against me, using all the leash he's got to push his body briefly against mine, his mouth grazing my lips in a light kiss before he slumps, dragged back to the bench by his fixings.

I stare down at him, blood racing.

And in the next second, I'm on him, grinding my mouth against his, shoving my tongue into his willing mouth. My hands rip his tunic open—a shoulder clasp goes skittering across the floor.

I grunt with satisfaction when my fingers encounter his smooth, bare flesh.

I break the kiss, panting. His eyes are wild and glittering.

"For the record, I wouldn't let you fuck me," I inform him. "I don't let anyone fuck me."

"Why?"

"Because I don't."

"Whatever," he says, impatient. "Pull my cock out, then. You can blow me instead."

For a moment, we stare at each other, gazes burning, but the command in his voice is as strong as any steel.

In the end, I do as he says. A deep thrill of primal satisfaction thrums inside me as I wrench one of the blades out of my vest and slice his silky briefs from his body, exposing his beautiful, rosy dick and tight balls.

I sink to my knees beside him.

"Suck it," he demands, and I do, driving my hot wet mouth down over the musky flesh, inhaling his scent greedily.

I work him relentlessly, sucking and slobbering all over his dick. My own cock is so hard it almost hurts.

Soon enough, his panting cries are almost sobs, and his bent, suspended legs are shaking in their bondage. "Jesus, that's...fucking intense," he gasps. Then, "Stop. Get up here and show me that cock."

I pull off and clamber to my feet. The easy access leather pants come into their own as I rip them open, revealing my own massive erection.

Kit asks, "Out of interest, do you have any lube?"

I swallow hard and shake my head. "Like I said, I don't let guys fuck me."

He rolls his eyes. "Yeah, you said. But I like it both ways, and I would love to have you fuck me like this."

I groan at that. "God, *Kit*—"

His smile is wicked. "My very own stud to service me."

Just the thought makes my dick pulse and leak. What am I doing?

"Never mind," he says. "No reason you can't still please me. Done well, I like frottage just as much as fucking. Bring that big dick up here and show me what you can do. And Will?"

"Yes?" I husk.

"No hands, and no coming till after me, understood?"

Heart racing, I nod mutely, stepping between his legs, ignoring the distant voice in my head telling me to get the fuck out of there.

I consider my options briefly before carefully climbing onto the bench and draping myself over him, holding my weight off him with my arms even as I settle my groin against his, our cocks bumping, sliding, snagging, making us both moan and strain for more.

I start grinding against him, searching for a good rhythm. I know when I hit it from the pleased murmur that rumbles out of him.

I take him all in with my body, enjoying the thick log of his cock, warm and hard against my own. I would give him anything right now.

No coming till after me...

His command rings through my mind, doing wild things to my libido. *Understood?* I slow at one point— deliberately—going more slowly than I should, wanting him to correct me, command me.

"Will," he hisses bitingly. "Don't you dare play games."

Don't you dare... Just that and I nearly lose it.

I step it up, nudging our hips together, giving him what he wants.

I settle my mouth on his, then, and kiss him—almost pleadingly.

He allows it.

That he lets me kiss him like this fills me with something that feels uncomfortably like joy. My tongue in his mouth and his in mine. My fingers, tunneling into his long, silky hair as my hips drive against his.

Friction. There's almost too much friction, with just a little precum to ease the way between us. But it's good too, that friction. The stuttering snag of skin on skin. The blunt butt of our cockheads. The driving thrust and parry of our hard shafts. And God, Kit. Kit, licking at the seam of my mouth—when did I close my lips? I open them again, welcoming him inside, relishing his moan of approval, my name murmured against my own lips—

"Will..."

I pick up speed, driving harder with my hips, making worshipful love to his mouth. I can feel the strain of his wide-open body, the build of tension in his limbs, as his orgasm begins to churn.

"Kit," I gasp against his lips.

"Don't stop. Just keep...moving."

I grind against him and bury my hands in his hair and kiss him like I don't think I've ever kissed anyone else in my whole life. I don't even know why.

When I feel the first pulse of his release between us, I moan.

"Kit," I beg. "Let me come. *Please.*"

"All right," he gasps as he jerks against me. "Since you've been...such a good...ah, boy, you can come."

And I do. Like a goddamn geyser.

CHAPTER TWELVE

Kit

He collapses on me. The weight of him feels hard and good. I love that he lost himself to this. Despite the danger. Despite my men who could find us any moment. Despite his partner who could walk back in. He fucking lost himself.

We both did.

Already though, he's shaking off the after effects, raising his head, gaze distracted. Realising he's wasted precious time.

Hopefully enough precious time for Polzin to have packed up and left Cage.

Poor Will. He'll be seriously fucked off.

But what else was I to do? Let him take out the man I've been protecting for the last two years at all costs? Worse, let him walk into the middle of a guaranteed suicide mission? Because that's what it would be. Fucking suicide. He'd be lucky to stay alive two seconds after popping Polzin. My only other option would be taking him out myself—which of course is exactly what I should be doing. But that's not something I can even bring myself to contemplate.

As he levers himself off me, I say, voice soft and teasing, "You can't look at me now?"

Immediately, he turns his gaze on me. He looks...regretful, and for some reason, that fucking kills me. Stupidly, I find I very much wish my hands were free, if for no other reason than to stroke his hair. To let him know how good this was—he was.

How good he *is*.

How good, how pure, how loyal, how very uncompromising. He has no idea how rare his loyalty and steadfastness are. Well, he wouldn't. It's all part of the package.

I find myself filled with some strange emotion. Not wanting, precisely, though there is that, but something more. Yearning maybe. Longing.

Longing. Jesus Christ, is that what it's coming to now? Like I'm some fucking consumptive Victorian poet?

Disgusted as I am with my own sappiness, I still drink in his dark, burnt umber gaze with a pang in my chest. He's such a principled fucker, this Will, so very different from me. Even when I'm trying to do the right thing—because, yes, that's how I started out—somehow I end up on ugly, twisting, downward paths. Over the past few years, my good intentions have left behind a staggering amount of wreckage.

Tonight's just another episode on my ruinous primrose path. Already, I can't stand how much I've polluted what happened between us. Within a few minutes, he's going to be feeling sick and wishing he'd never met me.

Again.

He'll realise I've used the chemistry between us to help Polzin get away. That I've betrayed the gift of trust he just gave me when I demanded his obedience. His service. I hardly know this man, but I can tell he's all trust, all uncompromising principles. Those things are his strengths, but they're his Achilles' heel, too. There for somebody like me to exploit.

They'll be what gets him killed in the end, too. And the worst of it is, I'm not sure he even cares about that, so long as Polzin pays. The way he took me down earlier? That was fucking suicidal recklessness.

He must've loved his men a lot, to go after Polzin so hard. I bet he was a damned fine leader to them. Brave and fair. Somehow—I'm not sure how yet—Polzin was instrumental in Will's men getting killed, and Will's here to make it right. That's how he sees it, I bet—making it right. I called him a bull earlier, and yes, he's like a bull, seeing red, insensible to the dangers lurking in the shadows, the people in his way who might not be so pure and good. The people who aren't direct like him, but twisted up and compromised beyond repair.

People like me.

He doesn't know—or more likely, doesn't care—that a bent, twisted-up, deeply tarnished sword can kill just as readily as a straight and true one. Sometimes more readily, because men like Will don't see it coming.

"You need to stop, you know," I blurt, surprising myself as much as Will.

His mobile mouth twists in a sly grin. "You didn't want me stopping a minute ago."

I don't smile in return. "You know what I mean."

He looks at me, steady for a moment. Then he says, "I can't." He levers his big body up and away from my bound and aching one. He's covered in cum. He glances down at the mess, then looks around, his gaze searching. Already his mind's moving on.

"Cleanup stuff's in the wooden cabinet by the door," I say, as much to bring his attention back to me, as to help him out.

He just nods without looking at me and makes his way over there, the crotch flap on his leather trousers hanging loose, gorgeous cock still half hard. He opens the cabinet door and, out of view now, rummages inside.

It's here it occurs to me that it's possible I'm being over-confident about Polzin having left. Dmitri could've missed the message I sent him ordering him to herd Polzin out of Cage when I had Will in the back passageway. Even if he did get it, Polzin could've been difficult. He's hard to manage when he's in the middle of an assignation like this.

A little more delay would be no bad thing.

"Hey, you better clean me up before you go anywhere," I grumble loudly. "Your jizz is beginning to itch."

He just grunts, but a few moments later he emerges with a pack of wet wipes and comes back to stand over me, expression neutral as he opens the seal and fishes inside. I've lost his attention now. I can see his mind's wandering back to the job he's supposed to be doing.

He cleans me up briskly with a few cool swipes, removing all traces of our mingled come. It's all pretty matter-of-fact, but for some reason I feel stupidly, weirdly emotional about it. Just the fact he's actually doing this, despite everything. Because I asked him to. Or maybe he'd have done it anyway.

This man and his straight-down-the-line, honest-to-God, do-the-right-thing principles.

My eyes prickle, and I blink irritably. It's the wipes, I tell myself. They're probably meant to be lavender or something, but they have the harsh scent of toilet chemicals.

When Will's done, he pulls my skirt over my groin, hiding my nakedness below the waist. He covers my chest too, yanking the fabric of the tunic back up, though he can't fasten it in place—I lost one of my shoulder clasps during the sex. Luckily it was the left one.

"That's better," he says, not sounding convinced as he eyes my bound form uneasily. He stands and casts the used wipe aside, quickly plucking out a few more to clean himself up with. "I'll come back, Kit. After I deal with Polzin, I'll come and untie you. Okay?"

I hiss out an impatient breath. Is he really that stupidly principled?

"Do you have no sense of self-preservation whatsoever?" I ask, my words dripping acid. "The things I've done to protect Polzin would turn your hair white. Would you really mistake me as your ally? Your friend?"

He ignores me, his expression calm as he turns his attention to his pants, snapping himself back up. "I'm not thinking friend, exactly," he drawls.

"Correct. I'm not your friend. You'd do well to remember it."

"Whatever you say, boss." He finishes putting himself back together, snapping the snaps. I study his generous features. If I painted him, it would be a study in blacks and browns. The richest browns—umber and sienna. Everything elemental. "But I'm willing to bet you wouldn't kill me."

He's an idiot. A certifiable idiot.

"That would be a mistake," I warn. "A very dangerous mistake."

He slides my platinum piece inside his vest. Puts his Glock where he can get it. My blades go in his side pockets.

All of sudden, I find his Zen-like calm utterly infuriating.

"Do you honestly think they would want you to do this?" I demand. "If you could reach out to them? If you could ask them?"

His gaze snaps up to mine. I'm talking about his men. He knows it.

"Would they want Polzin dead?" he snaps. "Damn straight they would."

"Forget Polzin. Would they want *you* dead? Charging after him like this, over and over? Eventually, it'll get you killed—you know that. It's absolutely *fucking* senseless."

He shrugs. "It's not senseless if I succeed."

"And what if you don't succeed? What if Polzin lives and you die? Your men are already dead, Will. You can't bring them back. And if you could ask them, I bet each and every one of them would tell you the same thing. They'd tell you to move on."

His jaw tightens. "You don't know shit."

"You were leading them how long? A year? Two? Three?" The cant of his shoulders tells me I'm warm there. "Enough for them to respect you. Trust you. Maybe even love you."

He fixes a hard gaze into the corner of the room. That's part of the pain, I can see. They trusted him, and he thinks he let them down somehow. I say softly, "They'd want you looking toward the future. Not trapped in the past like this. Fighting until you die, too."

He cuts me a sullen look. "I'm thinking I should've put that red ball in your mouth," he says. "That's what I think." He shoves the last of his weapons into his outfit. Ready for the kill. "You want me to come back here afterwards to free you or not?"

"No," I snap. "I can free myself, thanks."

His eyes narrow. All told, I reckon we've been in this room alone together, what? Twenty minutes, tops?

This time when he turns away, his step is swift, and he doesn't look back as he leaves the room. I hear the click of the door to the hall passageway. His footsteps, jogging, growing fainter.

Dmitri better have gotten Polzin out of there—he's had fucking long enough.

I tip my head toward my right shoulder and, reaching toward the remaining clasp with my tongue, eventually manage to press the catch and hit the button to call for backup.

While I wait, I remember how Will's mouth felt on me. His tongue. His cock. The rich timbre of his voice and the way it cracked when he begged. His fingertips skating over my skin when he examined my ankle bracelet, how much I loved the feeling of his hands on me, though I can't say I loved him looking at my lucky charm.

I shouldn't wear it, but it was my mother's, and it reminds me of her. Of them. Her and my dad.

I need that sometimes. To remember why I started this, even though I'm doing it for different reasons now. Now that I know what I know.

The first time I saw the charm was the week before the bombing. My father had brought down a box of stuff from the attic, and we were sitting round the kitchen table of our little house in Clapham. There was a map of Wisconsin in the box, and he spread it out, pointing to a swath of blue above the state, and when you looked closely, you could see small islands above it, spraying out into the blue of Lake Superior. He pointed to the largest of them. *Madeline Island,* he'd said. *The only way you can get to it in the winter is by snowmobile. It's only for us to know about, though. A secret.*

I'd asked him whether we were going on holiday there. I'd been hoping for Disney that year. Theme parks and swimming pools. He'd seen my disappointment and had brought out photos from the box—ones taken before I was born—to show me how great the island was. My mother in a rowboat. The two of them in a restaurant, heads together, grinning at the camera.

I remember it was the first time I'd seen my mother smile in ages, that night, as she looked at those old pictures. In her last weeks, I used to see her looking at my father with this sad expression all the time. But that night, at least, she'd been happy.

My father's grin as he pulled out the charm. *Remember this, Mandy?* A silly present he'd bought for her. She'd idly played with it for a while, then set it aside. It hadn't been put away with the other things.

I found it on the kitchen floor the next day and put it in my pocket. I was glad about that later. A lot of the stuff from the Clapham house got taken away after the bombing. Archie managed to recover quite a lot of it, but the Madeline Island box wasn't among what was left.

Maybe MI5 kept it, or maybe my father disposed of it—he seemed to be disposing of a lot of things in those last days. Looking back, he obviously knew things were going south at that point, that whatever he'd done was about to catch up with him.

Madeline Island was their getaway place. I see that now.

I often wonder what would've happened if we'd made our move that night. People always think they have more time than they do. It seems my parents were no exception.

Perhaps we would've spent the years that followed as wholesome island people, snowshoeing and chopping wood. Swimming in the summer months under endless, blue skies.

My parents would be growing old now. Maybe I'd visit them for holidays and long weekends and we'd sit around the fire talking, arguing even. My mother loved to bake— she'd do a lot of that, I bet.

In this fantasy world, I imagine myself walking around with a clean conscience—stupidly clean. No flashing on the eyes of dying men. No sickening thoughts about how easily flesh and tendon give way when a freshly sharpened blade is pushed gently into a man's neck.

I picture the heart of this other Christopher Sheridan, inside his chest, red and healthy, beating strong and true, instead of the twisted dark thing I have now, with its hidden veins of ochre and olive.

That Christopher would go to sleep at night with nothing more on his mind than his art.

His world would be brighter. It would contain more primary colors.

Gleb finally strolls in, mouth twisting in an amused smile as he takes in my predicament. I'm glad, now, for the pulled-down skirt and pulled-up tunic. It's bad enough him seeing me bound.

"Is Polzin gone?" I snap.

He nods his square head. "He was angry."

Yes, he would be.

"Get me out of these chains," I say in Russian. "Key's on that hook." I signal it with my eyes. Gleb knuckle-walks over and retrieves it, then starts unfastening one wrist.

I don't like him seeing me this way. Such an easy thing for the guards to laugh about later. As he unlocks me, he mutters a saying in Russian, the general equivalent of my being in a pickle.

"*Idi nakhuy*," I spit, startling him so badly he drops the key. *Go fuck yourself.* So much harsher in Russian. "Give me that key." I gesture impatiently at the place where he dropped it with my now free right hand. "I'll do the rest myself."

Obediently, he picks the key up and places it in my waiting hand, eyeing me warily.

As I begin unfastening the rest of my bindings, I let myself rant a little. "In a pickle? In a *fucking pickle*? Christ, you've got a nerve. You got us in this mess, you and fucking Dmitri, but can you get us out of it? Of course not. As usual, it's me who has to pick up the pieces."

"We didn't—" he starts, but I don't let him finish.

"You didn't check the layout," I snarl, half in Russian, half in English. "Did you even know about the back passages?" I get to my feet, suppressing a groan as my cramped muscles protest. Gleb is not a man to show any vulnerability to. "Hey? Did you?"

I wait until I have my *nyet*. He delivers it, eyes downcast.

"That's right, you didn't know." I spy the other shoulder clasp on the floor and grab it, clipping my tunic back in place. "You think it's funny I got chained up? I put myself in front of that guy's gun to keep Polzin alive. I use my fucking *head*—" I jab myself in the temple. "—to stop him from putting a bullet in me. Hell, I even managed to get some intelligence from the guy while I was in chains. And what the fuck did you do?"

Gleb keeps his gaze on the floor.

I make a disgusted noise and pull out my phone, scrolling quickly through the messages.

"Let's go." I head for the door without sparing him another look.

I stride down the hall, Gleb keeping pace beside me, glancing my way from time to time. That big ox would gut a man fast as you can blink, but letting himself be chained? That's a place he couldn't go. He might be dumb, but he knows he wouldn't have a hope of coming out of a situation like that alive, much less with information in his pocket.

When you work with guys like Gleb, you need to be able to impress them. Dominate them. Lucky that comes naturally to me, even when the guys in question top me by a head and outweigh me two to one.

Well, the bigger they are, the harder they fall.

"Where we going, boss?" Gleb asks.

"Back to the townhouse," I say. "Polzin wants a debrief."

CHAPTER THIRTEEN

Will
One week later
Baltimore, Maryland

"Just tell me who it is," Wagner says.

"A person of interest," I say, shoving the photograph across the desk at her.

She takes it. "Where'd you get it?"

"Can't say."

"Come off it, Will," she says. "I'm the intel, you're the muscle. Not the other way around."

"Okay," I say, pulling it back.

She slaps a hand over it. "Russian?"

"British."

"Connected to Polzin?"

"That's the question."

She squints at the picture. "He looks familiar."

"Are you going to run it?"

She sighs. "Yeah I can run it. We'll set the group as UK males, ages 25-40...go from known convicts and criminals, then widen it out. Sound good?"

I nod.

She writes it up. An assistant appears at her office door, and she goes to him, handing it off, speaking to him in low tones.

I thought the fucking Marines was bad. I've never seen so many assistants and layers to an organization as at the CIA.

I grit my teeth. This has to work.

I was gutted to find Polzin gone. Fucking gutted.

While I was losing myself in Kit, he was working on Polzin getting quietly lost.

I spent a good amount of time beating myself up about letting my dick get in the way of finding justice for my men. My men gave their lives. They deserve better than what I gave them in that sex club. They deserve better than me, maybe, but I'm what they got.

That's not the worst of it, though.

In the endless hours I spent on that plane riding back home across the Atlantic, nothing to do but sit like a big ox trapped in a small crate, it wasn't my men I was thinking of. It wasn't my failure to kill Polzin that burned me.

It was Kit.

It was knowing that for Kit, sex with me was just stalling for time, a ploy to get his employer free and clear. Just the job. I shouldn't care about that—it's all part of the game, and he's one of the best.

I did care, though, and the countless tiny bottles of Jack Daniels I consumed on that plane only made me feel worse.

But the sex club wasn't all a loss.

After I'd verified Polzin had flown the coop, after I headed out with Wagner and saw her retire to her hotel room for the night, I snuck back. Alone. I broke in and copied that night's CCTV.

Was it a bull-in-a-china-shop move like Kit would say? Fuck yeah. But I wasn't going to leave without something to work with, some clue about him. And checking that surveillance was all I could think of.

I took the stick back to my hotel and stuck it in my laptop. Eventually I came upon a decent image of Kit, heading out with one of the Ruski thugs, shooting the big bruiser a look of icy fury. He wore a long black men's coat, and he looked really fucking pissed. He was no longer the poised, elegant girlfriend of Russian billionaire Sergei Polzin, but someone more human. Someone more real.

I sat there in my hotel room and stared at that picture for a long, long time. The Kit in that shot was still lean and blond and beautiful, still made up like a socialite despite the coat, but I could see the real Kit now, the fierce warrior.

When I'd gone back to that club for the surveillance, I'd just been thinking about finding a clue to lead me to Kit.

But now that I thought about it, I saw Kit was the key to so much more.

To Polzin.

The CIA had run background on Polzin's girlfriend Kate already, but only on Kate as a woman. They'd never thought of running her as a man.

Because they didn't know. But I did.

We could track Polzin through Kit. It would give us a new angle on Polzin, maybe even an element of surprise.

If only I could ID Kit.

That night, I sent that surveillance still to my dad. It gave me a kind of twisted satisfaction, seeing as how Kit thought it was so funny my dad was a sketch artist. Well, Kit wouldn't be laughing if he knew what I held in my paw now. I had my dad use his sketch artist expertise and a photoshopping program to redo that scowling picture of Kit, transforming him into a man, the way I'd seen him at the hotel after that first night. I told him to take out the long hair, eliminate the makeup and jewelry, all the little things that created that untouchable persona of Kate.

Funny though. When I looked at the photoshopped picture, I realized it wasn't the feminine touches my dad had removed that made this picture so different. Not really. It was that mask—the mask was gone. Smooth, expressionless, *beautiful* Kate Nelson had been ripped aside, exposing the warrior under the surface.

A warrior with a toppy, superior look that had dropped me to my knees twice already.

This was Kit.

And he really must look different, because Wagner didn't make the connection when she looked at the picture.

She didn't see Kate Nelson.

"You hungry?" she asks.

We head out for burgers.

The results are back when we return.

Nada.

"No," I say. "He's somebody."

"You sure?"

"Run it wider. Put more men in the set you run it against."

Wagner frowns. "Facial recognition ties up our techs— it's not just a computer. They don't like us tying up the techs just for fishing."

"I'm sure. Run facial recognition. Expand it to all UK males under 40."

She calls back the assistant.

I spread out my hands on her desk, thinking about the way Kit let me kiss him that night, the way he felt—the way the buzz of his touch lit every corner of my body. I close my eyes, and I remind myself it was all a ruse, none of it real—not for him, anyway.

Sure, he came, but what does that mean? Just friction. Objects rubbing together.

It was different for me. Maybe because of the way he put me on my knees—no one ever did that to me before. Nobody ever made me want it. Now it's all I can think about, as if my whole brain chemistry changed.

Wagner and the assistant are going back and forth on the details. The assistant's not happy. Something's got to give. They talk in vague terms about other priorities. Wagner's gaze flickers to me and back to the assistant; I catch the tiniest hint of warning, reproach even, before she turns to me. "You look beat. Go back to your hotel and get some sleep. I'll call you when we've got something."

"How long?"

Her gaze is steady. "As soon as I can make it happen. We're looking at a pretty goddamn big pool here, Will."

I nod and get slowly to my feet.

She's right about one thing: I am beat. But when I leave the building, I don't head back to my hotel. Instead I go to a bar where I nurse a glass of whiskey and search sex clubs on my phone. A few hours later, I'm walking into a dive called Leather & Lashes.

It's open, but only just. There's a little desk area at the front, a bar beyond. The desk is deserted, but a heavily pierced chick in a leather bustier and jeans behind the bar spots me and strolls up to find out what I want. I tell her I'm looking for some action. She nods and pulls out her phone.

"Hey, boss. Membership query at the front desk," she says, then hangs up. She invites me to take a seat while I wait, but I feel antsy, so I stand, examining some artsy black and white photos on the wall. People getting hit mostly.

The guy in charge emerges from a side door near the desk. He's tall and built, bald with a goatee. He wears black but no leather. Businesslike but with an edge. He introduces himself as Master Tom. I have to bite back the urge to snicker at the title.

Master Tom leads me into a little office. He riffles around in a filing cabinet in the corner, then shoves a pile of papers in front of my nose—a heap of house rules. A bunch of forms I'm supposed to sign. I hand over a membership fee.

"What are you after?" He looks curious, like he can't work me out.

"I wanna try submitting." I make myself say it plain, though it makes my face burn.

He looks dubious. "Really?"

"Yeah," I say, my tone a little belligerent.

"To a man or a woman?"

I pause, thinking. I'll fuck either, but the only person who's ever dominated me is Kit.

"A guy."

He frowns at that. "I'm not sure I have anyone who's got the balls to try and top you," he says. "You strike me as something of an in-charge type."

I give him a look, cruising him blatantly. "What about you? You seem like an in-charge type."

His laugh is dirty, but he seems to be thinking about it. "Okay. Why not?"

Master Tom takes me into a space he calls a playroom. Somewhere along the way he's put on a cap—it's in the style of a cop's hat, except it's leather and there's a chain above the brim. It's like the one the stylist was trying to get me to wear to the London sex club. I thought it was stupid.

I still think it's stupid.

Master Tom talks at me for way too long about safe words and consent and shit. I'm only half-listening; the rest of my brain is thinking about Kit and what he'd make of Master Tom.

The guy drones on, showing me the equipment, explaining the way stuff fastens together and the fancy techniques he uses with his whips and crops. He makes me test how the blows feel on my denim-clad thigh, giving me the grand tour of the equipment like a shop clerk playing daddy.

Kit would have none of this. He'd know what he wanted—what I wanted—and he'd get right down to business. His authority is quiet but completely real, a core of certainty underlining every word.

Let's see that big cock of yours. Oh, and Will? No coming until I say so. Understood?

I'd be on my fucking knees before he finished the command, wanting whatever he'd be prepared to give me, a kiss or a caning—wouldn't matter which. I shiver, just thinking of it.

I'd take anything he wanted to give me, I think.

It's humiliating, but it's the truth, and I'm not in the habit of lying to myself. Even now, even after Kit hoodwinked me like he did, I'd go on my knees for him. He could have me panting like a dog, begging for his touch, pain or pleasure.

Just the thought of his palm on my rough scarred belly makes my mouth dry up.

Or his pale, clever fingers gripping my chin as he forces me to look into his amber eyes. He'd deliver some command in that chilly tone he uses that makes me so damn hard. Giving me instructions. Telling me what he needs.

Except no—Kit doesn't need anything from me. That's the thing I need to remember.

He only needs me not to kill that scumbag Polzin. Not much to build a relationship on.

"Hey. You listening? You with me here?" Master Tom asks. He's making all the right noises—firm, deep voice. Eye contact. But I just don't...believe in him.

Fuck.

"Can we just fucking do this?" I say. "Can you just tie me up and beat me now?"

Master Tom straightens up. Raises one eyebrow. "You think you're in charge here?"

I'm thinking *yes, a little bit,* but I give him the benefit of the doubt. "No."

He stands and points at the floor. "Assume the position." He hits a crop against his palm. "Now."

I make myself obey, getting on my knees. He walks around me, touches the end of the crop to my knee. "Hands there. Don't make me tell you again."

"You didn't tell me a first time, buddy."

He touches the end of the crop under my chin, urges my head up. I meet his eyes. He looks irritated. "You'll address me as master, and only when I request you speak. Understood?"

I suppress a sigh. "Yes."

"Yes *what?*"

"Yes, master," I force out. God, I sound bored. Hell, I *am* bored.

"I see. You want to make this hard on yourself. Fine. Up."

I stand. "What? What'd I do wrong?"

He gives me a look. "You know what. You think I'd let you take that tone of voice with me?"

I frown. Sure, it wasn't the *Yes SIR!* type response you'd get out of a boot camp recruit, but that's not what he asked for. His directions were unclear.

Kit's never unclear. You always know what Kit wants.

Put those shoulders back a little more—and get that chin up. Really display yourself to me. And spread those thighs more too...

My cock stiffens at that memory, and I shift uneasily. I say, "You didn't specify a tone of voice."

The guy eyes my crotch with interest, probably drawing exactly the wrong conclusion.

"Yes, master," he says, firmly and clearly. "That's the tone of voice I'm looking for. Now let's try this all over again."

He hits the floor—hard. Something goes through me. I want it to be lust, but it's more like resentment. I know what he wants, though, and I do my damndest to give it. I asked for this, after all.

I go to my knees, hands on my thighs.

He circles around me, once, then again, and then he touches the crop under my chin. "Let's hear it."

I suck in a breath, wishing we could get to the beating part. "I'm not feeling it."

Again I get the raised brow. "This won't do at all." He strolls over to the rack and puts the crop back in its place. He makes a show of picking out a large cane. He cracks it against the wall. "Usually I escalate my toys, but you're going right to the top of the class. Now strip," he says.

I do it. I don't much mind stripping in front of him. Plenty of guys have seen me naked. But I've lost my stiffie, and I don't like the idea of him seeing me soft—it'll be an insult to him after all his work.

If he minds, he doesn't show it, though. He directs me to the St. John's Cross. I step up to it and allow him to buckle me in. The cuffs are thick leather, the buckles solid steel. I should feel helpless once I'm strapped in, but I don't. I don't feel like this guy has any power over me at all, yet Kit was able to bend me to his will even when *he* was in chains.

Master Tom slides his hand over my back, pausing over the various scars, then continuing on down to the ancient exit wounds on my right side. "I don't give a fuck who you are," he rasps in my ear. "Or what a tough guy you might be. You'll call me master, and you'll mean it, and we don't stop until you do. Understood?"

I close my eyes, thinking about using my safe word— "iceberg"—just out of sheer boredom. But I stay, because surely that big motherfucking cane will be able to do what he can't. If he hurts me enough, maybe I'll be able to feel just a tiny bit of what I felt with Kit.

I need to know that Kit's not the only one who can make me feel alive.

He hits me square across the ass with a decent amount of force—no warning—and I grunt. I have the impulse to praise him, to tell him he managed a damn fine hit, but that's exactly the opposite of what's supposed to be going on here. So I wait, hoping he's got a bit more.

He does, as it turns out.

He makes it hurt, makes my flesh sizzle, all across my back, my ass. Now and then he asks me whether I'm okay, whether I understand. I'm supposed to say *yes, master* in a way that convinces him. But it's not in me even to try. The words come out robotic.

The pain is good. It doesn't bring me to my knees the way Kit does, but it feels right in a different way. It's nothing to do with the guy delivering the blows and everything to do with the pain itself. It might as well be a machine wielding that cane for all it matters to me.

It's just—punishment. Pure and simple.

The crop comes down on my shoulder.

Craaaack.

Pain spreads like a tonic.

Splack.

Again and again.

I close my eyes, remembering the sound of the explosion that took my men, all in one go. I should've thought. I should've known, I should've sensed something off, but I had to charge in there alone, the hero, ready to take all the fire.

Except it was my men who took it.

Crrrack.

If only I would've stayed back with them—just a few minutes longer. Been with them for the end. Gone up with them like I should've.

I should've perished with them.

Crrrack.

You never abandon your men.

A voice. Angry words. I open my eyes and find myself face to face with Tom. Master Tom. He's panting. Sweaty.

"I said, I'm going to unbuckle you now."

"We're done?"

"Oh, we're *definitely* done." Tom moves around behind me, undoing the buckles and straps with rough efficiency. "And you're done here. Whatever you're looking to buy? We're not selling."

CHAPTER FOURTEEN

Will

I show up at the concrete bunker-like building that goes for a CIA satellite office bright and early with two coffees in hand—one black, no cream, no sugar, and one mocha half-caff cappuccino, heavy on the froth, shot of vanilla.

I get in the elevator. My whole body aches from the licking I took two nights ago, but my step is light. I'm feeling something like hope—Wagner called me last night. She's got something.

Not done with you, I mumble as the metal cell begins to rise through the guts of the building. *Not by a long shot.*

It's not until I get off on the fourteenth floor that I realize I haven't given a thought to finding Polzin all morning—it's all about finding Kit again. I scowl. Well, I have to find Kit to get to Polzin, right?

Wagner grins at me when I reach her open doorway. She looks tired. "Aren't you Johnny-on-the-spot." She puts aside her office mug.

"That's me." I hand over her cup.

She waves at her visitor chair.

"I'll stand," I say, casually leaning against a filing cabinet. Sitting down is still a challenge.

She opens the lid of her coffee. "Tell me again why you had me run that photo."

"Hunch."

"Tell me where you got it."

"Can't," I say. "Gotta protect my sources."

"You're a freelance field agent, not a journalist, Will." She blows on her coffee, then fixes me with a hard stare. "Spill. Or you get nothing."

I stare at her, calculating. I don't want to give her this. I trust Wagner with my safety, but I don't trust her with Kit's. Still, I need to give her something to get what I want.

"I went back to that Cage place after we left that night."

"You went *back*? What time was this?"

"Around two." I gesture at the file she holds. "I saw the guy in the picture leaving with some Russian guy. I figured they were connected with Polzin. The blond's accent is British, and he was definitely in charge."

Most of that's true. My lies are mostly of omission.

Wagner frowns. "Just because one was Russian?"

I shrug.

"Jesus, Will. London's full of Russians. There's probably more oligarchs there than in Moscow." She runs her hands over her face. Yawns big. "Okay, there's kind of a weird coincidence here," she says. "But from what you're telling me, my gut says it *is* a coincidence."

"What?" I say. "Who is this guy?"

"He's nobody. That is, he's not *nobody*, but he won't lead us to Polzin." She comes around her desk and sits on the edge with her iPad in hand. She swipes a few times, then enlarges a photo and hands it to me, watching my face.

I nearly drop my fucking coffee. It's a photo of Kit in a paint-covered jeans and T-shirt, hair tied back in a loose ponytail. He's got a rag in his hand, and something else—a pencil or a paintbrush, maybe—that part's a blur. But his expression isn't; he's glaring at the camera as if he's been disturbed. And he's fucking beautiful. A lion in his natural habitat. This is him. The real Kit.

He's surrounded by easels displaying paintings in different states of completion. The paintings are dark and blustery, mostly figures, lines strong and bold and a little bit wild, as if created in a frenzy, but nothing's haphazard. The curve of an arm, the line of a leg, a cheek, the gesture of a hand—they're not life-like, not photographic, but more real, somehow. More true.

"Wow," I say.

"Yeah," she says. "This guy is all kinds of *hot*."

I straighten. Grit my teeth. "He's an artist?"

She looks at me. "Christopher Sheridan. Heard of him?"

I shake my head. "Art's not really my thing."

"I guess you'd call him an *enfant terrible*. Famously reclusive. He won a big international art prize a few years ago and didn't even turn up to receive it. No one knows where he lives, but judging from this, I'm guessing London. He has no social media accounts. No friends apparently. His work fetches big money, but there are only two official photographs of him floating out there. Well, three, now, if you include yours."

"Three photos. This one and mine are two." I look up. "You gonna show me the third?"

"This is where it gets interesting."

She swipes again, and I'm staring at four people. Two men, a woman, and a little boy standing in front of some river, boats in the background. The men are in suits—one in thick-rimmed glasses, the other balding, with a lean, spare frame.

The woman's blonde hair blows to the side. She has Kit's cheekbones and that lithe, tensile build, but she's older—early forties, maybe. Her hand rests on the little boy's shoulder. He's five or six, but he stares out at the camera with a deeply serious, almost grown-up look. Amber eyes that I'd know anywhere. A chill runs down my spine.

Kit.

"This was taken twenty-some years ago." She points at the screen. "The kid is Christopher Sheridan. His parents, Amanda and Leonard Sheridan." She moves her finger to the balding man. "Archie Reynolds."

I can hardly breathe. I say, "And the interesting part?"

"You're looking at spy agency royalty here. You'll almost never see a shot like this. Amanda was CIA. Middling-successful agent—till she met and married Leonard. Leonard and Archie were best friends at school—they went into British intelligence straight from university in the late '70s—both high-flyers. Between the three of them, they put away a hell of a lot of people, especially Leonard and Archie." Her voice softens. "Made a lot of enemies, too."

She pauses. "Amanda and Len were killed a few years after this. An embassy bombing in Sudan. He was working, she just went along—she was out of the game by then—luckily, they left the kid behind. There was no other family, so Archie stepped in and raised the kid. Some old-timers here reckoned Archie wanted Christopher to follow in the family business, but Christopher wanted nothing to do with it. Well, I guess I don't blame him. Besides, with artistic talent like that, why would you do anything other than paint?"

This is where I should correct her assumption, let her know Kit—Christopher—has definitely entered the spy business, but I just...don't. Instead I ask the glaringly obvious question that would explain why Kit is involved in this. "Was Polzin tied to the bombing?"

"Nope. Polzin features nowhere on the list of suspects. I hunted around to see if there's any connection between Polzin and the Sheridans, but Polzin's one of the few players the Sheridans *didn't* run afoul of in the '80s. They probably didn't even cross paths. The Sheridans were mostly operating in North Africa and the Middle East. Polzin was KGB back then, based in Europe. Then along came *Perestroika*."

I nod. I'd read Polzin's background file—or at least what the agency was willing to show me. Polzin had seen the writing on the wall of the Soviet Union early and had started positioning himself as an information broker through the reform years. Soon after the Soviet Union was dissolved, he'd begun to rise, accumulating seemingly vast wealth out of thin air.

"So," I say slowly. "In a nutshell, this Christopher Sheridan isn't connected to Polzin other than by the fact that his parents were Western agents around the same time Polzin was a Soviet agent."

"Yeah," Wagner says. "Well, and he was seen leaving Cage the same night Polzin was there—but we think we know why he was at Cage."

I glance at her sharply. "Why?"

"Why do you think?" she asks. "He's kinky."

My throat feels like there's a fucking rock in it. "How do you know?" I ask faintly.

She turns back to her iPad, swipes a few times, hands it back to me. "Since this is from his prize-winning show, I'm willing to bet."

The tall, narrow painting takes my breath away. There's a naked guy lying on his back, chained to a bunch of rocks. His big muscled form strains against his bonds, and his cock lies half-hard against his thigh. He wears the marks of violence on his body—bruises and lash marks—and he looks broken, hopeless. A huge bird, an eagle maybe, perches on him, its razor-sharp talons sinking into the flesh of his belly. The bird's gaze is a very intent and predatory amber. It reminds me of Kit.

I search the page for information. The painting's called *Prometheus Bound*.

CHAPTER FIFTEEN

Kit
London

In the days following the Cage debacle, Polzin is impossible. He demotes Dmitri, bringing in two new guys above him. Gleb gets sent back to the motherland on some other mission. As for me, my position is unaffected since I, at least, managed to salvage the situation, but he doesn't seem to have the same confidence in me as before.

He's also become obsessed with taking out Nero. He's worked out that's who came looking for him in Cage but thankfully hasn't linked him to my supposed ex-boyfriend from the party in New York. To my vast relief, Cage's assurances that they don't run security cameras in the playrooms turns out to be actually true. The only CCTV available of Will is of him entering and later leaving the building, and there's not a single image of his face. Somehow he contrives to be out of shot or looking away from the camera the whole time, without appearing the least bit shifty.

The female he's with isn't so fortunate. Polzin quickly identifies her as Agent Taryn Wagner of the CIA and deduces from this that the US government is bankrolling this hit. I'll have to tell Archie to pick up with his guy in the CIA about moving Wagner off the case.

"You need to neutralise him," Polzin tells me. He's in the midst of getting a massage so he's speaking to the floor, his head held stationary by the face-hole in the massage table. The masseur, a huge Turkish guy, is pummelling his back so hard it's making me wince. "I get you because you say you are best," he goes on. "So why is this American still walking around, eh?"

I'm glad he's not looking at me, glad I don't have to worry about my expression, only my tone of voice.

Patiently I say, "Like I said, we're working on ID'ing him, but from what he said to me the other night, I'm pretty sure, first, that he's ex-military and second, that from his side, this is personal. So, tell me: Can you think of any US military personnel who might have a grudge against you?"

He swears in Russian. Something impatient. "How old is he?"

I suppress a sigh. I've told him this half a dozen times already.

"I'm guessing thirty. I'd put money on his having been some kind of commander. A leader of some sort...but he lost his men. Two, three years back, maybe?" I pause. "Anything you can think of that falls into that category?"

He's quiet for several long minutes, then just when I'm beginning to wonder whether he's actually fallen asleep, he shifts, dismissing the big guy in Russian.

"Anything?"

He hops off the table and reaches for his robe. Sergei Polzin is in his mid- to late sixties with a stocky, barrel-like frame, short, strong legs, and a pelt of silvery chest hair. Silvery sideburns too, though the rest of the hair on his head is improbably black. All in all, he's kind of bear-like, lumbering but somehow effective.

Polzin crosses the room to the fridge while the masseuse packs up. He pulls out a bottle of chilled Bison grass vodka and pours himself a generous shot, which he immediately necks before pouring another large one and putting the bottle away. He doesn't offer me a drink. He's graceless like that.

Once the door finally shuts behind the masseuse, Polzin says, "There was an incident a few years ago. Unavoidable." He glances at me, eyes flat and shark-like.

I keep my face neutral. "Hmm. What happened?"

Polzin takes a seat on the big leather couch in the middle of the room and sips his vodka. "You know my new summer home on Black Sea?"

I narrow my eyes, not liking this already. "Of course," I say. It's a palace more than a home, obnoxious in its grandeur. He's very proud of it. It was recently featured in some high-class magazine article on contemporary Russian architecture.

"You know the marble there. The walls and floor."

I do indeed. White with onyx-black and gold veins running through it.

"This was the last marble of its kind from Herat, in Afghanistan. Very rare. Very difficult to acquire."

But not for somebody like Polzin.

"This marble, it was essential, the centrepiece of the home. Called for by the architects. But of course, the war." He flings his hand. *The war.* As if it was being fought purely to cause him annoyance.

"Fighting delayed mining operations," he complains. "And once they had my stone on the truck, the road was out. My construction people, they sat on their asses waiting for weeks. Every week I had to pay them—for nothing! As if they were toiling away. Finally the marble was cleared with the shipment papers. And then—the Americans came along." He nearly spits that out. "They took out the man who had assured passage."

"He was Taliban?"

"Who else up there? I had to deal with a new leader. Stupid Americans. You take out one—you just get another. This new one, he wanted intel on Army movements. He wouldn't let my shipment out. He had me by the balls with that marble." Polzin sighs.

"You couldn't use a different marble?"

He looks at me, affronted. "It was mine, paid for! The entire house was designed around that marble—how it looks at a certain orientation to the sun. You've seen it. Anyway—" He shrugs here. "—it was just intel he wanted. Nothing of consequence."

"Like what?"

"A meeting location. Time and place. The Americans were pulling a collaborator out of there. Very secret." He laughs, holds up a finger. "But nothing is secret from me, is it?"

"So these Americans were ambushed." Distantly I'm amazed by how calm I sound when my heart is thudding and my blood's pounding so hard in my veins it feels like I'm about to have an aneurysm.

Polzin responds to my question with a careless wave of his hand. "What can you do? The Taliban is crazy— there's no guessing what they'll use information for. The Americans know this."

I work to school my features as I parse the rest for myself. If he'd only say, *I knew men would die for my marble, and I didn't care,* it would somehow be less vile than pretending he had no idea what a Taliban warlord would do with that kind of information. But then, Polzin is a bully, and bullies always imagine themselves as the biggest victims. Even now, years later, he's clearly still furious about the money he lost, despite the fact such sums would have been small change to him.

I think about the gleaming veins of gold running down the walls and spreading across the floors of Polzin's big, tasteless palace, how he loves to show off the photos he carries on his phone.

I say, "So, what happened?"

"The Americans went to the meet. They imagined it was safe. Very foolish—even deep in your own territory, you should never think things are safe. They pull up and the leader..." He wags his finger back and forth. "This leader senses something about this building. He tells his men to stay in the truck. He'll go in alone and see if there's trouble."

Polzin catches my eye, and then, as if he's delivering the punch line to a joke, he says, "This leader goes in—like a cowboy. And *ka-boom!* His trucks go up behind him. It's the trucks that were not safe. Twelve men." He sniffs. "They should be more careful in territory such as this."

Jesus Christ. Twelve men for some marble.

I look away, thinking about the bleak rage in Will's eyes when we spoke about his men before. Will told those men to stay behind. He was willing to risk his life to keep them safe.

Instead he signed their death warrant.

"Twelve men." The words are out before I can I stop them, and when I glance at Polzin, it's to find him eyeing me.

"My Katerina does not approve?" he asks silkily.

Somehow, I keep my face devoid of expression, saying dryly, "I'm not here to tell you how to build your summer house."

No, I'm here to kill you.

Polzin chuckles. "They're all crazy down there."

"That they are," I agree. The whole fucking world is crazy.

I take out my phone for something to occupy me, staring down unseeingly as I swipe at screen after screen with my thumb, manufacturing a semblance of purpose even as my mind races and my gut churns.

I shouldn't be as shaken as I feel right now. I know Polzin's vile. I've always known it. There's another dozen stories as bad as this one I've already heard, so why I should I be so affected now? The white of this room—the walls, the curtains, even the fucking towels—feels suddenly too bright. Everything too bright.

I sense Polzin's gaze still on me. I've entered very dangerous territory, nearer to breaking character in this moment than I've ever been with him before. The things he'd do to me if he knew my true purpose...Christ, if he even *suspected* my true purpose.

But I can't stop thinking about it. Will, steeling himself to go into danger, to take the hit for his men. Hearing the explosion. Running back out to them. Falling to his knees as their screams die inside an inferno too hot to approach.

The horror of it gnaws at my belly.

Gold-veined marble from Herat. A normal man would feel sick just looking at all that marble, knowing the lives it cost, but I'd be willing to bet the deaths of those men only make the marble that much more beautiful to Sergei Polzin. Like an elephant's tusk. Beautiful and rare—and with an amusing story behind it.

I told Will he was like a bull in a china shop, the way he was going after Polzin, but the truth is, he's more like a bull in the ring, maddened and bloodied by the picadors' lances, except in Will's case, the lances are the guilt and rage he feels over his men. Right now, he's running at Polzin as wildly as any *toro* at a crimson cape. It's foolish, and there's no art to it. But there's something deeply honest about it. Something honourable and pure.

All my life, I've been trying to capture something pure like that—maybe because I lack such a quality myself. Both as an agent and as an artist. But Will—God, Will with his loyalty to his men and his pain and his stubbornness and the way he submits to me...

He takes my fucking breath away.

If I were a better man—a man like Will—I'd run at Polzin right now. I could kill him five different ways, and he wouldn't make a sound. It's shameful that I don't. Truly, it's shameful.

And yet I don't.

The cool, calculating part of my brain stops me.

Maybe I'm just as twisted as Polzin with my rationalisations and games. Protecting him because Archie and I have decided that some horrors are preferable to others.

Maybe Polzin and I are just two sides of the same snakeskin.

I picture the just-begun canvas standing on a lonely easel back in my sunny London studio. The piece I started before this whole nightmare with the Roc file began. It was meant to be the second part of my triptych, a continuation of the work I'd just shown. This second canvas would be *Prometheus Unbound*. But I'd left it, unfinished.

When I first started working for Polzin, I'd imagined that, with the skills I'd been taught, with the way I'd been training, that I'd find the file quickly and easily. I thought I'd be back home within weeks—a month tops. Back to my work, my father's name cleared.

I can barely believe the hubris of that now, thinking Polzin would hide the file where somebody could find it.

Christ, all the things I've done to get here, and for what? To discover that there's no way a man like my father—an agent in the game—could ever be the man I'd once so innocently thought him?

I understand so much more now. Mostly that there are no good agents.

No one who does what we do could ever be described as good. Maybe not even human. I certainly don't feel human, not anymore.

So why don't I just stop? They say when you find yourself in a hole, stop digging. But I have to keep digging. It's not just about my father, anyway. There are dozens of names in that file. Undercover agents, collaborators, informers. They'll all be in danger if the file is released.

Polzin doesn't care—those people are commodities to be traded, bit by bit, for the things he wants. The CIA doesn't care, either, apparently—to them, it seems, they'll be collateral damage to be borne if Polzin's to be taken out and his death prompts the file's release.

I can't stop now. I need to find that file.

As I'm lying in bed late at night, I still sometimes think about that half-finished canvas, collecting dust in my studio. A figure study in umber and sienna, straining muscles under tight chains that are just beginning to break. The human form suffused with agony and ecstasy, on the verge of freedom.

The purity of naked suffering. The purity of the maddened, bloodied bull.

I used to think of that canvas with a kind of longing, wanting so badly to get back to it, as if returning there would get me back to my normal life, my honest life. Back to something good. As if I would regain my better self.

Now the longing I feel when I think of that canvas, of that life, isn't a longing to get back; it's a longing for a place I can never return to.

It's a longing for lost things never again to be found.

"Poor Katerina," Polzin says. He's making a fake pout, but his flat, shark eyes are keen, watching me. "I've disappointed you, have I not?"

"Well, you know..." I shove the phone back in my pocket and fake a yawn. "That sort of marble is a bit...last decade, don't you think?" I say it dryly, almost bored. Hitting him where it hurts—Polzin's vanity is immense.

This is what I've been reduced to, scoring cheap points off a narcissistic psychopath to distract him from my abject horror.

Christ, I loathe myself.

And the worst of it is, it works. It does distract him. He frowns, thinking. "It was pictured in *Contemporary Architecture* four months ago."

I give a short laugh. "Well, there you go." As if that proves it's unfashionable. As if it's the ultimate mark of mediocrity.

With sudden clarity, I realise I can't do this much longer. I *need* to find those files. If I don't, I'm liable to lose it, in which case, either Polzin will see through me and take me down, or I'll snap and kill him. And then where will we be?

If anything happens to Polzin, those names will be released, along with details of everything my father did. And as much as I need to know the truth of that, I'm not sure I can bear that ugliness being exposed to the world. I know it's absurd to feel so protective of his memory, but when I think of what it might mean, it's as horrific to me as exhuming his grave and raking through his bones.

Not that he had the luxury of a grave. There's not much left of a person after a bombing like the one my parents were in.

Fuck.

I need to get a grip on myself. Stop thinking about what happened to Will and start concentrating on achieving the mission. Retrieving the file.

I'll start with the new potential lead I just identified. A safety deposit box I've uncovered in Rio—a city Polzin visits pretty regularly. It's not much, but it's a new lead, and it's the best I've had in a while. I'll work it like I worked the others. Pray I might find the file. If I do, I'll need to secure it before I do anything else. Protect those agents and informers.

I imagine how I'll kill Polzin once the files are in my custody. A blade in the belly can be very painful. Twist it in, pull it out. Twist it in again.

"Enough about my house," Polzin snaps irritably, dragging my attention back to him. "Concentrate on what you're good at, Katerina: getting rid of my problems. Now, you will neutralise the American, yes?"

"I won't just neutralise him," I say, though it's Polzin I'm imagining at the business end of my Sig, not Will. "I'll make him suffer." I lower my voice. "He'll never see me coming."

CHAPTER SIXTEEN

Will
Two weeks later

I sit in a rental car across from Archie Reynolds's Kensington house, looking at an image of the man on my phone. It's two decades old, but I'm sure I'll recognize him easily enough. He was losing his hair already in that old picture—he'll be totally bald now. The shaggy eyebrows are likely the same. Deep, expressive eyes.

When I knocked at the door earlier, nobody answered. An elderly neighbor passing by thought he'd stepped out with the dog.

So I wait.

Agent Wagner says he was a father figure to Kit. A stand-in after Kit lost his parents. She says Reynolds is retired.

It's this last bit of intel I question. I'm thinking Reynolds is something more than just a father figure to Kit. I'm thinking he's his handler. Running Kit as a spy. It's the only thing that makes sense. Maybe he groomed the kid from an early age to be really deep cover.

I shudder, thinking of that photo with Kit as a boy. Those too-serious, too-grown-up eyes. Were they training him to be a spy even then?

Finding out who Kit is gives me everything I need to neutralize him, to get rid of the one person standing between my blade and Polzin's chest. My plan is to kill Polzin nice and slow, to look into his eyes as I recite every last one of my men's names so he understands exactly why he's dying. Give them the justice they deserve before I cut out his heart.

If I were a cutthroat CIA agent like Taryn Wagner, I'd just send an anonymous letter to Polzin suggesting he take a closer look at his favorite bodyguard. That would be the path of least resistance. I'd enclose that picture of Christopher Sheridan in his art studio. Polzin wouldn't need anything more than that to connect the dots from Kit to UK intelligence.

The CIA wants Polzin's blackmail file out in the light, but the UK intelligence or whoever Kit's working for doesn't want that. There's dirt in there that they don't want out. Why else protect a scumbag like that?

Kit protecting a man like Polzin finally adds up. It's not Polzin he's protecting after all. Christ, maybe Polzin even has dirt on the Sheridan royal spy family itself or whatever Wagner called it. Or maybe good ol' Uncle Archie.

Would Wagner blow Kit's cover? She's cheerful and helpful with me, a friendly, efficient partner and sometimes a grumbling ally, but underneath that, she's a fucking high-performance agent who knows exactly how to win the game.

Wagner wouldn't lose a wink of sleep over a dead body-guard if it cleared the path to killing Polzin.

Not me, though. I can't do it. Especially not with the agent in question being Kit.

I can see how playing it the way Wagner would play it would leave Polzin vulnerable for a few days—give me my best possible chance to kill him.

I could take advantage of the chaos and distraction caused and walk right through those Russians. Hell, I already *have* walked through those Russians.

But I know what a man like Polzin does to people who cross him. Kit's good, yeah—but Polzin knows that. He wouldn't underestimate Kit. He'd probably have his guys disable Kit in his sleep. And he wouldn't kill him fast.

It's only right that I warn Kit that I know who he is now. That his work with Polzin is finished. I want to give him a chance to get out of there before I make my move. Once Kit's out of there, *then* I'll take out Polzin.

I tell myself again that it's not about me thinking with my dick here, though I'll admit, it's been hard to get him out of my mind. Real hard.

Sometimes I do actually manage to shut him off, but then I wake up in the middle of the night drenched in sweat, hard as rock, mind racing with images of Kit standing over me, Kit issuing commands in that icy-hot tone, so clever and worldly, gaze like a lash through the gloom.

Or specific memories will repeat in my brain like movies on rerun. Like the heart-stopping moment when he pulled up his gown that first night, the sight of his junk bulging out of those silk panties—I get that one over and over. He was so motherfucking hot. He tasted so damn good.

And I'll never forget the amazing goddamn feeling of being on my knees in front of him, waiting for whatever he would think up next. I can't believe how bad I got off on that, and how bad I crave it. How deeply I trust in it...and in him.

The thing is, you get a sense of a guy when you're kneeling for him, waiting for him to give you what you need. Just like you get a sense of a guy when you're fighting alongside him.

Or *against* him.

Fuck.

It would be easy to read too much into this. Yeah, Kit makes me come harder than any guy I ever met, but that's not why I'll give him the heads-up. There's a thing between combatants like us—a code. Rules of war. If you don't have that, you don't have anything. And that's the reason I'll warn Kit off.

I couldn't look at myself in the mirror the next day if I didn't.

Then, once I've tipped Kit off, *then* I'll kill Polzin.

Except I still have to find him.

And I'm thinking Reynolds will know where Kit is. The trick will be getting the old spy to let it slip to me.

Yeah, it's a fuck of a long shot.

But I've gotta try.

Information about Kit's alter ego, Christopher Sheridan, is all over the internet, lucky for me. After a degree in fine art, he studied painting at the Royal College of Art, later working and exhibiting alongside a group of artists known as the Strayhorn Collective before breaking off after some disagreement.

His first solo exhibit, at the age of twenty-four, thrust him into the spotlight, gaining him critical attention and sky-high prices for his work. Two more shows followed, the last being the one that included the painting Wagner showed me.

There are online photographs of that last exhibit. I studied the shots a long time, enlarging them to get a better look at these paintings of Kit's. I don't know much about art, but I like Kit's paintings. They're of myths, the write-up says. Kind of an old-fashioned subject, but there's something fresh and confident about the bold lines, the straining muscles, the wild-looking animals with fierce eyes. They have the intensity and quickilver brilliance that Kit himself has. It's no wonder he's a sensation. Well, was a sensation.

That exhibit was three years back. Nothing since then.

I don't expect Reynolds will just hand over Kit's location to me. But maybe he'll let something slip to an old friend of Kit's.

I spot him when he turns the corner onto the street where I'm parked. He's carrying groceries, and he's got a small dog on a leash—a Jack Russell terrier, from the looks of it. He has a slight but noticeable limp. It strikes me as an injury he's had for a long time.

He goes inside. I wait ten minutes, then I head up to the door and grasp the brass knocker, giving it two quick raps. The dog barks, and eventually Reynolds comes.

I'm wearing a simple black jacket and dark jeans with a white T-shirt underneath—it's the kind of outfit the men in his artists' group seemed to wear in the pictures of them. I picked up a dark knit cap, too—a few of the guys wore those—but I pull it off as soon as Archie shows, twisting it in my hands as I introduce myself as Henry Dewsbury. Dewsbury was in the collective but never pictured that I could see. I'm banking on Reynolds not being that up on Kit's friends of that era.

"Christopher and I used to share studio space," I explain. "He'd sometimes talk about you."

Reynolds cocks his head slightly. "An American." It's barely afternoon, but he smells like booze.

I smile sheepishly. "Not much I can do about that." Because trying to fake an accent is the last thing I'd do. Kit can probably fake dozens of accents perfectly.

For a long moment he just stares at me, then to my surprise, he shrugs and invites me in, even turning his back on me to lead me into the house.

I follow him down a narrow, fancy hallway, all carved, polished wood and leather and brass doo-dads. He shows me some sort of fancy room that probably has a special name, like a study or drawing room or sitting room or something. Maybe it's a library. It's got a lot of books, that's for sure, plus a whole lot of heavy wood furniture. Table in the corner. One of those big globes with liquor bottles inside.

The glassware clinks when he opens it up. "Whiskey?"

I smile. Is this guy a little drunk? "Why not."

He pulls out a bottle of expensive-looking scotch, sloshes some into a heavy crystal tumbler, and hands it to me. I sip. It's smoky. Fishy even.

"So," Reynolds says as he puts away the bottle and closes the globe. "You're looking for my godson."

"I have some pieces of his," I say. "And since I'm moving out of my place, I need to get them back to him, but nobody knows where he is." I smile stiffly, feeling stupidly fake. "Probably not a surprise to you. He's very...elusive nowadays."

Reynolds cocks his head, eyeing me. Does he suspect something?

"So you tracked me down," he says, smiling thinly. "However did you manage that?"

My face feels hot. "Christopher, uh, had me send some of his things here once—I still had the address, so I thought I'd drop by and see if I could get a forwarding address."

Reynolds raises a brow. "As you already seem to be aware, Christopher is very protective of his privacy—I'm sure you appreciate that I can't give out his address to anyone who comes calling."

I clear my throat. "Oh no, of course not. I understand. I was just thinking, maybe you could get in contact with him and see where he wanted me to send his pieces or something. He left the group on...well, not that great of terms. But it seems a shame to toss them out." I trail off weakly.

Reynolds watches me. Does he know he's making me sweat? I feel sure he does. Wagner warned me not to try field work. I could be blowing everything with this.

It's then I spot the painting across the room, over the fireplace. I know instantly it's Kit's work. It's a blonde woman in front of a brownstone. She holds onto a vertical pole of some sort—maybe the bottom part of a street sign. It could be she's in the act of spinning around it— her hair and yellow sundress flutter sideways. Or maybe it's just windy.

And she's beautiful.

I go nearer, mesmerized. It's Kit's work, I'm sure, but it also looks like Kit. At first I think it maybe is him, dressed as a woman again, until I get closer and see that the body is way too feminine and the face too mature. The features are subtly different from Kit's too, the nose a little smaller and more pert, the lips a little fuller. Her gaze, though, is challenging and amused. Yeah, the gaze is all Kit.

"The resemblance is amazing," I say, almost in a whisper.

Reynolds joins me in front of the painting. I feel his eyes on me.

"Christopher's mother," he says at last. "She died when he was a child. There was one summer—I think he was nineteen or twenty—he did nothing but paint her. Dozens of canvases—sketches too. At the end of that summer, after he'd left for the new university term, I found all of it piled up outside on the street, waiting for the rubbish collection." He sighs. "Most of it's in the attic now. I just keep a few bits and pieces down here."

My gut twists at that little story. *Christ, Kit.*

"So like him," I whisper. "Even her expression..." I should be playing it cool, but I can't seem to keep the admiration out of my voice.

A loaded silence falls over us. So fucking loaded that I finally have to glance over at Reynolds—that's how much I'm sweating it. He's frowning slightly, and I remember here what Wagner said about there being hardly any photographs of Kit out there. What an enigma he is.

It occurs to me that I've just proved to Reynolds that I actually know what Kit looks like. So that's something.

"A friend, you say." Reynolds's expression is calculating, like he's speculating on me. Deciding something. Lightly, he adds, "Or maybe a lover?"

My face heats like a goddamn inferno. "Just a friend," I mumble self-consciously.

Reynolds's lips quirk, not quite a smile. "I'm not shocked, Mr. Dewsbury. I'm well aware of Christopher's orientation—you're far from the first of Christopher's lovers I've met." He chuckles then, though without much humour. "And I doubt you'll be the last. He's very much like his mother in that respect, I'm afraid." A twist of his lips. "Easily bored."

He throws back his whiskey and turns away, heading back to the globe to refill his glass, his limp a little more pronounced than before.

"Did you say you have a few of these pieces down here?" I ask. "I'd sure love to see them...if it's not too much trouble." It's true—I really do want to see them. I also need to keep Reynolds talking. Because so far, I haven't learned shit.

Reynolds sloshes more whiskey into his glass, then glances at me, a question in his eyes, shrugging when I shake my head no.

"All right," he says. "Why not? The canvases are all packed away but I've a folio of other work you can look at here."

He shuffles over to a cabinet on the other side of the room. It's got one of those drop-leaf desks with a row of drawers underneath. He pulls a key out of his pocket and unlocks the top drawer after stabbing at the keyhole a few times. Inside, there's a large black folder. He pulls it out and takes it to the table in the corner.

"Have a seat." He nods at one of the chairs. I settle in to watch as he undoes the black ties holding the thing together.

"After his parents died, I stored away all their personal things. Before that summer, he never really looked at them. But once he started going through the boxes, he became obsessed. He poured over everything—and Amanda was a bit of a hoarder, so there was a lot of stuff. He watched every bit of video too—Len had taken a quite a bit of film of Amanda with Christopher when he was a baby. It's how he was able to capture her in his paintings, I suppose. She was a woman of great charm. Great humor. That comes across in Christopher's paintings of her, I think."

He opens the folder, and the first thing I see is a fleeting sketch of Amanda laughing. Just a few lines on the page, but there's so much life to it. It blows me the fuck away.

Reynolds stares at it, somber.

There's a pencil stuck into the fold, and Reynolds picks it up. There's Japanese writing up the side. "You probably recognize this."

"Yes," I lie. "Well, wouldya look at that."

"You wouldn't believe how quickly he goes through them."

I smile and nod. "Blast from the past."

"It's one thing he's not fickle about." I glance at him. He's holding the pencil, but he's not even looking at it. His gaze is still on the sketch of Amanda Sheridan. He sets the pencil down and shoves the whole folio toward me. "Here." He stands. "Look for yourself. I've seen it a hundred times." He limps over to the window and stands looking out as I shuffle through the pieces.

They're mostly sketches, mainly of Kit's mother, Amanda, though there are several of a thin, sensitive-looking man. Kit's father. Leonard. I can see Kit's bold, clever touch in every piece, and it makes me really want to just see him again, even though he made such an idiot out of me that last time.

I go through piece after piece. I should be pressing Archie, looking for clues, but I'm not sure how to without rousing his suspicion.

So instead I go through Kit's drawings. I get absorbed in them, I guess you could say. I feel different about him, seeing these pieces. Closer to him. Or maybe closer to who I think he might be.

After some time, Reynolds's voice interrupts my thoughts.

"As pleasant as this has been, Dewsbury, I have an appointment later today, which I really ought to get ready for, so you'll have to excuse me. If you leave your number, I'll pass it on to Christopher."

I close the folder and stand. "Of course," I say. "Thanks for the drink." I fish in my pocket and pull out a card. It just has the number of an untraceable burner phone Wagner gave me on it—I scrawl "Henry Dewsbury" on it and hand it to Reynolds.

He doesn't even look at it before putting it in the inside pocket of his jacket.

I emerge back into the daylight, squinting. I get into my rental car, driving from the passenger side, and get the fuck out of there. Archie didn't tell me anything, but I'm not completely empty-handed.

At a stoplight, I take the pencil from my pocket and study the Japanese writing. Wagner would probably be able to read what it says.

I'm more interested in how the writing got on there, because it's the kind of writing that's painted on, not factory stamped. This is some kind of really fancy, fussy pencil.

It was risky to nab it, maybe, but it was what Reynolds said—*It's one thing he's not fickle about.*

Does he have a thing about these pencils? If they're rare, it could be a lead—at least, if he's still drawing.

And he has to be. No one who draws as beautifully as Kit does would just stop. It would be like cutting off an arm. Something about those pictures of his mom, especially the pencil ones in there. It wasn't just about drawing something pretty; it was a way of knowing her, of interacting with her.

One summer—I think he was nineteen or twenty—he did nothing but paint her...

I search for art supply stores and find a pretty big one fairly nearby, but when I show the sales clerk Kit's pencil, he doesn't even recognize it. He suggests half a dozen different kinds of pencils. I tell him no go. Eventually, he sends me to another store, smaller, pricier.

Forty minutes later, I'm showing it to a clerk there, and this clerk is all over it. "This is a Taka. We do stock one of their more popular sets, but it's at the basic end of what they do..." Frowning, she unlocks a glass display case and pulls out a wooden box with the same kanji symbols etched on it as are on the pencil. There are three pencils nestled into red velvet, but it's the price tag that has my eyes popping out.

I look up to find her watching me, smiling. "Pricey, right? There are artists out there who swear by them. They sharpen well, and the wood is springy, or at least, that's what the diehards say." She compares Kit's pencil against the three in her set. "You'll probably have to go to Sakura Studio in Camden for an oddball grade like this."

"This is an oddball grade?"

She points to a small letter and number near the top of the pencil. "Yeah." She goes online and gives me yet another address.

Sakura Studio turns out to be a small, run-down storefront with a window so full of plants, you can barely see in. The sign on the door says "by appointment only." Nobody answers my knock.

I go up the side of the alley and step up on a crate to peer in the window. It's dirty safety glass behind a few rusted bars. I can see in, though. There's a workbench and a lot of tools. Toward the back is a shipping area with a laptop. The screen is lit, a screensaver image bouncing around from corner to corner.

You wouldn't believe how quickly he goes through them.

Wouldn't I though? All those sketches...

Those fancy pencils need to get to him somehow.

I yank at the bars on the window. They're rusted but firm. I run my thumb around the bolts holding the bars into place. I could loosen them up with an adjustable wrench and a whole lot of elbow grease. I could pop the window without breaking it. I could be in and out with nobody the wiser. I could take a copy of what's on that computer. The pencils are shipped from here. I could find addresses. We have addresses for Polzin's past locations, but none specifically for Kit.

Kit could have an account.

I decide to make a quick trip to the hardware store. I'll come back when it's full dark. A shopping list forms in my mind.

CHAPTER SEVENTEEN

Kit

It's been three months since I've been to my studio. Too long.

The times between visits are getting longer and longer these days.

When Archie first sent me on this mission, it sounded like it was going to be quick and easy. I'd known about the cloud of suspicion hanging over my father for a while by then and had undergone months of training while Archie put the machinery in place to get me into Polzin's inner circle. He arranged to have me set up as Polzin's new head of mobile security—shortly after the guy before me conveniently fucked up, and promptly disappeared.

I was told my job would be to look after Polzin while he was on the road. It sounded perfect—I'd have access to Polzin's heavily fortified residences while being able to follow him around the world. Such a convenient perch from which to find and snatch the Roc file. Not to mention the fact that I wouldn't have to live with the psychopathic fucker day-in, day-out.

A month, I thought. Two tops, and I'd be done with it. File secured, my father's name cleared and all my questions answered.

But here I still am. Two years later, and with more questions now than when I started out. Questions I'm pretty sure that file won't answer.

I had this idea that Polzin would spend most of his time at one of his homes, being looked after by his domestic security team. After all, how much time can any one man spend on the road?

Turns out, quite a lot. Polzin is inherently restless and rarely stays put more than a week at a time. I'm perpetually on call and have to jump whenever he decides he needs me—and this is a man who has a pathological need to yank chains. But every now and again, just occasionally, I'll get a few precious days to myself. Like right now. He's got a new toy, and he's taken her to his Black Sea palace for a week of "play." So I've come here, to my refuge.

Archie doesn't know I come here—he'd be furious if he did. He taught me that to have any kind of connection to a place or person is to have a weakness.

Remember: A man like you needs, above all things, to be unfathomable. A home, friends—these are luxuries you can't afford until this is over.

For the most part, I've abided by Archie's rules. I've abandoned my home, isolated myself from every friend I ever had, including the talented, generous artists I worked alongside at the collective I helped to found. That was hard. But I couldn't not have this one thing—my art. I just need this last touchstone to the man I used to be. One last link to a road that might lead me back home one day. No matter how fucked up my life gets, knowing I have this bolthole makes it somehow bearable.

The arrangements I've set up to pay the rent for this shithole studio are ridiculously convoluted. The money tracks through half a dozen accounts before it finally reaches the letting agency, and there's no identifying information available about the tenant. The buzzer is marked "D Smith," and there's no landline listed. All utilities and property charges are covered by the letting agency, a service for which I pay a substantial premium. The building has no CCTV. No security. No cleaners even.

What's more, when I come here, I'm very careful. I don't let down my guard until I'm safely inside the studio with the door locked behind me—that's my cardinal rule. I never take a straight route to get here. This morning I left Kate's London flat in a dress and heels. Five hours and two changes of clothes later, I'm climbing the stairs to the studio in the nondescript hoodie and jeans of an anonymous young male, my bright hair completely hidden under a knit hat.

The studio is four floors up and cramped as fuck. The view's terrible—just a grey urban sea stretching in blocky waves as far as the eye can see. But the light's magnificent.

That's what I care about—the light.

And the solitude, of course. Even though the whole studio is no more than a single room with a tiny shower-room off to the side, it feels like the wide-open plains to me. It's the only place in the whole world with enough air for me to breathe.

Today I feel particularly bad. Three months is a long time to be cut off from my work, and by the time I reach the front door, I'm shaking with a mix of anticipation and relief. I can't wait to get inside and get my hands on my supplies. I have a half-formed idea for a picture in my head. A bull, all driving, aggressive masculinity. Unthinking power. My fingers have been itching to form the lines of the image in my head, and, as I open the door of the studio and cross the threshold, I'm debating whether to start with charcoal or pastels.

I drop my rucksack to the floor and turn to lock the door behind me.

"I was beginning to wonder if you'd ever show."

I freeze.

Will.

I whirl around, and there he is—standing in the doorway of the shower-room, Glock in hand.

I stare at him, stunned. My gut's a knot of snakes, a twisting morass of fear and excitement and something that feels crazily—stupidly—like happiness.

He looks tired. Good, but tired.

He smiles at me, his gaze a little curious. "How've you been, Kit?"

The way he says it, it sounds so ordinary, so everyday. Not like a sarcastic spy question: *So, Mr. Bond, how have you been?* But like he's really asking. Like he really wants to know.

And suddenly I feel so...alone. Or maybe I felt alone all along, and his question just threw that reality into relief.

I feel frayed. If I were to answer his question honestly, that would be what I'd say. As would, *all the better for seeing you.* I'm seized by the sudden overwhelming desire to tell him how twisted-up I've been lately, how hard it's felt to keep up my facade with Polzin, as if Will is an old friend rather than my most formidable enemy.

How did it come to this? That of all the billions of people in the world, I feel closest to *this* man, who has every reason to kill me?

Which, come to think of it, is probably why he's here.

Somehow, I manage to prevent the flood of words from pouring out. I give him my coolest smile instead. "Will. What a pleasant surprise." My lips feel numb, but I sound collected enough.

"You look good," he continues conversationally, as though I haven't spoken. He steps closer, regarding me for a moment, his gaze taking me in thoroughly, head to foot and all the way back up again.

Give him nothing, I remind myself wearily. How did I get so fucking tired?

"You know," Will murmurs, "Much as I love when you dress like a woman, the dude-look is growing on me." He reaches out, sliding my knit hat off my head and tossing it aside. "You shouldn't cover up the hair, though."

I was covering it up for a reason, and we both know it. But I don't say that. Instead I say, predictably, "How did you find me?"

He shrugs. "I can be tenacious. I called in some favours, took some stupid chances." He grins then. "Fuckin' worth it for the look on your face. Not many guys get the drop on you, huh?"

I just stare at him, still struggling to take it in. *Him.* In my studio. "Why are you here, Will?"

He tips his head to the side, watching me. "Why do you think?" He seems honestly curious.

I say, equally honestly, "I don't know. I'm guessing, to kill me?"

His blunt features tighten into an expression I can't quite read. "That's what you think?"

I raise a brow at him. "You *are* aiming a gun at my heart. Is it such a surprising deduction?"

He snorts. "The gun is for my protection, Kit. I just want to talk. Can't have you trying to take me down while I'm saying my piece." His mouth kicks up at one side. "Think of it as a listening aid."

I don't know why, but I find I want to laugh. I must be hysterical. I scowl at him instead. "Can I at least sit down while we have this conversation?"

"Sure." He gestures at the lumpy sofa bed with the weapon. "Take a pew."

I settle in and lean back, arms crossed over my chest, gaze on him. Already I'm looking for a chink in his armor, and he knows it. Hence the Glock—I suppose he's got a point about needing it. "Okay, then," I sigh. "You've got something to say. So talk."

He eyes me. Then he says, "Okay. Tell me this: Why's it so important to you to keep Polzin alive?"

"It's my job," I say flatly.

He stares at me, expressionless, and as the seconds tick by, a strange dread starts to build in me.

At last he says, "It's not your main job, though, is it? Not your real job."

Fuck.

I feign amusement. "What are you talking about, Will?"

Calmly, he says, "You're not a mercenary. You're Christopher Sheridan. Your parents were Amanda and Leonard Sheridan—both killed in an explosion in Sudan when you were ten. "

Horror begins to gnaw at me. He knows who I am.

"The explosion was a suspected act of terrorism, though the culprits were never identified. You were taken in and brought up by your parents' friend, Archie Reynolds, a senior British intelligence officer, like your father."

No one has ever made me—*no one.* "How did you...?"

"Like I say, I'm a tenacious motherfucker." His voice is matter-of-fact, as though he's reading a grocery list and not taking a sledgehammer to the spun glass of my mission. "You made a name for yourself in the art world some years ago. Among other things, you're known to be reclusive—that must've proved helpful when you made the decision to join British intelligence yourself. Two years ago, you secured a position with Sergei Polzin as a senior member of his security team, working deep cover. So deep that not even the CIA knows who you are. Probably not even many of the Brits, I'm guessing. Polzin sure as hell doesn't know who you are."

"No, not Polzin," I agree, adding flatly, "Until now, I'm guessing?"

Will's expression softens. "He doesn't know yet."

"*Yet* being the operative word, I take it?"

"Let's just say, I wouldn't recommend you turn up for work on Monday. I'm guessing you don't want to be around when he finds out who you really are." He meets my gaze, his own serious. "And if you go back there, he *will* find out, Kit. This is the only warning you're going to get. Right now, you're the only real obstacle standing between me and him—and I want him dead."

"That's why you came here?" I say. "To warn me off?" My tone is calm, but inside I'm panicking as I contemplate what this means. Two years' work, gone. All of it, for nothing. I fight back panic, quelling the urge to put my head in my hands. I can't give up. There has to be a way back up.

"That's about the size of it," Will agrees, but he doesn't move. Which has to mean that warning me off isn't the *whole* size of it, whatever Will might be telling himself. The very fact that he came here to do this means something. If his objective is to get me out of the way, there are far easier ways to do that, starting with telling Polzin who I am and then sitting back to watch as the man dispatches me, leaving himself briefly vulnerable for Will's move.

Isn't that what I'd do?

"Let me see if I understand you," I say. "You believe that with me out of the way, you're going to kill Polzin?"

Will's eyes twinkle. "With you out of the way, I can kill him just fine. Those other guys of his are just goons. Easily dealt with."

I feel sick, thinking of all the pieces of my soul I sold over the past two years to keep Polzin alive. For nothing.

Gritting my teeth, I say, "You can't just kill him, Will. He has insurance—information that will harm countless people will be released if he dies."

Will's gaze narrows. "Is that your mission? Retrieving that information?"

"You mean you don't know?" My tone's caustic. "And here I thought you had all the answers."

His dark, fathomless gaze is unsurprised. And right then, it occurs to me that he knows more than I've given him credit for, a thought that's confirmed when he says, serious now, "I take it we're talking about the Roc file?"

His words drive the breath from my lungs, leave me gaping. At last I manage to get out, "What do you know about the Roc file?"

"Not much," he admits. "Possibly a bit more than you, though."

It's late afternoon, my favourite time of day here because of the way the light streams in from the west. I've never seen Will in natural daylight before, but it suits him, bringing out new richness—hints of sienna in his dark hair, an unexpected shade he probably doesn't notice or care about. The scruff on his cheeks has it, too. He's not as black as he paints himself. He's not wearing his usual all-black outfit either—his jacket is more grey than black, hanging open over a white T-shirt, a casual ensemble that does nothing to conceal his muscular build.

"What could you possibly know about the Roc file that I don't?"

He regards me steadily and silently. Does he know something? Is he actually thinking about telling me? He may not be here to kill me, but he has little reason to trust me. I wait, studying the tiny lines on the outer edges of his eyes, more obvious in this light. He laughs a lot. Or he used to, anyway. I see also that he had freckles as a boy. Wholesome as apple pie—isn't that what the Americans say? A perfect Boy Scout. Not like me. I was pale and fey and delicate as a child. Will was probably playing football in the sunshine with the other boys while I was alone in my bedroom, feverishly sketching out my adolescent desires about them.

Will says, "You believe Polzin has the file, don't you?"

I stiffen. "He doesn't?"

Will shakes his head.

"No," I whisper. "That can't be right. He's released information from it."

"He's *bought* information from it. He doesn't have it, though he likely knows who does. Though he probably doesn't know where to *find* that person. If he knew that, they'd likely be dead."

My heart punches against my rib cage as I try to absorb this new information. "The CIA knows this for a fact?"

"A fact?" He shrugs. "I don't know about that, but it's what they believe. Pretty strongly. If the CIA believes it, I'd imagine they've got their reasons."

Of course they do.

I've been working for Polzin for the past two years with two objectives: firstly, to protect him and thus prevent the release of the file on his death; and secondly, to allow me to search for it. If Will is right—if Polzin doesn't actually have the file—that's all been for nothing. It's a thought that fills me with despair. I might as well have been banging my head against a brick wall all this time.

Fuck, I *need* that file.

I get up from the sofa bed and step toward Will. Desperately, I say, "Listen, *please*, give me a week. Before you go after Polzin, I mean. That's all I ask, Will—just one week."

For a long moment, he says nothing. Then, quietly, "What do you need a week for?"

"To give me a head start at finding the file."

"You've had two years to find it already," Will points out.

"True, but I thought Polzin had it. Now I know different."

"You don't even know where to start. What can you do in a week? Besides..." He shrugs, the very picture of careless power. "...when Polzin dies, the file will come to light. Killing Polzin will bring it out into the open—that's what my CIA buddy tells me anyway. Maybe they think whoever has it will turn around and sell it on the open market or who knows. They think it shifts things enough to bring it to light—"

"And that's the last fucking thing I want!" I exclaim. My desperation is showing now, but I don't even care. Abject pleading's all I've got left, and I throw it into the mix too. "Do you want me to beg?" I demand. "Hell, I'll beg." I drop to my knees, hard, lifting my head to gaze up at him, hands on my thighs. "I'm begging you, Will. Let me have this one chance to get that file."

He looks away. As though seeing me on my knees offends him somehow. "Tell me why," he says, his tone hard, jaw hard. Even the cords in his neck seem steelier, somehow. "I need to know why."

I close my eyes, bowing my head, grinding my teeth. I'm on my knees, demonstrating my need in the most physical, visceral way I can. Can't that be enough for him? Does he have to prise my innermost secrets out of me too? They're all I've got left, now that even this studio, pathetic refuge that it is, has been discovered.

"Wanna know what I think?" he asks.

I look up at that, regarding him warily.

"I think this is about your parents. I think there's something in that file about them you want to see or—" He watches me, standing over me, calculating behind narrowed eyes—" or that you're worried about leaking out. You not wanting the file coming out into the open is personal, isn't it? Is it something you know for sure is in there, or just something you suspect?"

I want to close my eyes against that penetrating gaze, but I force myself to stay looking at him, to face everything head-on. "There's a lot of information in the file," I say. "And yes, I think some of it could be about my parents, but that's just one part of it. There are a lot of other people who could be hurt by that file getting into the wrong hands."

It's true. What I just said is perfectly, undeniably true, but in that moment, I realise something important about the file—*I don't know what I'm going to do with it.* All I know is that I need to see it. To know what it says. But after that, will I hand it to my superiors? Bury it? Destroy it? I don't know, and that's all I have right now. All I have till I finally get it in my hands. I feel like it's only then that I'll know—and that I'll find out what kind of man I really am. I press my advantage. "One week," I plead, keeping my gaze fixed on his, difficult as that is. I'm not in the habit of confession, and he's pushing me to places I don't want to go, a new country where things feel unpredictable and dangerous.

After a moment, he says, "The woman I've been working with is a real career agent. You probably know the type." He smiles at me, though it's not quite a real smile; there's too much world-weariness in it; the lines outside his eyes remain unaffected. I can't read him, suddenly. And I badly want to.

"Right now, her orders are to get rid of Polzin. So they bring me in and pair us up. From what I can tell, five years ago, Polzin and the agency got on just fine. Now they're on the outs. Who knows, in a month or two, things might be okay between them again."

My stomach sinks. What is he saying?

"What it all comes down to," he continues, "is that her orders could be countermanded any time, and that's okay with her, because she's in the game too. Just another player." He pauses. "But it's not okay with me. I'm not a player, Kit."

I know that, of course; I've known it since the first. What I don't know is what it means. How far astray he'll go. He's been given a mission, just like me. Would he disobey his orders? My voice, when it comes, sounds hoarse to my ears. "You're not?"

I watch his Adam's apple move, his throat working; his gaze is heavy on mine. The air between us feels impossibly thick. "Nope."

I wait, heart pounding, wanting him to say more, *needing* him to say more.

"If they told me to stop going after Polzin tomorrow, it wouldn't matter. I'd still go after him. I'd still kill him. They'd have to kill *me* to stop me." He pauses, seeming to consider his words carefully. "And you know what? I think that's how you are too. You're not chasing this file for MI5, you're chasing it for you. We're the same like that."

We're the same...

Slowly, Will reaches out to me, there on my knees gazing up at him. He strokes my hair, his fingers infinitely gentle. I make an odd, embarrassing noise in my throat, part pleasure, part plea, as I turn my face into his hand. His palm is slightly rough, and warm, and dry. He strokes his thumb over my cheekbone. That tiny gesture of tenderness is almost unbearable. I can't remember the last time anyone was tender with me. My childhood perhaps.

Helplessly, I kiss his palm.

I hear the thud of the Glock as it falls to the floor. He's on his knees beside me, his arms going round me, our mouths coming together in a kiss of pure desperation. He holds nothing back, and neither do I.

Distantly, I'm aware that I'm panting his name between kisses, saying *Please, Will, please,* and it's not because I want to come quicker—though I do want to come, like, *now*—no, it's because I want something from him that I've never wanted from anyone before, and I'm petrified of what that thing is.

We're the same...

We slide to the floor, kissing frantically and pushing each other's clothes aside. In every encounter we've had, Will has let me master him—and oh God, I've loved mastering him—but this isn't about that. Not today. There's no master here. Only two lovers and a desperate need that's been denied too long.

Will shoves my jeans and boxers down over my hips. We're lying on our sides, facing one another, our mouths still locked together. My fingers are buried in his soft, thick hair, and I just can't breathe enough of him in. When he takes hold of both of our shafts in one big hand

and begins stroking them together, I whimper in my throat.

The pleasure is intense. The light snag of that slightly calloused palm working me, the smooth stroke of Will's stiff, velvet-skinned cock against my own, the occasional bump of his cockhead when he pulls back too far and loses the perfection of his grip, only to regain it an instant later. His mouth, devouring me. His need and his pleasure, surging to meet my own.

And that thing—that thing that petrifies me. That thing that yawns and aches inside me. That thing that made me turn my lips to his hand. That made him cast the Glock to the floor. It's been there since the beginning, small and insistent at first, but growing since then, and at such a pace...

We're the same...

We climax together, our mingled cum pulsing warmly, wetly over our bellies.

And then, together—wildly, improbably—we begin to laugh, huffing astonished mirth into each other's mouths, only to resume the hungry press of our lips a moment later.

Gradually, we calm, easing back to look at one another's faces again. I don't want to speak. Words can only spoil this.

Will has no such compunction.

"All right, Kit," he says, his voice tender and rueful. "One week. But I'm coming with you."

CHAPTER EIGHTEEN

Will

I watch Kit's amber eyes as he absorbs this, the whole world sideways except for the two of us.

I wait. I can't read his expression, and I really want to.

Say yes, I think. *Say yes.*

Seen from his point of view, I guess it looks like I'm holding all the cards, calling all the shots. I am, I suppose, but that's not how it feels. I never feel like I'm holding all the cards with Kit; if anything, I feel out of control.

Out of control isn't a feeling I usually enjoy, but everything is different when it comes to Kit and me. This thing between us feels as powerful as dynamite, and just as dangerous. Maybe alliances between adversaries always feel like that. You're always playing with something combustible.

Adversaries. I guess that's what we are still, wanting different things. No point shying away from that. But we can work together on this one thing—finding the Roc file. At the back of my mind, I'm astonished that I want to. It means I want it more than I want to kill Polzin, at least for now.

I try not to think about that too hard; instead I take a lock of Kit's bright hair and slide my fingers down it, letting it fall in a shining ribbon that drapes over his jawline and under his chin to brush the floor. He was wearing it tied back before, but somewhere along the way, it came undone. I love it like this, loose and shining.

"You can't be serious," he says.

I'm putting it all on the line here, but I don't care. I pull his face to me, pressing my mouth to his, kissing him good and hard. I find his lip between mine and give it a little suck and his whole body responds, sliding up against mine.

This guy.

"We'll help each other," I say into the kiss. "Go all in."

He pulls back to get a look at me. He's got that sparkle in his eyes he sometimes gets—interested. Amused. "Go all in," he repeats. "*Help* each other?"

The way he says it, I think he's a little bit warm to the idea, and my heart swells. "I have a line into the CIA and whatever they know," I say. "You have a line into Polzin."

He studies my eyes, right, then left, then right.

I don't know what he thinks is in that file about his parents—or about anything. Maybe I should ask him. But the truth is, it doesn't matter, because we're the same deep down—I meant it when I said that. I may not know what's inside that file, but I know what's inside him.

"How do you know you can trust me?"

I try not to smile at that. Does he even realize he didn't ask how he knew whether *he* could trust *me*? Like that part's not a question.

"I have a feeling I can," I say. "And hey, we've gotta switch something up here, right? Turns out we're shit at stopping each other." I try to bottle up my smile, but it's hard. I like the idea of us working together, traveling together. It feels so fucking right.

"So, let me understand this," Kit says. "We're going to work together, first to recover the file, then to go after Polzin. That's your plan?" He's on his back now, his hair splayed across the cheap, scratchy carpet like a lopsided fan. And he's beautiful.

I prop my head up on my hand, looking down at him, getting my fill of him. "Yup. That's my plan."

"And which of us do you propose kills him? Because I have to tell you, it's something I've been rather richly looking forward to."

I get suddenly that he's teasing me here. He knows how bad I want to do it.

"Me. Non-negotiable," I say. "I got a few things to say to him first, too."

The shadow that comes across Kit's face tells me he knows more than I realized—about me and what happened with my men in Afghanistan.

"Names, in particular," I add. "I tell him their names while I kill him. So he knows why he's getting it."

"That's a little dangerous," Kit says. "Killing a man slowly, keeping him conscious enough to hear your whole recital of names. A lot safer and cleaner to outright kill him. In and out."

"It's how it's gotta be."

His expression is tender. "You think it'll help?"

I pause here because nobody ever asked me that. Nobody ever gave a shit. All those shiny CIA guys with their pretend sympathy that they roll out when they want a guy like me to go on a hopeless mission.

He's waiting—waiting for an answer.

"I don't know," I say. "This isn't about making me feel better. It's not like I'm expecting that."

Solemnly, Kit says, "I'll help you, Will. I'll get you to him."

I nod. We're two guys putting it all on the line for each other. Two leaps of faith. Meeting in the middle. I'll get him that file, and he'll get me Polzin.

A surge of excitement, of certainty, swamps me.

"You're away from him now," I say. "How long until you have to go back? Is it a week? Is that why you asked me for a week to find the file?"

He sighs the way he so often does. Even that sigh—I find I like the sound of it. "I never really know. A week is a guess. He's ensconced in one of his vacation homes with a woman. As soon as he gets bored with her, he'll probably call for me."

I frown, not liking what he's getting at.

Kit sputters out a laugh. "Oh, please. For *protection*," he says. "Because he'll want to go somewhere else at that point."

"Right, I didn't think..."

He raises a brow at me, haughty like he gets. "Oh, I think you *did* think it for a second there. Really, Will?" This last he bites out scoldingly. Then he runs a hand down my chest as though he's tracing my muscles. Carelessly he roams his fingers around the contours of my chest, a young prince surveying new lands. I roll my shoulders back a little. Christ, I'm *displaying* myself to him. A weird mix of excitement and embarrassment unfurls in my belly.

Kit pauses over a scar on my belly, fingertips whispering over the puckered skin. "Shrapnel?"

"Yup," I get out, my voice husky.

"Did they get it all out?"

"So they say."

He slides his hand up and up, drifting past my collarbone, my throat. Eventually, his fingertips light on my lips, to the scar there. It's so pale, so faint, most people don't notice it. I forget about it more often than not, but Kit sees it. Kit sees a lot. It's the artist in him, I suppose.

"This one's my favorite, I think. It's right on the bow."

"You like that?"

He smiles. "You'd look far too pretty without it. How did you get it?"

I kiss the tip of his finger.

His eyes flash as he draws it away. "How?"

"Grade-school rumble."

"Were you stealing some poor child's lunch?"

"Hey, I'm a good guy!" I protest. "It was over a dodgeball game."

"*Dodge*ball?"

Jesus. The perfect, cut-glass way he says that. Like he's never heard of dodgeball. And maybe he hasn't.

"You don't want to know."

Kit chuckles, and suddenly I decide he knows exactly what dodgeball is. I have this sense that he likes playing up the fancy Brit stuff for me because he knows it makes me smile.

We're quiet for a bit, hanging out in each other's arms, then Kit says, "How does the CIA know Polzin doesn't have the Roc file?"

I shake my head. "I don't know."

"It would be helpful to know. That's where we start."

"I can work on Agent Wagner to find out. Though if I get anything out of her, it'll be in person. She's got some expressions I noticed, some tells—at least with me, anyway. I need to get back there and get face to face with her. A week's not a long time."

"Right," Kit says. "I'll come with you."

My heart lifts. It's the only way I want to do this thing.

"We have to be ready to move and act fast from here," he continues. "The file could be anywhere in the world. We'll take whatever you get and put it together with what I know or what I can get from Archie. I don't know what it could be, but I'll know it when you tell me. You might need to go and see Wagner more than once."

"What if Polzin calls for you while we're out there?"

"I can stall him a day or two," Kit says, rising and heading for the bathroom. "Any more and he'll get paranoid, and he's already the most paranoid man you'll ever meet."

* * *

Seven hours later, I'm walking down the aisle of a Boeing 777 looking for seat 13B, which turns out to be in the last row of the business elite class. The man in 13A looks up briefly from his paper and nods as I stow my luggage. He's wearing a tight cashmere sweater and his blond hair is caught back in a manbun. He looks so hot I almost swallow my tongue. I take my seat and pass on the beverages the flight attendant offers to get for me.

It's a direct flight to Dulles Airport in Washington, DC. We stay quiet until well after takeoff. I order a scotch once we get to cruising altitude. The man in 13A orders a gin and tonic. He turns to me once we've got our drinks—he's wearing a little bit of eyeliner and a silver ear cuff I can't take my eyes off of—and introduces himself as Chris. He offers a seductive smile and adds, "But you can call me Christopher."

"That's what you want me to call you?"

He waves an airy hand. "It's what my friends call me."

He proceeds to entertain me with a monologue about his supposed life as a PR executive in London and all the celebrities he knows. It's a campy routine, with lots of innuendo and sexy looks from under his lashes. He's like a whole other person. The kind of guy who does nothing to hide his sexuality. I find myself wondering how close this is to the real Kit. If he's acting a part or letting me see a glimpse of something true.

After a while, I lean in close. "I like this look." I let my lips graze the delicate outer edge of his ear, the silver cuff. Fuck, he's sexy.

He turns to meet my gaze. Our faces are so close, I can feel his breath against my lips.

"You like it, do you?" His voice, quiet as it is, is very distinct and my gut twists to hear it.

It's his Kate voice. And with the eyeliner, the jewellery, the way his hair's gathered at the back of his head—for a moment, he *is* Kate. My pulse races.

He notices my reaction and something in his expression shifts so that he looks wary. "You know," he says, "sometimes I wonder if you like me best when I'm dressed as a woman."

I startle, surprised. "What do you mean?"

He gives a little huff of laughter. "What do you think?"

I stare at him, unsure what he's getting at. "Why do you do it?" I ask at last. "Dress as Kate, I mean." We've never spoken about this. "Do you do it out of personal inclination? Or is it just for the job?"

He eyes me. "Would it bother you if it was just for the job?"

"*Bother* me?" I eye him, fascinated. Could he possibly be insecure about this? It seems crazy to me—he's *Kit*. "How could you think that? Why would it bother me?"

"Because of how much you like it." He searches my face. "I don't *mind* doing it, but it's not, you know, part of my identity. And you're bi, aren't you?"

I frown, not sure what he's getting at. "What does that have to do with it?"

"I don't know," he shrugs. "Maybe you'd prefer if I *were* Kate."

I glare at him, mad. "That's not how it works. You know that, right?"

He holds my gaze with a glare of his own, then the anger goes out of him and he looks away. "I know. Sorry."

"Hey." I slide my hand discreetly under the hand rest to touch his thigh. I burrow my pinky underneath. "The truth is, yeah, I like you in a dress. And in a suit, and like this. I like you however you want to be. Because it's about *you*—the person. Not you as a gender." I lean in, voice husky, "Though if I do sometimes get a little excited when you're in women's panties—well, Jesus, what do you expect?"

"I guess it is a little hot. With *you*. How you react." He seems to bite back a smile. "You should've seen your face, Will. That first night?"

Heat steals up my neck as I think of him lifting his gown and revealing himself to me.

"Your expression," he continues. "So fucking priceless—"

"Excuse me?" a voice intrudes. "Could I ask you gentlemen to fasten your seatbelts, please?" We both jerk our heads up to find one of the cabin crew leaning over us. He offers an apologetic smile. "We're about to hit some turbulence."

Which brings our little talk to an end just as it was getting interesting. And maybe that's a good thing.

We buckle up and ride out the bumps. No sooner is that done than the announcement comes that the cabin lights will be switched off in a few minutes.

Kit heads to the bathroom. While he's away, I think about what's ahead. It's midnight London time now. The agency usually puts me up in their favorite Hampshire Inn near their main office, but Kit got reservations at a small boutique place across town. Different names again. Real spy shit.

The cabin goes quiet.

Kit and I figured out this whole elaborate plan back in his studio. I'll go see Agent Wagner again. I'm supposed to tell her that a man named Boris came to me with a piece of intel to pass along—that Polzin's found out where the Roc file is and he's en route to get it. The idea is that I need to get to the file first and intercept Polzin. That's my supposed reason for going to her—to find out where Polzin's headed.

The CIA doesn't know where the file is, but we're hoping it inspires her to give me a bit more of what they do know.

Boris, it seems, was once a guard of Polzin's who had some grudge against him and did actually pass intel to the CIA. Kit tells me Polzin killed him for it, but the CIA won't know that for sure. Kit figures the CIA would absolutely believe that Boris went into hiding, and that he might come out to deliver this tidbit.

It's a good plan. Simple. Believable too, since that's pretty much what I would do if I got intel like that from this

Boris. Hoof it over to Wagner and pester her for information. She won't be surprised.

They want the file. Hell, they'd be thrilled if I found it for them. Not so thrilled if I turned it over to Kit, but that's what I'll be doing.

When Kit gets back, most of the passengers have got their standard-issue blankets and are huddling under them, trying to sleep. Kit settles into his seat and pulls out our blankets. He hands me one, shakes out his own. I pause for a moment then I follow his lead—it *is* pretty cold in the cabin.

Once we're both covered up, I feel the edge of my blanket stir, followed by the soft creep of Kit's hand across my lap. Tensing with excitement, I wait for his hand to graze my crotch, stroke my shaft. I'm exhausted and dubious that I'm up for what Kit wants, but I'll sure as hell give it my best shot.

It doesn't happen.

Instead Kit's hand keeps fumbling... till he finds mine. When he does, he threads our fingers together and goes still.

I sit there for long minutes, hardly breathing, waiting for a move that never comes. Eventually I realise Kit has fallen asleep beside me, his hand still in mine.

My heart clenches, a painful twist of almost unbearable happiness.

I rub the back of his hand with my thumb till I fall asleep too.

CHAPTER NINETEEN

Will

Wagner regards me from the other side of her desk. I just gave her the Boris story, and she sat through it, stony-faced.

"When did Boris approach you?"

"Yesterday morning."

"You didn't see fit to call me?"

"He didn't want that." I fight the fidget. I'm not cut out for all this pretense. I'd rather square off with an opponent any day of the week.

She narrows her eyes. "And he said Polzin was going *when?*"

"Soon." I shrug, sticking with my story. "That's all I got."

"When Boris said *soon*, did you have any sense of what it meant?"

I shake my head.

Wagner sits there studying me closely. It's unnerving. Is she sizing up what I told her? Or is she sizing *me* up? Does she suspect? Does she know Boris is dead?

It's possible. This is the CIA, after all—they're not dipshits.

My pulse kicks up a little. I'm traveling and working with Kit now. Kit, who is Polzin's bodyguard. Looking at it from their angle, I'm literally *working with the enemy*. They could jail me for that.

My gut tells me to trust Kit, but on paper? Yeah, this thing looks like every kind of wrong.

Wagner opens up her laptop and clicks around, then taps away for a while, giving me the silent treatment. Is she really interested in what she's working on, or is she trying to make me sweat? If she's trying to make me sweat, she's doing a damn fine job of it.

More smoke-and-mirrors shit. I want to demand she tell me what she's doing on there, what she's thinking. Is she playing some kind of game? Usually when I don't like something, I let a person know.

But I can practically hear Kit in my head: *This is no time to be a bull in a china shop.*

Kit would be cool and thoughtful. No—strategic, I decide. An equal player with her. He'd have finesse—that's what he thinks I'm missing.

Finesse.

I make myself relax, sitting back and crossing my legs, like everything's perfectly under control, trying to channel Kit and his finesse. He'd have a good laugh if he knew what I was doing, but I instantly feel better.

The *whoosh* of a sent email sounds out from Wagner's computer, and the hairs on the back of my neck prickle, but I keep channeling Kit.

She shuts the thing, eyes fixed on mine. I want to fill the silence with some kind of question or reassurance. I smile serenely instead.

Kit does that sometimes—puts on a serene Mona Lisa smile. A little bit icy. And sitting there wearing Kit's smile, I have this realization that underneath it, he's carrying a hell of a lot of weight—probably more than I can imagine. I feel this wild rush of affection for him. More than that, even. I want to be part of it. I want to help him carry what he's carrying.

Wagner finally wraps up the staring game. She rises from her chair and goes to the filing cabinet behind me. She flashes a plastic card that she wears on a lanyard around her neck at a reader on the side of the cabinet. With a muffled click, the drawer locks release. She opens the second one down and pulls out a slim file of papers in a buff folder, carefully closing up the cabinet again after, tugging on the drawer to make sure it's secure.

She sets the file down in front of me.

"I'm going to get some coffee. I'll be back in fifteen minutes, but—" She holds out a hand. "—I'll need your cell before I go."

That's not an idea I like, and Kit wouldn't much like it, either. I want to tell her *hell no*, but that's too emotional, too reactive. *Finesse*, I remind myself.

I reach into my pocket and pull it out without handing it over. It's not so unnatural for a man not to want to hand over his phone, is it? I give her an easy smile. "How about this—you can lock it in the cabinet."

She says nothing for a long beat, then she nods. I hand the thing over. She flashes her lanyard at the filing cabinet again and puts my phone carefully inside. Then she leaves the room, shutting the door behind her.

For a second, I stare after her, then I open the file. The sheet of paper at the top of the file has a title in all caps: THE NEST.

An executive summary of sorts follows. It seems the Nest is a small group of agents, and Polzin is the only known member. The sheet says that at least one other Nest member is CIA and one has links to British intelligence. These agents pooled classified information. Sold secrets to the highest bidder.

They were traitors. *Fuck.*

There's a list of names and incidents with dates next to them—most from the 1980s. A few I recognize as bombings I heard about when I was a kid. One assassination. I'm guessing these attacks have the Nest's fingerprints on them and that's why they're listed. A lot of people died on the back of the information they traded.

There's not much more to the file—a bunch of support documents that take a lot more space to say the same thing as the executive summary. A few photocopied documents with handwritten notes in the margins—dates, initials.

There's a folded-up sheet of paper stuffed in the back. I pull it out and spread it on the desk. It's marked "A2" at the top, and it's all scribbles—some sort of mind map in Wagner's telltale scrawl.

I pour over it, frowning, trying to understand how the information's being organized. She's used different shaped boxes and colors to show connections. I don't get what they all signify, but in some places, it looks like she's linking information leaked to outcomes and victims. I get the idea that she's trying to work out who the information was leaked to—who would've had an interest in the incidents.

There's a long list of names on the left of the page, some highlighted in different colors, some crossed out. Each one of the highlighted names has an arrow coming off it going into one of three boxes at the bottom of the page headed up "Sirin," "Griffin," and "Phoenix."

"It's not the easiest to follow," Wagner says from the doorway. She's carrying two mugs of coffee. She sets one down beside me, shuts the door, and retakes her seat.

"I think I get the gist," I say. "You're trying to find the other members of this *Nest*, right? Which one is Polzin?"

"Polzin is Sirin," she says promptly. She sips her coffee. "We've known that much for quite a while."

"And Griffin and Phoenix—those are the British and American members of the Nest?"

"Right."

"So, I'm guessing the Roc file tells you who the Nest guys are—and that's why you're so keen to flush out the owner?" Another thought occurs to me. "Or maybe the owner is another member of the Nest?"

Wagner's smile isn't altogether friendly. "The latter," she confirms. "Of course, it's possible the Roc file contains some helpful information too. The truth is, no one's entirely sure what the file contains."

I blink, taken aback. I assumed she knew the contents, that she'd assessed the risk of it getting out. But no. She just...doesn't care. I think of Kit, and his warning about the people who could get hurt if the Roc file was released. According to the papers I just read, it was a specialty of the Nest to sell information on undercover agents and informers. If the file gets out, those people will be in danger—even more danger than they're already in, given their information could be traded any time.

When you come down to it, that's what happened to my men. They died because someone sold information about us—our location—to Polzin, and he turned around and sold it again. Does the CIA care about that? MI5? Course not. All those people on the ground are just collateral damage to them.

But not to me. And not to Kit. Somehow that thought fortifies me.

I say, "Aren't you worried that by flushing this guy out, you might cause the file to get into the wrong hands?"

Wagner's look chills me. "It's already in the wrong hands."

I say, "So what can you tell me about its whereabouts?"

"Not much," she admits. "Well, there's this." She pulls the file back toward her, all business now, shuffling through till she finds a page I'd skipped past. It's a densely populated spreadsheet. There's a column of IP addresses and another of coordinates. To the left of this, Wagner has written place names like "Paris, France," "Klerksdorp, South Africa," "Spring City, Maine." It's a single sheet, but every single-spaced row is filled. There must be for-ty-plus rows on the list.

"What is it?" I ask as she turns it around to face me.

"We managed to hack Polzin's private email about a year ago. We didn't get far before he closed us out again, but we found a few messages from someone we think is Phoenix."

"That's who you think has the file? Phoenix?"

"I'm sure of it."

"And this list—"

"A bunch of relays," Wagner says. When I frown, she adds, "It's a way of sending something like an email through layers, like layers of an onion, except it's a series of network nodes. All any one node knows is the previous relay and the next relay, which makes it hard to trace if there are lots of nodes. That's how Phoenix stays anonymous when emailing Polzin. And this is as close as we ever got."

She stabs the sheet with a glossy purple fingernail in a way that makes me think she's spent a lot of time with it.

"There was a vulnerability in his browser three years ago," she continues. "It let the agency see a lot of the relays that were being used at a given time. Not the order they went in, but we got the locations. That's what this list is."

"So you narrowed it down to forty or so computers?"

"No, these are the *routers*. A ton of different computers in an area will use a single router. So...thousands of phones and computers, including public ones."

Fuck.

I swallow back my disappointment, forcing myself to focus on what we've got. "But Phoenix was for sure in one of these places three years back?"

"Well…" Wagner winces. "There are nodes we didn't get."

I stare at the list again, dismayed. "So, Phoenix *was probably* in one of these places three years back."

Wagner sighs. "Yeah. It's not much. We poked around in a lot of these places, but nothing ever came of it. But this intel of yours—that Polzin's heading for the Roc file—this is good information. I've got a junior analyst setting up alerts with private airports around all forty-three of those locations right now. The second Polzin lands in any of these localities, you and I are there."

"Here's hoping it's not…" I lean over and read from the list. "…Yagodnoye, Russia. That's Siberia, right?"

She rolls her eyes. "That's not as far-fetched as you might think. You check into the Hampton yet?"

Shit. "Not yet," I say.

Her phone dings, and she picks it up, reads the text. "Good, we're all up on those airports. Excellent." She starts texting back.

She doesn't know that Polzin's in his Black Sea resort for the time being, playing with his new toy, but watching all these airports will keep Wagner and her friends busy. Hopefully keep their attention off of me and Kit while we…what? Visit forty-three places in the next six days?

That's all we have, though. Phoenix in one of forty-three places. *Three years ago.*

I wait for Wagner to finish her message. It's an effort to bite back the despair that's filling me. All around the globe, from South Africa to Siberia, from remote villages to densely populated cities. Six days.

And then Kit will go back to Polzin.

I hate that idea. Things are dangerous for him. If I learned his identity, anyone could. In fact, thanks to my interest and the way I've been stirring everything up, it's more likely than ever that Wagner or somebody else will put the pieces together. Wagner would tip off Polzin in a minute, just to create a little chaos. A bit of an opening. What would she care if Kit paid?

And Polzin would put Kit through unimaginable pain if he knew who he was. Two fucking years undercover with Polzin—Kit has steel *cajones*, no question about that.

I think of Kit, his face lean and beautiful in the lamplight as we agreed to work together. Would he see something in this file that I don't?

"Can I take a copy of this file?" I ask when Wagner finally puts down her phone.

"What?" She's surprised.

"Just to study it. See if anything clicks. You know..." I have this feeling that the incident list, all those locations and dates, would be really helpful for Kit to see. And I want that place names list, too.

She looks at me like the request is outrageous. "This is the product of years of field work...different agents...I can't. No."

"Yeah, okay." I shuffle through. The executive summary I have memorized. I hit the incident list again, read it over, try to commit things to memory. There are little notes all over it in different handwriting. Of course she can't give me that. Then I go back to the place names... "How about just the list of places? These nodes? It's just a computer-generated list, right? Would this be a problem?"

She frowns, always a good sign with Wagner. She's thinking about it.

"Just to familiarize myself. Keep my ears open going forward. You never know what I'll pick up out there."

She watches me for a moment, then she goes to the filing cabinet and extracts my cell, setting it on the desk. Keeping her hand on it, she says, "If this list spurs anything for you, you call me. Immediately. Agreed?"

I meet her cool gaze. "Agreed."

CHAPTER TWENTY

Kit

The Nest.

I've never heard that name before. I was familiar with the group, though—Polzin and his two accomplices. I'm not surprised to hear the CIA thinks it's the American agent, Phoenix, who holds the file. What I am surprised to hear is that Agent Wagner had nothing to say about the British agent, Griffin.

I suppose I've been obsessed with Griffin for so long that I assume everyone else regards him as the critical player. But of course, the CIA would be more interested in their own traitor.

I study the torn sheet, covered with Will's scrawl. It's as much as Will memorised of a list that Wagner showed him of incidents that the CIA connected to the Nest. Dates beginning in the late 1970s.

Will watches me carefully. "No surprises, I take it."

"Not really."

"I wish I could've remembered more."

"This is a lot. It's helpful."

"I've got one other thing. It's not good news." He draws out his phone and swipes at the screen till he finds the picture he's looking for, sliding his finger and thumb apart to magnify the image before he hands it over.

I take the handset from him and stare at the close rows of information. "What's this?"

"It's a list of possible locations of Phoenix three years ago," Will says. "Those are IP addresses. They show routers—from what I understand, they're locations from a communications relay network. The CIA hacked Polzin's private email last year and got all of this off a message they think Phoenix sent a few years before that. Some kind of temporary vulnerability let them see the relays. Something like that."

"Helsinki, Albuquerque, Happy, Texas...I can't say this exactly narrows it down."

"Yeah, I know," he says. "Needle in a haystack, right?"

"I'd say so. I don't think we can—"

And then I see them—three very familiar words about two-thirds of the way down the handwritten list of names.

Madeline Island, Wisconsin.

Just like that, I'm back in that terraced house in Clapham, looking at that map of the Midwest with my father, my mother next to us, cross-legged on the couch. So serious. So sad.

Madeline Island. A secret place just for us. Even now, I can feel his hand, brushing back my fringe. *You're so good at keeping secrets, Christopher. This is one you mustn't ever tell.*

My mother's sad gaze. I didn't know why she was so sad— not then, anyway.

Later I realised, of course—she was going to have to start over, leave behind the new life she'd worked so hard to establish in England with my father and me. She'd loved that little house in Clapham. They'd bought it just before I was born—she'd stopped working by then because she wanted to be at home with me—and she'd filled it with all sorts of tat she'd picked up in local antique shops and markets. She would've hated having to leave all that behind to live in the wilderness.

Anyway, she never made it. Neither of them did. Or so I'd thought.

I stare at the screen of Will's phone. Had I been wrong?

No. They couldn't still be alive. They wouldn't have left me. They loved me. Hell, my mother *adored* me—she'd die before she left me alone in the world. And my father? No, I'm pretty sure he wouldn't have willingly left me, either.

"What is it?" Will asks. His voice is sharp.

I swallow hard, staring mutely at the words on the screen. It's a coincidence, I tell myself. But objectively I know it can't be. Madeline Island's population is three or four hundred people, tops. There's no way this can be a coincidence.

"Kit?"

I look up. Will is concerned. Serious.

"We're going to need tickets to Wisconsin," I say.

"Why?"

I force a shrug. "A hunch."

He frowns. "No. You saw something."

I shake my head. "I just need to..." What? Go and find out whether my long-dead father—the father I've been suspecting may have been a traitor—is in fact alive and well in the back of bloody beyond?

My heart nearly bangs out of my rib cage with the implications of it. I've been aware for a while now that my father isn't the man I once thought him. Hell, he was an active field agent for two decades. You can't do that job and stay squeaky clean. But the possibility that he's still alive? That's new. New and difficult to contemplate—my own father, letting me think he's dead all these years. Leaving me alone in the world at ten—supposedly orphaned and grieving, while he hides on the island we were all supposed to go to together.

While he sells secrets to Polzin.

Christ, the idea that my own father was once allies with a man like Polzin? That he may still be? I sink onto the bed. My father. Still alive. A traitor. It's the only explanation.

Madeline Island. A secret place just for us...

You're so good at keeping secrets, Christopher...

Yes, I think bitterly. I'm very, very good at keeping secrets. One of the best.

A wave of nausea comes over me when I think about what I've turned myself into for my father—for the chance to vindicate him. Or maybe just protect him.

"Kit. Talk to me."

Will. He sits on the bed next to me.

I toss his phone on the mattress between us and stand up, yanking my own phone out of my pocket. I open an app and start looking for flights. I don't want to be near him suddenly. I don't want honesty right now. I feel too raw.

He stands too, steps into my space. "What did you see?"

I keep my eyes on my phone, my fingers rapidly swiping as I select destinations, times. "A place to begin, that's all. An instinct. We have to start somewhere."

"Kit," he says in a heavy voice. "I thought we were partners."

"We are," I say. "Thanks to you, we're making great progress." I wave my hand at his phone, lying there on the bed. "Good job getting a copy of that list. Did you talk Wagner into letting you snap it, or did you do it on the sly?"

He eyes me, not concealing his disbelief. Then he goes and picks up his phone from the bed. The glass catches the light, the thing so slim and sleek in his big muscular hand. He's scrolling through the list now with his thumb. He knows I stopped near the bottom. That's where he's looking.

It's ridiculous not to tell him which one of those locations I fixed on—it's not as if I can keep our destination a secret. "It's Madeline Island, if you must know," I say, unable to banish the note of resentment from my voice.

He looks up. "Madeline Island? Wisconsin?"

I see the moment he makes the connection, when the faint puzzlement in his eyes transforms to understanding. "The charm on your ankle bracelet," he murmurs. "With the picture of the boat..."

I force a chuckle. "Yes, in Cage, when you tied me up...like a *Christmas ham*, as I recall?" I can see he doesn't buy my levity. That's the thing about Will: Once he zeroes in on something, he won't be distracted. He saw my reaction when I looked at the list, and he wants to know why it affected me.

He says, "You said you'd never visited there."

"That's right, I've never been there." I turn back to my phone. We can catch a ferry to the island from Duluth, which unfortunately is a small airport without a lot of traffic—and things are really booked up. The best I can do is a connecting flight out of Minneapolis tomorrow afternoon. I finalise the ticket purchase. "We fly out of here at six in the morning."

I tuck my phone away and fight the urge to shove my hands into my pockets—that's where the charm is at the moment. I touch it sometimes, rub the raised design of it like a good-luck trinket or a talisman, an artifact from a life I never got the chance to live—an alternate existence free of poison and shadows and corruption. A different world.

Will looks unhappy. It does something to me, his misery. Gets me in the gut. "I'm not going anywhere till you level with me."

Glaring, I turn on him. "You said you trusted me. We have a place to start now. Our agreement was to work together, not to share every goddamn detail that comes into our heads. There's no need—"

"Yes there is," he interrupts, stepping into my space. "I've never seen a guy who can shake things off like you can. Big things, even. But just then? When you saw that name? I need to know what caused that look on your face."

I step back. "It's nothing. A hunch."

He shakes his head and closes the distance I just put between us, big body moving with easy grace. "No way. I saw your face—it's not nothing."

I step back again, and this time my shoulder blades collide with the wall. I'm out of road. Will keeps moving forward till he's so close our chests are brushing.

"Tell me."

Christ, he's relentless, and I'm so fucking tired. Bad enough we've got to get a brutally early flight. Bad enough I don't sleep at the best of times. I'm running on fumes—I don't have the energy now to keep my secrets locked down as tight as I've kept them all these years. Sometimes it feels like my whole body must be trembling from the physical effort of holding them inside, and it's only going to take one little push to send the whole tower tumbling.

"Kit," he says softly. "*Please.*"

"It was a place we were supposed to be going," I blurt. "Me and my parents—before the bombing."

He's silent, watching me. At last he says, "What do you think we're going to find there?"

Already, regret is swamping me at having let even that much out. I look away, avoiding his gaze. I can't say more. I don't want to speak my worst suspicions aloud. It'll make them more real somehow.

"I have no idea," I lie. "But it's as good a starting place as any. I think we should go there and see what there is to see."

Silence. Then Will says, "Kit, we're partners on this now. I need you to level with me."

"There's nothing to tell!" I snap, shoving him away more roughly than I meant to.

Will staggers back a step, but he quickly regains his footing and closes in again, stopping me from striding away with a hand to the centre of my chest.

"No. Here you are twisted up like a pretzel off the name of this island. There's something to tell, Kit, and you're gonna tell it."

I open my mouth to tell him to fuck off, but nothing comes out. It's like all those secrets in me, knotted up so tight, are backed up in my throat and I can't get a word out.

"What do you think we'll find on that island?" His tone is soft, but his dark gaze bores right into me.

I look away, eyes stinging. He takes my chin in two fingers and turns my face back to him. I push away his hand and fix him with a hard look. The chin thing. Just no.

"Your parents had friends there? A place?"

"No—I—" I break off, heart banging so hard it's like I've been running sprints.

"You think we'll find the Roc file there, is that it?"

I shake my head, adrenaline thrumming through me. "Maybe. I don't know..." It occurs to me that this might be how a deer feels when it freezes in the middle of the road, pinned in place by a pair of headlights. "I think..."

"What? What do you think, Kit?"

"I think—" Everything in me stills. "I think I might find my father there."

Will's gaze stays steady—staring, assessing. The moment stretches on. Then he says, "I thought your dad was dead."

"Well, me too, but you know how these things go." I smile bitterly. "Those crazy fucking secret agents..." I suck in a breath, steeling myself before I go on, as breezily as I can manage. "Madeline Island was the safety valve, you see. The ticket out. When I saw it on your list—" I gesture at his phone, still lying there on the mattress. "—I thought, *Oh right. Maybe Dad made it there after all.*" I give a hollow laugh.

Will doesn't think it's funny. His face is like a mirror for how gutted I really feel. Weirdly, it helps that he's so affected. Like, at least there's one person in this world that's in this with me.

Slowly, carefully, like I'm a dog that might bite, he moves toward me again. When he's close enough, he lifts one big hand and slides it into my hair, till he's cradling the back of my head in his palm. It feels really good. Warm and solid and reassuring.

Gently, he tips my face up, making me meet his dark gaze. "Let's say your dad is holed up on that island. What do you think he's doing? You think he has the file? You think he's selling secrets to Polzin?"

He says it almost disbelievingly, though it's obvious that yes, that's exactly what I think. Hearing it said aloud is still difficult, though, making the vague possibility that's been lurking at the back of my mind for months suddenly real. Official.

"Maybe," I whisper. "Yeah."

Will's gaze softens, and his voice gentles. "God, Kit—"

His sympathy is unbearable. I pull free of his hand and move away, putting a few feet between us. "Don't look at me like that. Like this is—I don't know—like I never suspected till now. I mean, yes, the idea of him being alive, that's new, but him being—a traitor?" I swallow. "The truth is, I'd been wondering about that."

Warily, I glance at him, expecting disgust, but all I see is concern. I don't want his pity—I really don't—but I'm fucking relieved he doesn't seem to hate me. Not yet, at least.

"How long?" he asks quietly.

"A while. I accidentally discovered my parents were under suspicion by British intelligence a few years ago—my father suspected of treason and my mother of aiding and abetting him. That's why I became an agent myself. I wanted to clear their names, prove their innocence. They were my heroes, you know? I fucking worshipped them."

Will just watches me, expression sombre.

I go to the window to look out at the rooftops and the grey clouds hanging low. Dots of drizzle speck the glass.

It's nothing much as far as views go, but I can't bear to look at him as I spit out the rest. I press my hand to the cool pane, stalling, I suppose.

I can feel him waiting back there. He wants to know the kind of person he's fallen in with. And it's only fair to tell him, even if that changes the way he looks at me. Will's a good man. Maybe the Christopher Sheridan who grew up on Madeline Island chopping wood and snowshoeing would have deserved a man like Will.

"Once I was in the game, I began to see everything differently," I say. "You have to compromise your principles so much when you're an agent. Do a lot of twisted things. And yes, I've done my share." I pause. "It's not just the stuff you actively do either, it's the stuff you don't do. The sins of omission. Just...allowing evil to happen. All of it—God, it *corrodes* you. Eats you up, from the inside out."

"Kit." It's not a question, not a protest. Just my name, and his voice heavy with sympathy.

I take a deep breath. "Somewhere along the line, I had to face up to the fact that my father had to have done some pretty awful things—he was a field agent for almost twenty years, after all, and I know what I've had to do in just two. Even if he had nothing to do with the Roc file, he had to have been at least as corrupt as I am now." I pause. "Once I knew what he was capable of, I realised that becoming a traitor wasn't really such a big step. After that, it wasn't about vindicating him so much as just *knowing*. Knowing the whole, ugly truth."

Quietly, Will says, "Do you have any concrete reason to suspect him of treason? Besides the fact you're so disillusioned with him?"

I shake my head. "Nothing concrete. Just little things I remembered from when I was a kid. Until I saw Madeline Island on that list."

"That could be a coincidence," Will says, but he doesn't sound any more convinced than I was.

I give a harsh laugh.

"What're you gonna do with the file?" he asks. "If you get it?"

"I don't really have a plan," I say wearily. "I should turn it over to MI5, of course, but sometimes I think maybe I'll just bury it somewhere. An unmarked grave. Maybe no one needs to know the truth but me." I look at the rain dots on the window, improbably colourful on the field of grey. "I suppose that would make me a traitor too. Well, why not? Why not go the whole hog and sell out my country, eh?"

"Fuck, *Kit.*" I turn to find Will moving toward me. I feel winded by the hurt I see in his eyes, like my confession has caused *him* pain. "You're not *corrupt.*" His voice breaks on the word. He pulls me away from the window and into his arms. "You're fucking amazing," he whispers. "Brave."

I open my mouth to contradict him, but he stops my words with a swift, hard kiss that sends me reeling, big hands cradling my face.

"Will," I whisper when he finally breaks free. "If you knew the things I've done..."

"If I knew the things you've done?" His words are fierce, challenging. "I know that most people in this world don't have the guts to face the truth of things. They want an easy life. Want to pretend they're okay, that everything's okay. But some people—they've got to know the truth of things. They'll die getting it if that's what it takes. That's the kind of man you are."

I stare at him for a long moment, unsure I've heard him correctly. I've spent so long loathing what I've become that it's difficult to comprehend that Will can see anything to admire, much less find *amazing*. I'm baffled. Grateful. Scared.

I can't think what to say. In the end it doesn't matter, because Will covers my mouth with his again. This time the kiss ignites into something fierce.

Our tongues tangle, hot and hungry, while we claw at each other's clothes. Will muscles me over to the bed, toppling me onto my back and climbing over me.

"Kit," he mutters, trailing kisses up the side of my neck. "I want you to fuck me so bad."

I still. "You said you didn't let anyone fuck you."

"I don't," he gasps. "Only you."

His words thunder through me. He wants *me* to fuck him. Only me. It tears my heart out and puts it back bigger.

"Will—"

"Please," he begs.

I flip us over so he's on his back and I'm covering his big body with my leaner one. I stare down at him, and he looks so fucking desperate and hungry. So eager to please me. Submit to me. There's some emotion shining in his eyes that I'm not quite sure I recognise. Or maybe I'm not quite ready to recognise it. My heart beats faster just looking at him.

He swallows hard, his gaze eating me up.

I drop my head and take his mouth again.

CHAPTER TWENTY-ONE

Will

It's not like I struggle with my bisexuality. I like dick and pussy both and I don't have a problem going down on either one. But opening myself up like that to another person? How could I ever trust someone enough to let them right inside me like that? To dominate me like that? I could never relax enough to enjoy it.

Until Kit.

Well, it turns out Kit's pretty much the exception to every rule I ever made, and right now, as he tongue-fucks my mouth and shoves my T-shirt up to expose my chest, all I can think is that I want him in me, fucking me hard, making me feel every stroke of his beautiful cock.

I want everything with him.

Everything you can do with another person, I want it with him.

Kit breaks the kiss to draw my shirt off my head, then yanks his own shirt off too, exposing his smooth chest and pale brown nipples. My mouth waters just looking at him. He's not as obviously muscled as me, but he has the lean, compact strength of a gymnast. He looks beautiful, straddling me like this, half-naked, pale hair loose around his shoulders.

244 | JOANNA CHAMBERS & ANNIKA MARTIN

His gaze finds mine, and it's like a searchlight, fixing me in the darkness. His eyes are more golden than amber right now, and they never waver. He's as still and focused as any bird of prey. I feel his gaze on my skin.

I think back to the painting Wagner showed me—the man chained to the rock with the eagle on top of him, claws digging right into his belly. I feel like that guy right now. About to be torn into.

And I want it. Bad.

"Christ, you're beautiful," Kit murmurs, running his hands down my sides.

I'm raw to his touch, skin strangely sensitive, defenses stripped bare. I arch toward him, growling low in my throat. He says, almost regretfully, "But we'd need lube for this."

"There's some in my pack," I say voice hoarse. "Side pocket. Condoms too."

He pauses, perched there atop me. I almost laugh. Yeah, I brought lube. The guy who doesn't let other guys fuck him. Who am I kidding?

He moves off the bed with efficient grace and retrieves the lube and condoms, tossing them onto the mattress before swiftly removing the rest of his clothes. I watch him, transfixed. His cock is beautiful, red-tipped and throbbing, jutting up at a hard angle.

I yank off my jeans and underwear.

When I'm done, I find him standing over me. I like the way he looks at my body, surveying me, like I'm his and it pleases him.

There's something objectifying, even, in the way he looks me over. Why that should make it somehow easier to let him inside my body than if he whispered sweet nothings at me, I have no idea. He looks at my body like it's an instrument he's going to play, something he's going to draw a performance out of, and it makes me want to be perfect. Perfect for him.

The best.

"Spread your legs, Will."

His voice is low and quiet and very certain. I obey, shifting my thighs wider.

"Hands behind your head and bend your legs. Knees up for me."

His gaze is a fucking laser on me. So concentrated. I do what he says.

He looks me over. "Now," he says, "let your knees drop to each side."

This time, I hesitate. Meet his pitiless gaze. He raises a brow.

I swallow hard, then I do as he commands. I feel the stretch on my inner thighs—I'm not the most flexible guy in the world, and this position is ruthless. There's something satisfying, though, about the physical discomfort of it, and how completely it exposes me, opening up the most intimate part of my body to Kit's gaze. Like it's a trial I'm undergoing for him.

It bothers me that I can't read him, though. What is he thinking? A hard flush heats my face and neck, and I think, *The best? Really?* Maybe I'm not as good at this as I thought.

Kit's gaze is a laser beam on me.

At last he says, "I like this very much, Will. Can you guess why?"

I give a slight shake of my head, mute with embarrassment and mortified pleasure.

"Because you find it hard, but you do it anyway. That struggle—for me—is everything."

A moan escapes me, and I don't know whether it's pleasure or something else, but when he says that, it's like he just read my mind or maybe he just *gets* me. Gets me in a way no one else ever has. Like he found the one convoluted path that leads to this secret part of me.

Kit smiles, then he climbs on the bed and reaches for the lube. He flips open the cap and drizzles the stuff on his fingers.

"Let's get you ready," he says softly, and I moan again. I want to reach for him, but he told me to keep my hands behind my head, so I do, clutching my own goddamn wrist in a vise grip.

His wet fingertips drift up the cleft of my ass, just grazing me, no real purpose yet. My thighs shake with the effort of holding still. Allowing this.

Kit's fingertips drift upwards, bypassing my hole, brushing over my taint. He leaves a trail of cooling lube in his wake.

"Lift your hips," he says, upending the bottle again. I do as he says, shifting my hips up as though I'm offering him my cock. He drizzles on more lube and chases it with his fingers and this time he does touch my hole.

I gasp and clench up, just off that one glancing stroke. He grins at my reaction, his gaze eating me up, all restless appreciation.

He begins a slow, circling caress, touch patient, as though we've got all the time in the world.

"You're very tight," he murmurs. "Have you done this before?"

"It's been a while," I gasp. A long while. Like over a decade.

His fingers still. "You don't have to do it."

"I *want* to." He has no idea how much. Well, he probably does now because my voice sounds so fucking desperate.

His answering smile is wicked. "All right then."

He starts his teasing caress again, gradually increasing the pressure till I feel the tense muscle begin to loosen. By the time he finally breaches me, sliding a finger inside me, I'm incoherent with lust, gasping his name and begging for more.

"*Kit.*"

He lowers his head and laps at my balls, suckling them carefully into his mouth as he works another finger inside me and begins a maddening thrust-withdraw-thrust rhythm as he searches for, then finds, my prostate.

"Oh Christ *fuck*—"

He finger-fucks me mercilessly, grazing that sweet bundle of nerves over and over till I'm babbling out pleasure-soaked pleas—for more, for less, for mercy, for destruction—I'm barely coherent, especially once he pushes another finger inside me—or at least I think that's what he's done.

Whatever it is that he's doing to me, it's driving me insane.

After a while, he releases my balls from his mouth and moves up, licking a stripe up the length of my cock before driving his lips down my shaft. I yell out, nearly sobbing at the intensity of the sensation of his mouth, soft and hot and clasping, on my dick. The sudden space at the back of his throat as I go deep makes me groan and coincides with his fingertips nudging my prostate again.

I nearly come off the bed.

"You're gonna make me come before you can get inside me," I gasp.

He pulls off my cock with a loud slurp and looks up at me. "Well, we can't have that."

He rises up on his knees and reaches for a condom, tearing the packet open with his teeth and sliding the rubber into place with ease. Another drizzle of lube, on himself this time.

I catch his eye. "You want me to turn over?"

He shakes his head. "I want you like this. Pull your knees up for me."

I don't feel like I've got any shame left as I put my hands behind my knees and open myself up to Kit. I'm not embarrassed anymore, and even if I was, the lust in his eyes would chase the feeling away.

Lust. No, it's more than that—it's desire, and it's stunning on him. He's not even touching me, but his desire warms me, covers me, makes everything right.

He shuffles close, then, and lines his cock up with my body. Carefully, he presses his shaft against my hole and begins to guide himself inside.

In one smooth thrust, he fills me.

He's worked so much lube into me, finger-fucked me so goddamn thoroughly, that his big, hard shaft just slides home. Not that I don't feel it—*God, I feel it*—but that first thrust is smooth, and I'm ready for him, and he feels amazingly good. I'm being fucked, owned, possessed in the most earthy and intimate way possible.

For the first time in my life, I'm loving it.

He pulls out and slides in again, then again and again, building a relentless rhythm. After a few more strokes, I let go of my legs, wrapping them round Kit's waist instead, and he drops down to me, capturing my mouth in a fierce kiss. I kiss him back—wildly—pressing my heels into his ass, wanting him as deep inside me as he can go.

He fucks me faster. Deeper. He grips my sides hard. There'll be bruises where his fingertips press into my flesh. I think of the eagle in the painting. I want him tearing into me like that eagle.

"I'm gonna come," I breathe against his mouth, almost disbelieving. He's only been in me, what—a minute? But Christ, I was so ready for him.

I've barely finished saying the words before my orgasm is on me, barrelling up my shaft and exploding out of me. I throw my head back as Kit fucks me through the shocks of intense pleasure. My cum spills between us, warm and viscous.

As my climax tails off, Kit's begins. He takes my mouth again, snarling against my lips as his hips pump. His strong fingers intensify their grip.

It's wild and animalistic. And I love it.

Kit's civilized demeanor has fallen away completely, exposing the passion that lies beneath the cool, icy surface.

His rhythm gets choppier as he comes. He's giving me everything he's got. I take it—and like a champ, if I do say so myself, given how roughly he's fucking me now. I'm usually sensitive post-orgasm—painfully so—but I can't get enough of Kit right now. I relish every last thrust.

Finally, he collapses on top of me, utterly spent, his lungs heaving.

"Will," he mutters. "Christ in heaven."

My heart is pounding—I can't speak, can't articulate what I'm feeling. Instead, I turn my head and find his mouth again.

It's a lot easier than finding words.

CHAPTER TWENTY-TWO

Kit

We settle onto the couch with several dishes of a room-service dinner spread out before us. We both ordered steak. Rare fillet for me, well-done T-bone for Will with a baked potato, onion rings, and 'slaw. I tease him mercilessly about his choice. He's so American, I tell him, with his big overcooked slab of meat and sides. He tells me I'm a food snob and starts drinking his bottle of beer with his pinky up in the air. It's weirdly easy and comfortable. I feel happy in a way I can't remember feeling for years.

Once I've satisfied my immediate hunger, I become transfixed by the way Will's eating. He tears into his meal with gusto, enjoying every bite.

"What?" he asks when he catches me staring.

"Nothing." I fork up some shoestring fries—casually—as though I wasn't just thinking he's the most beautiful thing I've seen in a very long time. Even scarfing his criminally overdone beef, he's beautiful.

It's good to see him like this. Being normal. Just chilling out in our hotel room with room service.

Maybe he thinks the same about me. Like two ordinary people.

I'm not an easy man to know, but somehow Will just *sees* me. Like when he caught my reaction to seeing Madeline Island on Agent Wagner's list.

Maybe he sees me better than I see myself.

When I confessed the worst of my truth, his response was that I was *amazing*. The idea that this good man could look at the despicable life I've been leading and see anything but darkness spun me around. *That* was amazing. That and the way he gave himself to me after. Let me in. Wanted and trusted me so completely.

Only you.

He pulls the gold foil off of a pat of butter and smashes it into the centre of his baked potato. He unwraps another and smashes that on, too, and then another. His gaze lands on the two unused pats on my side plate.

"By all means," I say.

He looks over at me, lips turned up at one side in a way that tells me he didn't know I was watching. He likes when I watch him. "You sure?"

"Please."

He unwraps them, big strong fingers working deftly, and smears them onto his potato.

"Should we ring for more?" I ask dryly.

He pauses and inspects my eyes—the left, the right, as if he doesn't know I'm joking. Except he *does* know. I can see the smile he's hiding—it's a match for my own, which I've veiled behind a raised brow and a deadpan look.

"Nah," he says, smashing his concoction with his fork. "This is good."

A pang of happiness flashes through me, sweet and painful at the same time. It's the ordinariness of it. Watching him butter his baked potato. Teasing him about it. When we first met, I'd never have imagined I might one day find myself doing this boring thing with anyone, let alone Will. Domestic and boring and—unexpectedly wonderful.

Will.

What struck me about him that first night was just how single-minded he was in his determination to kill Polzin. Even if that meant his own suffering, his own death. I'd thought of him as a bull, blind with rage and the need for vengeance, still charging even when he was rent with arrows. A warrior who would stop at nothing to avenge his men, fully committed to his enemy's destruction, even if it brought about his own death. I thought there was a kind of awe-inspiring purity to it. A beauty even. Not many men will walk into a hail of bullets without blinking, not caring what the outcome might be.

Now, though, Will's callous disregard for his own safety horrifies me. I know he feels guilty about his men, but does that guilt go deeper than I realised? Suddenly I can't stop thinking about it, wondering whether there's more to his obsession than just a desire for vengeance. Maybe even a sort of death wish.

He's like the subject of my Prometheus painting, bound to his mission by chains of guilt. Reliving his agony over and over.

And, Christ, there's *nothing* pure or beautiful about that.

I close my eyes, trying to shake out the darkness. When I open them, I see that he has his potato spread open into a kind of patty, fully and evenly slathered with all that butter, and he is raining a hailstorm of salt onto it. And digs in.

Will. He's so fucking vital. It's difficult to reconcile this side of him—this earthy, sensual man who revels in the stuff of life—with the man who runs into the line of fire without caring whether he even survives.

Maybe it's just that he does nothing by half. That he's so certain of what he wants.

I do love his certainty. He seems so sure of everything—even the way he eats his dinner is full of purpose, for God's sake. But that certainty bothers me too. Will's not a man to be turned from his purpose.

Slowly, the intense enjoyment I felt just from watching Will eat—from watching Will be Will—has become tinged with dread and fear.

If he's Prometheus, what does that make me? The eagle? Perched on his belly, taking what I please as he suffers?

It's a horrible thought, and much as I'd like to shake it, I find I can't.

This evening is the first time we've been together for any length of time where we've not been sparring. Until now, I was enjoying myself, but the truth is, I've been fooling myself, thinking of this time together as a holiday when the truth is, this is just us passing time till it's time to get on with the job. Our quid pro quo. He helps me, and I help him.

A little voice in my head asks, *Help him? Really? What* exactly *are you helping him to do?*

I think of him chained to a rock, with the eagle perched on his torso, feeding off him, *living* off him. Is that me? Am I using him? Using his guilt?

No, I tell myself. He'll get something out of this too. I can help him get to Polzin—that's what he wants—what he *needs*. I can do that. But as I think about it, I feel only dread. Anxiety, even.

It's then I realise—I don't want to help Will.

I want to save him.

Jesus Christ.

I've met quite a few men like Will over the years, men driven by some deep, festering thing inside them. I've seen the look in their eyes when you try to reason with them—that look that shows they don't hear you or see you or even know that you're there. They just keep on going. Whether it's drink, bullets, whatever, they just keep stumbling forward, hearing only their demons. You can't save a man who doesn't want to be saved. Or thinks he can't be.

I stare at my half-eaten dinner, heart flooded with despair, and find I suddenly can't even look at Will.

"Your dinner okay?" he asks, a puzzled note in his voice.

I clear my throat. "Perfect," I say. "I'm just not especially hungry."

I force down the last of the steak, then push away my half-full plate, glancing at the clock on the wall. It'll be getting on for midnight in London. I should really check in with Archie. It's been five days since we touched base—I don't usually leave it that long. He'll be wondering what's going on with me.

Will stacks up our dishes outside the room and comes back in. He does a circuit of the suite, checking the doors and windows again, then he settles back down on the couch and picks up the remote. He flicks on the TV and starts surfing around channels, pausing every time he hits a basketball game or American football. He's still alert; still watchful. Even so, it's all so oddly normal.

After a while, I sigh and say, "I need to call Archie."

He slides his gaze to me. He's silent and expressionless for two beats, then he says, "You sure?"

I frown. "Of course I'm sure. I need to call him anyway, and he could give us some perspective, maybe. Another hint."

"What more hints can he have? He must've given you everything he's got by now."

"Madeline Island could mean something to him. That's new information for him."

I need every advantage I can get now, every step of the way—including after I get the file. Whatever Will thinks, I don't intend to leave his side until Polzin's taken care of. I've decided—I'm going to find a way to save Will.

Will mutes the TV and fixes me with a serious look. "You never told Reynolds about Madeline Island?"

Suddenly I feel uncomfortable, and I'm not sure why. "No."

"Why not?"

I can't read him, and it bothers me. "I don't know." Even to my own ears, I sound unsure. Quickly I add, "It never seemed important."

"Maybe we should just see what there is to see up there," Will says. He sounds...careful. "Before you call Reynolds, I mean."

I stare at him. "Archie's on our side."

Will stares right back, but finally his expression softens, and he says, "I don't know that he's on my side."

When I realise that's what he's worried about, relief floods me. "More than anything, Archie's on the side of getting that file, and that's what we're working on now," I say. "And anyway, I should've called him before now. He'll be wondering what's happened to me."

Will looks away. He's still not happy.

"Listen—" I shove his thigh with my foot, and he glances back at me. "I know he was probably off-putting to you. But that's just how he is—and he's protective of me. Anyone who turns up asking about me isn't exactly going to get a warm welcome. I know he's a bit of a cold fish, but...well, he's the closest I've got to family."

Will doesn't respond to that, but he frowns in a way that makes him look sad rather than angry. He doesn't say anything else, though, just reaches for my phone on the table and tosses it to me.

I catch the phone one-handed and select Archie's number, getting up when it starts ringing, wandering toward the dark bedroom.

Archie answers, voice low and relaxed. He's probably settled into his chair by the fire, a Glenlivet or two under his belt, the cards laid out on his desk, Radio Four on in the background.

"Kit. I was wondering when you'd call," he says. "Where are you?"

I sit down on the bed. "In the States—we've made a bit of progress actually. There've been some unexpected developments."

That's what I expect Archie to pick up on—the unexpected developments, or maybe the fact that I'm in the States—but no, it's the pronoun he seizes on.

"We? What do you mean, we?"

I pause. Then I say, "Nero and me. We've...worked something out."

"What?" Archie's voice is no longer the low, lazy timbre of an old man relaxing at the end of a long day. I hear him set a glass down sharply, the disturbance as he rises from his chair. "Are you mad?" Footsteps. He's pacing now, his words tight and sharp.

I explain that Nero located me, that we agreed to work together to find the file, that he offered to give me CIA information on it. I leave out most of the details, of course, keeping my language concise and unemotional, like he taught me when I was a boy.

Just the facts please, Christopher. We don't draw any inferences until we know all the facts.

He doesn't like that I've aligned with Nero, not even when I explain that Nero dug up a lead from deep in the CIA offices that we'd never have gotten otherwise.

"Get rid of him," Archie insists. "You've got the lead now. What more do you need him for? He's a risk, Kit. You can't know what his real purpose is."

I don't bother telling him that I'm pretty sure I know Will's purpose. Or that Will might be the first person I've trusted in years.

I don't bother saying anything at all, and the silence stretches far. Too far.

"Kit," Archie says at last, and there's a sigh in his voice. Like I'm a trial to him.

"Okay, listen," I say. "I wanted to ask you something..." I pause, unsure how to put it. I hear drawers opening and closing on the other end of the line. Is Archie tidying up? "How confident are you really that Dad is dead?"

"Christopher," Archie says slowly. "You can't be suggesting that your father could have survived?"

"Why not?"

"Because it's ridiculous!"

"Just think about it," I urge. "The DNA, the dental records, did you actually *see* any of the hard evidence that put him among the dead? I know it sounds outrageous, but here's the thing—Nero says Polzin doesn't have the Roc file."

Everything on Archie's end stops. Complete silence. Then, "What did you say?"

"Apparently the CIA is confident Polzin doesn't have it. They think somebody else does, and that person is selling Polzin the pieces. They believe it's a former agent they call Phoenix, but I think it might be Dad."

The silence continues until at last Archie says calmly, "Let's take a step back. Where does the CIA get all this from? What are the *facts*, Kit?"

"The CIA believe they've intercepted emails between Polzin and this person. Not only that, they have a number of possible locations for him—a browser glitch made the trail transparent at one point."

"So, that's why you're in the States," Archie says flatly. "You're at one of those locations." It's not a question.

I pause, undecided about my next question. Then I think, *fuck it.*

"Does Madeline Island in Wisconsin mean anything to you?

I'm almost disappointed when he immediately says, "I can't say it does. Why?"

"It meant something to Dad. It was a getaway place. A someday place—they talked about it, toward the end. We never made it, of course, but it came up on this CIA list Nero got. A remote, sparsely populated island in the Great Lakes of North America—"

"They talked about it—Len and Amanda?"

"Mm-hmm." Into the silence that follows, I add, "We have dozens of locations for Phoenix on that list, but this is the one...I feel it. We're heading up there tomorrow."

"Tomorrow?" he exclaims. "Christ, Kit, you're supposed to keep me informed of your progress."

"And I am."

"Only after the fact!" He sounds agitated—it's unlike him.

"It's not after the fact," I point out testily. "And anyway, what if it was? I've done plenty of stuff and told you after. Why are you so bothered about this?"

"Because *I'm worried about you*!" After a few moments, he lets out a long exhale and adds more quietly, "Look, just promise me you won't take this Nero with you. It's reckless beyond words."

I soften a little at this rare display of concern, but even though I've got my own reservations about taking Will with me, I can't do what Archie wants. More gently, I say, "Just trust me. We want the Roc file. I'm getting us the Roc file. And then Polzin dies. It's paying off to have Nero on our side. This is the most headway we've made in ages and—"

"Assuming any of this information he's feeding you is even genuine!" Archie interrupts. "For Christ's sake, Kit, this is a man who hunted you down—and how did he even find you?"

"An old art crowd friend of mine called on you recently," I say dryly. "Remember him?"

"Him? That was Nero?" He's obviously taken aback. "But he didn't—I didn't get any sense of him being a player."

"That's because he's not. He's not in the game, he just wants Polzin."

"Well, if that's the case, you've all the more the more reason not to take him with you—someone who doesn't know the rules? He'll be a liability." Archie sighs heavily. "Kit, just wait for me, all right? I'll leave tonight, and I'll be with you in a day. We can retrieve the file together."

"We can trust him," I say. "It's fine."

"Christopher, there are things…" he pauses. "We don't know what's in that file."

"We can trust him," I say again, more firmly.

"I'm more familiar with the situation than you are."

I frown. "If there's something I need to know, something you've left out, tell me now, because I *am* going up there in the morning."

A slight chill crawls up my spine in the silence that follows. More drawers open and close on Archie's end of the line.

"What is it that I don't know?" I demand.

"Please, Kit," Archie says. "Just wait for me."

"Why?"

"Where are you now?"

Answering a question with a question. Now there's the Archie I've always known.

"We're heading up there first thing tomorrow," I say firmly. "I'm not waiting."

"Christopher, please! Don't play games."

"We'll have the file soon," I assure him. "We've been running this thing for years, but I'm almost there, I'm on the ground, and I'm close. Trust me to make these calls. Nero is an ally. It'll all be over soon."

He should be happy. He knows it too, because he actually tries to sound happy then. Even wishes me luck before we bring the call to an end.

But something feels off. After I disconnect, I stay there on the bed, phone in hand, wondering what just happened.

* * *

I wake up the next morning to Will's long, lazy kisses, and his hand on my cock. We tangle around in the sheets, exploring each other, enjoying each other. After a lazy orgasm, we doze off again for a while, then have breakfast delivered to the room.

This feels like stolen time. Waking up with Will, great sex, morning sun streaming through the windows. Eggs Benedict and coffee and an actual paper newspaper, delivered by the hotel.

When Will finishes the sports section, he meets my gaze and smiles wickedly. "Round two?"

He wriggles down the bed and starts kissing his way down my belly—too slowly, teasingly slowly—till he finally takes me in his mouth.

I grab his hair. "Like you mean it," I rasp.

He tightens his grip on my arse, takes me all the way in, takes me in like he means it.

"More," I bite out. "Let me feel it. Let me feel your throat."

I fuck his mouth relentlessly, show him the rhythm I want, and he lets me have at it. It's a gift, his trust, the way he opens to me.

"More," I say.

He shifts so he can take hold of himself as he sucks me. It throws him off for a few moments, but he scrabbles to get back into the rhythm I set, and it's the hottest thing ever, the way he wants to please me. I watch him, mouth working me over, right arm jerking with how hard he's yanking his own cock. I want it to be my hand touching him, my mouth on him, my cock inside him, and I want it to be just exactly this, forever. I want him in every way possible.

"Bloody hell," I gasp as his mouth clasps me in a hot, wet grip. I'm trying not to come, trying to draw it out, but when he groans, it's a velvet vibration on my cock, and suddenly I'm shooting into him, fucking his beautiful mouth, worshipping him with every breath.

Afterwards, I just lie there, blissed out. He flops down beside me, nuzzling my neck. His morning whiskers prickle me, and his lips are plump from blowing me. The room smells of cum, and I wish we could just stay here forever.

At length, I drag him up and into the shower.

"Don't we need to get going soon?" he asks.

I shake my head. "We have a little more time—it's three hours until boarding. Time for one more go before we leave."

"Good," he says, but his eyes are shadowed, and I feel sure he has the same sense I do, of walls starting to close in.

I wonder whether he shares any of my other thoughts. That maybe we could have this for more than one night.

That we could disappear from the world altogether. I can't think of any two people who would be more capable of falling off the face of the earth than us.

But could I walk away from finding my answers?

Could Will from finding vengeance?

I shove those thoughts from my mind, reaching around him to grab a small bottle of shower gel from the concrete nook. "Be still," I say as I pour a bit of the green stuff inside onto my palm.

He groans. "This again?" He's smiling though.

"You liked this, as I recall." I soap him up, learning the curves of his body with my fingers, my palms, painting him in lathery streaks. He stands still and tall for me, gaze steady.

"You are so beautiful," I say, brushing off the suds under the hot stream of water, so that it's just him. All him.

I stroke the place to the right of his belly button where the flesh is rough and scarred from his old shrapnel wounds. It's the same place where Prometheus had his flesh torn in my painting—strange to think that I'd not even met Will when I painted it. Sometimes, mysteriously, art reveals its truth later.

I kneel down in front of him and kiss the ridged scars.

He shoves his hands into my hair and pushes my head back so he can see into my eyes. His concerned gaze searches mine. He doesn't like me kneeling in front of him. He closes his fist in my hair and pulls gently, coaxing me off my knees.

I stay. I kiss him again.

He drops to his own knees beside me, getting down to my level. Slides a thumb along my jawline. "What's going on?"

I gaze into his eyes. Black with flecks of brown, like small chinks in his armor. Everything suddenly feels too raw. Too real. My heart pounds out of control.

I've faced down some of the most dangerous men in the world, and it wasn't half as terrifying as being naked under this pounding water and really looking into Will's eyes. Thinking, *We could have this.*

I feel like he can see everything inside me. As though we're completely open to each other. It strikes me that I've gone through my whole life never having truly looked another person in the eyes the way I'm doing now. Maybe I never wanted to before.

I'm not sure what Will sees when he looks at me, but as I gaze at him, so true and certain, that idea comes to me yet again. *We could fall off the face of the earth together.*

For a split second, I'm certain he's thinking the same thing, but then, abruptly, he lets go of me and clambers to his feet.

"We should get going," he says, and his words have an edge of something. Sadness, anger, maybe both. "We can't miss this flight."

"Will," I say. "Listen—"

But it's too late. He's already stepping out the shower and reaching for a towel. And I know I've lost whatever chance that moment held.

CHAPTER TWENTY-THREE

Will

Kit's distant on the way to the airport, and I know it's because of that weird moment in the shower. It messed me up a little, too. I'm still not sure what to make of it. What did I even think he was going to say? It felt like we were on the verge of something game-changing. Only I was too chicken to find out what it was. All I know is that it was too...*something*.

Maybe this is what happens when you fuck, or maybe I'm just not the man he thinks I am, I don't know. We fucked, and it was the best thing in the world, but I can't give him any more than that—I just can't. *More* isn't in the cards for me. I'm surprised that a perceptive man like Kit doesn't see that. Most other people see exactly what I am.

Gradually, Kit warms back up to me. We get coffee and breakfast sandwiches on the layover, then we go and buy books for the flight. I pick out a mystery. Kit picks out something award-winning and historical and giant. It looks good, but I tease him all the same. "That's some hefty reading for a plane."

"Not a bit of fluff like yours, you mean," he says with a sideways glance at my book.

I get up in his face. "There's gonna come a time on that long boring flight, Kit, when I'm excitedly flipping the pages of this bit of fluff and you'll look over and wish to god it was yours. But you think I'm going to lend it to you?"

He smiles his evil, beautiful smile, and my cock hardens right then and there. "Oh, I think you might," he murmurs. "If I ask very nicely—by which I mean, of course, not nicely at all."

I have to suppress a groan and turn away, pretending interest in a display of nonfiction as I wait for my erection to subside.

The flight is long and boring. We're flying coach, me at the window and Kit in the middle. There's an elderly lady on the aisle seat who keeps talking to Kit throughout the journey, ignoring his polite hints that he'd rather be left alone. It's kind of funny to me that this ruthless spy assassin can't quite bring himself to be rude to a Midwestern granny. Kind of sweet too.

I can't concentrate on my fluff-book during the flight. What's more, there's a crying baby a few rows back, so I can't sleep. It's a relief when we finally land and pick up our rental car.

Kit lets me drive, which is good. Call me a control freak, but I like to be the one behind the wheel. Of course he's a control freak too, so he's got a million opinions; he thinks ten miles above the speed limit is too fast, tries to tell me the rule of thumb in America is seven above the speed limit, that we need to stay under the radar. Yeah,

I've heard it before, but ten works for me. He also finds my lane changes abrupt—that's the word he uses. "Okay, Dale Earnhardt Sr.," I joke. "I'll try to do better." He doesn't know who that is. "NASCAR?" I try. He simply narrows his eyes, as though he barely knows what NAS-CAR is.

In any event, by dusk we're at the wharf of Bayfield, Wisconsin, just in time to catch the last ferry. It's full dark when we step off the ferry and onto the brightly lit pier of Madeline Island. We're part of a whole mob of people arriving for the weekend, and we deliberately stay apart for the short walk inland from the pier, toward the festively lit main drag.

Kit strolls on the other side of a trio of college coeds who noticed him back on the boat. One of them smiles over at him, and he smiles back, though less warmly. Politely discouraging.

We're in the same outfits we went to the airport in—I'm wearing dark jeans and a black shirt; Kit's all in blue—faded blue jeans and a blue flannel shirt. He probably has an artist's word for the color. Cornflower or something. His pale golden hair is caught back in a low ponytail, his ball cap pulled down low. He looks...American.

Within minutes, we're right in the middle of the action. It's a Saturday night in high tourist season, and people are out everywhere, sitting at sidewalk tables, lined up for ice cream, walking up and down the main street.

We don't have to coordinate; we both see the shadowy gap between buildings, the perfect place to observe without being observed. Kit slips in first.

He's been on edge about this trip; I know he's worried about what we'll find here, worried about his dad's role in all of it, but I wonder—not for the first time—if there was something more to that call with Reynolds yesterday. Kit says he trusts him, but I don't know.

I hang back on the sidewalk and hold up my phone to the scene as though I'm a tourist taking photos, though I'm really just looking at everyone, and specifically trying to get a sense of whether anybody is watching or following us. I don't see anything that suggests that's the case. Then again, the place is mobbed.

Eventually I join Kit in the alley. "What do you think?"

"People do like their ice cream in this country."

"Damn straight they do."

I pull up a map. We decide to head out of the touristy area and into a commercial district several streets away. There are a few bars—pubs, Kit calls them—that we should find more locals in. Kit wants to show his father's photo around. I'm supposed to follow him, and after a bit I'll show the picture around and Kit'll shadow.

He takes off. After half a minute, I follow. He's excellent at blending, even with his striking beauty. He's twice the spy I'll ever be and ten times the actor. Kit usually walks tall, head held high, but now his shoulders are hunched, head low. He looks young and somehow insubstantial. People don't even notice him. It's competence at a level

I'm really not used to, and a shiver goes over me like it sometimes does when I witness how proficient Kit is at this spy game. It's part admiration and even a bit of envy, but it's also part sadness.

Kit is an artist, after all. A man with an eye for beauty and a sensitive soul. A guy like me's cannon fodder, but someone like Kit shouldn't be able to blend like this or fight like he can. How the fuck did he get so lethal? Who's responsible for teaching a boy who dreamed of being a painter all of those lethal skills? Is it because he grew up with spy parents? Or did Archie train him?

Kit disappears into a townie tavern. He'll walk in as a stranger, but he won't stay a stranger. He'll earn people's trust and quickly. He makes people want to help him—already I've seen it on this trip, at ticket counters, at the car rental place. He wins people over.

This street is lonelier. A few cars. A few pedestrians.

My mind goes again to us in that shower, to the way Kit needed something from me that I couldn't give. And that thought takes me back to another failure. To the informant's house outside Kabul on that fateful day, grit in my teeth, the faint scent of cooking spice in the air. Instructing my men to wait in the vehicle. Then the growing sense of wrongness in the gloomy stone house, just before the deafening blast of the explosion, the searing brightness of the resulting fire.

That old familiar path always leads back to the same place—to me letting people down when they need me most. People who deserve better.

I shake myself out of it. I need to concentrate on Kit. On securing this environment for him.

Kit emerges from the tavern after a few minutes and ambles down the street. There's a small grocer up ahead, and he goes in there. I wait in the shadows, watching him through the brightly lit window. He's buying something from the looks of it—gum or something. Smiling. Laughing. He takes out his phone.

A few people go by, some cars, too. Nothing that sets off my radar, until. A familiar looking car passes. Small red Honda. Lost? Twice I've seen it.

Kit comes out of the store and checks his phone. I text him: *All good.* He pockets it and heads to the next place. We need to cover as many places as we can before things start closing.

Two blocks deeper in—just as Kit has gone into a restaurant to show around the picture of his father—I see the red Honda again. And this time it parks. Just one man driving, a block away from me and strategically located in a shadowy stretch. The restaurant is between us. I think about texting Kit to stay in there, but it'll just draw him out.

I pull my own ball cap from my pocket and cram it onto my head. Just before I set off, the man slips out of his car. He looks up and down the street, and it's then I recognize him—he's one of the Russians. Specifically, he's the huge guy Kit left Cage with that night. I watched that grainy CCTV footage so many times, I know his big square head like the back of my hand.

He slips into the shadows around the corner of the building.

Waiting for Kit.

I start walking toward him. I've got my phone in my left hand, and I feel for my weapon with my right.

This is crazy. I should text Kit. Coordinate with him. That's what we agreed. But this huge fucking guy, he'll be ready for Kit. Probably knows his moves. He'd have surprise on his side.

He won't be ready for me, though—that's what I tell myself.

I move down the sidewalk toward where he's standing in the shadows. I'm a tourist just ambling while staring at his phone. I go slower.

Slower still.

My heart pounds as I draw near him. My Glock feels slick with sweat.

I can feel his irritation, wanting me to speed up, get out of his proximity. His right hand is slightly behind him. Holding his own piece.

It's quiet here, but there are a few people around, coming and going farther up the street. I can't just shoot him, not without drawing attention, and I don't know how many other guys there might be. My mind flashes to the guy walking across the street earlier. Is he one of the Russians?

Fuck.

One thing at a time.

In one fluid motion, I swing into the shadows, piece aimed at his temple. His right arm flies up in the same instant.

He's got a weapon of his own.

I catch his gaze and smile. "Now what?"

"You don't know wh—"

I explode into action when he's midsentence—a quick kick sends his piece spinning out of his hand.

He exclaims in Russian and grabs for my gun arm before I can recover my balance, sending my weapon skittering to the ground, too.

I don't have time to see where it went before he's on me. I land with an *oof*—wind all but knocked out of me. I'm a big guy, but he has the weight advantage. He straddles me, starting in on me with those massive fists. The punches are hard, but in this position, he's easier to dislodge.

I buck my hips hard, angling myself to send him up off me over one shoulder. He's massive, but his technique is shit, and he lands on his back.

Just as quickly, he reaches into his boot and draws out a blade.

I scramble to my feet, and so does he. We circle each other, gazes locked. The big ape lunges at me a few times, forcing me to feint and dodge. It's on my third feint that I see a chance to get in close.

I slam in and grab his blade arm. It's caught between us now, the sharp point a couple of inches from the underside of my chin.

He laughs, like that was a mistake. Maybe it is—this guy could take me in arm wrestling any day of the week. But he's not taking me in this fight—not with Kit depending on me to secure the area for him.

He starts using his strength to move the knife upwards, inch by inch. I'm using everything I've got to keep that blade away from my body.

My muscles burn. We're both shaking, but the blade is going north—right toward my chin. Because this guy's a strong motherfucker. Soon enough the point is grazing the vulnerable skin under my chin.

His smile is cold.

I give it everything I've got and I manage to force his blade hand back down from my vitals, shaking with the effort.

I jerk my head up and to the side and shove him away. The tip of the blade grazes my chin on the way out, but there's no time to think about that; he's stumbling, and I follow him, on the attack.

I grab his arm and wrench it viciously. The blade goes flying from his grip. It clatters to the ground.

He dives after it, but I dive on top of him, both of us reaching for the blade at the same time. He gets it first and turns under me, aiming to slide it between my ribs. I feel the point scratching my belly.

I pull away and deliver a quick, vicious head-butt before I roll off. He's stunned for a moment. I go for the blade, but suddenly he's back on me.

Again we struggle, grinding and writhing as intimately as lovers. There's nothing elegant about this fight—we're gutter animals, the two of us. Messy. Bloody. Utterly vicious.

He manages to cut into my palm and the inside of my fingers. Distantly I'm aware I'm bleeding, but it doesn't matter—all I know is that Kit can't be ambushed.

We grapple for the handle with blood-slickened hands. It doesn't matter who has it—we both have it. It only matters where it's going.

"I'll kill you," he hisses as he strains against me, venom in every word, but it's not true, and we both know it. He's weakening. Hurt. Maybe it was the arm, the head. Who knows.

Finally I get the knife turned so the point's resting against the soft part of his belly. With a last desperate twist of his massive frame, he tries to throw me off, but it's too late. I thrust up, using the whole of my body weight to drive the knife into his belly.

It's eerie how smoothly it slides after all the struggle to get it there. The big Russian goes silent, his eyes widening. I pull the knife out and get off him, unsteadily.

"*Zayebis,*" he whispers. He lies still, blood slugging out of him.

I start looking around for the guns—mine and his. I find them on either side of the alley. I'm tucking the Glock away when a new voice startles me.

"*What the fuck?*"

I look up. Kit's standing in the mouth of the alley, staring at me in horror.

"Kit," I say as he moves toward us. "Wait. I need to—" I gesture at the Russian.

"What?" he says, then, "Gleb."

"—finish."

He looks up. "Finish what? Christ, you're bleeding like a motherfucker." He pulls off his flannel shirt, stripping down to his T-shirt.

I look back at the Russian—Gleb. His eyes are wide open and glassy. "He's dead," I say numbly. "Shit, that was quick. I only stabbed him once, in the stomach."

Kit whips off his white cotton T-shirt and puts the flannel shirt back on. "You must've hit something vital." Angrily, he rips the shirt into strips and drapes them over his shoulder.

I squat next to Gleb's body and press two fingers to his neck. Nothing. My heart bangs in my chest. I saw a lot of action in the service and killing still doesn't come easy.

"Come here." I go to him. He grabs my hand—the one that took the wrong end of the knife. "Bloody hell."

My hand really does look bad—red and slick as a skinned rabbit—and it stings like a motherfucker. At least it's my left.

He begins to bind it. "We'll wrap this hand, then move the body behind the dumpster," he says in a clipped tone. "Then we've got to get out of here. No way was Gleb alone."

His movements are harsh and efficient; his lips are pressed together in a furious line, gaze dark.

My heart pounds. Is he angry?

I look back over at the body. "Maybe I got his kidney."

"Maybe so."

I turn back to Kit, shocked by his icy tone. He tightens a knot on the top of my hand and pulls another strip from his shoulder. "What's wrong?" I ask.

"We had an agreement," he says. "You were to text me. We were going to handle any threats together."

"I saw an opportunity."

He grabs a new strip from his shoulder and binds my fingers, around and around. Even his movements are furious. He ties this new bandage nice and tight. "Saw an *opportunity,*" he bites out. "You *saw an opportunity.*"

"Yeah. To secure the area—for *you.*"

In a flash, I'm slammed up against the wall then, face to face with Kit's blazing fury. "Oh no, you don't," he hisses. "Don't you dare."

"Don't I dare what?" I frown, mystified.

"Don't you dare say that was for me! What you just did was reckless, and it certainly wasn't for *me!*"

"I wasn't being reckless!"

He gives a harsh, incredulous laugh. "You're unbelievable! It was so fucking *beyond* reckless." He's got me by the shirt front. He twists the fabric in his fist, knuckles pressing into my solar plexus, as he moves in closer.

I've never seen him like this—so wild and enraged, so unaware of our dangerous situation. He's usually so cool and untouchable.

"But that's the point, isn't it? That's your real mission. *You die.* Whether it's going after Polzin or securing the area for a fellow fighter, it doesn't matter. All that stuff about revenge sounds great, but this is about guilt. They died. You didn't. And you want to fix that."

"Fuck you!" I shove him off me.

He staggers back a step but comes right at me again, pushing me back against the wall, his forearm hard across my throat. "This is a fucking suicide mission," he snarls. "And you've been using me to get yourself killed."

"That's not what this is."

"That's precisely what this is. Wake up!"

"Bullshit, Kit." I shove him off. "I got us this lead and I secured the area—successfully—didn't I? I did my part and I'm still fucking here. And now we're gonna get you your answers. So I don't see what the fuck you have to complain about."

"No?" His eyes are wild. "How you almost getting yourself killed for no good reason? How about me almost having to bury the body of the only man I've ever loved? How about that? Can I complain about that?"

My blood races. "What?"

But just like that, the rage has gone out of him. He steps back. "Whatever. We need move Gleb and get out of here. Get his feet."

The only man I've ever loved.

"Kit—"

"I said get his feet." He's already moving toward the body. I sway as the enormity of what he said sinks in. He loves me?

And I...

For years, all I've thought about is taking down Polzin. The only future I've allowed myself to imagine is one where I take him down, maybe—probably—dying in the process. *Fuck.* Is Kit right?

"Will! Come on!"

"Right." I snap back to the mission and go grab Gleb's feet. If there's one skill I have, it's that—snapping back to the mission, no matter what. I can't grip with my cut-up left hand, so I use my good hand and my left arm like a lobster claw.

Grunting and panting, we get Gleb behind the dumpster. He really is—was—a massive guy. We prop him up so he looks like a homeless guy sleeping.

Kit grabs a bunch of flattened boxes and discarded paper tablecloths out of the dumpster to cover him. I help arrange it.

"Wait," Kit says when we nearly have him settled. He yanks out his phone and shines the light on Gleb's hands, turning them over to examine the bloody palms.

"What?"

He turns the left, and I see something's been written on the man's arm. It says, "Isle Bakery," and there's an address.

"He always did have a memory like a goldfish," Kit says. "Let's go."

.

CHAPTER TWENTY-FOUR

Kit

I check the address written on Gleb's arm on my phone.
"Isle Bakery. Looks like it's on the other side of the
island." I hand Will the phone and fish around in Gleb's
pocket until I find keys, then I cover him back up. "You
see what he drove?"

"Red one." Will points at a small car under a streetlamp.

We go over and get in. I take the wheel and Will navi-
gates from my map app, telling me the turns, phone cra-
dled in his bandaged hand—I wince just thinking about
his injury. That was some fucking slice. It must hurt. Not
that Will gives any sign. He just directs me. Left. Right at
the next corner. Up four blocks.

Working with him like this is easy. It's as though that
stupid outburst of mine never happened.

Jesus. What was I thinking? *The only man I've ever loved?*
That was not information I needed to share. What was it
Archie used to say?

*All information has value. Would you hand someone your
gold watch for no reason? Of course not. The same goes for
information.*

Telling Will about my pathetic feelings...Will isn't on the
same page as me, and I already knew that. He's only got
one thing he's loyal to, and it's his mission. There's no
room for anything or anyone else. And if there's one

thing I know, it's that people don't change. That's true of Will, and it's certainly true of me.

He's loyal and single-minded.

I'm corrupt and compromised.

I think back on what Will said to me after I confessed my suspicions about my father being a traitor. After I confessed about the lengths I've gone to in my attempts to get that bloody file.

Some people have got to know the truth of things...They'll die getting it if that's what it takes.

That had felt like some kind of acceptance. Maybe even absolution. Like Will could see the man I used to be, the Christopher Sheridan I lost sight of a long time ago. It'd felt like, if he could see that man in me, maybe I could find my way back there too. But now I wonder whether all he was really talking about was our shared purpose— that we're these two warriors, risking everything to achieve our respective missions.

That's how Will feels. It's how I used to feel too. But everything's gotten twisted up since Will came along. If someone told me the only way my mission could succeed was if Will died, I'd give it up in a heartbeat.

And yet here I am, driving toward fuck knows what, with him right beside me. And the weight of it on me—it feels like some kind of disaster is inevitable. After all, this is a man who walks into bullets out of loyalty and single-mindedness. A man who has total disregard for whether he lives or dies.

Of course this is the guy I'd fall in love with.

I glance over at him. His eyes are lowered, his face lit by the pale, bluish glow of the phone screen. I feel this rush of emotion for him. Of love. It's strange, but when it comes down to it, it doesn't really matter if he doesn't love me. It's not a tit-for-tat thing, like I'd have expected. I could live with him not wanting me.

It's the thought of him dying I can't bear. Of him no longer being in this world. That hurts like a motherfucker.

He looks up just then, and I fix my eyes back on the road, forcing my mind to what's ahead. Gleb's presence on this island means only one thing. "You realise Polzin's here. He'll be at that bakery, and he won't be alone."

"Yeah," Will says. He shifts the phone into his uninjured hand and flexes his bandaged fingers. His mouth tightens.

"Sore?"

"It's okay," he says. "How'd you think Polzin knew to come here?"

It's a reasonable question. if Polzin knew all along how to find Phoenix he would've gone after him long ago.

"I don't know," I say. "You were digging around at the CIA—maybe it touched off a ripple there. I used a credit card for the flights, though it's an account I was certain he couldn't track. Maybe he did, though. It's possible he had that list of email relays that we did. Maybe he couldn't narrow it down, either, but then he sees us coming here..."

I look over at my phone in Will's big hands. The phone, my shoes, my wallet. Could Polzin have been tracking *me?* I've always been so careful, but lately all the moving parts in this game have been shifting faster and faster, and yeah, I've done some stuff since Will came along that probably made Polzin look at me closer.

"Doesn't much matter now, I guess," Will says.

"No," I agree.

Soon we're in a modest business district. It's different here from the tourist side of the island. A line of shop fronts comes into view, all closed up for the night, but each has a sign above the door. There's a laundromat, a butcher, a coffee shop, and finally "Isle Bakery" written in white letters on a red sign, brightly lit by a lone spotlight.

I park well back and we slip out of the car, shutting the doors quietly, and steal up the street without talking. We stick to the shadows, though not in an obvious way, both of us keeping our gait unhurried. Consummate professionals. We don't even have to discuss this stuff—Will naturally seems to do all the same things I do, without having to be prompted.

I'm in the moment now, all my concerns stowed carefully away, though a distant queasy feeling remains.

The shop windows of the bakery are blocked completely by checkered curtains—no cracks or gaps. The sign on the door says "closed," but there's the glow of a light on inside.

I draw closer, all the way up to the door, while Will hangs back. I put my ear to the glass and hear a low voice. I can't make out the words, but the tone is pure Polzin. I reach up and check the doorknob, turning it quietly. Unlocked. I let it go.

When Will catches up to me, I glance at him, point, and mouth "Polzin."

"Listen for me back there," he whispers. "I'll make some noise coming in."

For a moment, I want to grab him and stop him from going anywhere. Order him back to the ferry terminal. In the end, though, I just nod, and he disappears. We'll surprise Polzin from both sides at once. It's a decent plan.

After an interminable few minutes, Polzin stops talking, like he's heard something. Then there's a crash.

Will.

I turn the knob again, and this time I ease open the door.

The place looks empty; there's a bakery counter full of pastries, a few wooden tables and chairs, a couple upended.

I slip in like a ghost and quietly close the door behind me. It's then that I spot the body.

Dmitri, dead near the back passageway.

Who killed him? Where is Polzin? Who was he talking to?

There's a crash in the back. Metal clanging. Trays, racks maybe. I'm about to head back toward the ruckus when a faint voice stops me.

"Christopher?"

It's a voice I thought I'd never hear again. I spin around, astonished.

She's in an unlit corner, half lying, half sitting, hand clutched to her chest, white chef's jacket stained with blood.

My mother.

My heart stops. Everything stops.

"Mom?" I choke out the old childhood name and the word seems to unlock my motionless feet. I rush over to her, my knees slamming the floor as I drop to her side. "*Mom.*"

Her eyes are wet with tears. She moves her lips. Nothing comes out. There are silver streaks in her fair hair.

I imagined Dad with grey hair, never her.

I press my hand to her clammy brow, to her neck above where her pulse beats faintly and erratically. "We have to get you to a hospital. Can you move?"

"Shhh, Christopher, no." Her breathing isn't right.

"We have to—"

"No time," she whispers faintly. "No hospital here."

Of course. It's an island. "We'll get an airlift, then." Will has my phone. "Will!" I call out.

She looks panicky at my raised voice. "Shhh. Just listen, okay?" She lifts her hand, seeming to want to touch me.

Wildly, I grasp it. "I thought you were dead—"

"I know," she interrupts. Her voice is so faint. "Listen—Christopher—I need you to know—I've done terrible things. Before I met your father...I was lost. My compass..."

"It's okay." The stain is spreading on her chest, the chef's whites turning red. "This needs pressure," I say, pushing

her hands aside and pressing down. "Are you hit anywhere else?"

She shakes her head, pushes ineffectually at my arm. "Listen, baby, you need to hear this. I was a *traitor*—they
called me Phoenix..."

I freeze. Lift my gaze from my bloody hands on her chest
to her white, stricken face.

"*You?*"

Her eyes close for a moment, and the delicate lids are
purplish against her very pale skin. When she opens
them again, her eyes are inexpressibly sad.

"When I met your father, I was so messed up. They re-
cruited me when I was young and hurt and angry. I was
sure I was evil to the core—that I couldn't be redeemed—
but he changed me..."

"Mom—" My voice is hoarse.

"Your father..." She pauses, seeming to gather energy.
"...he started the change in me, but it was you who completed it. I wanted to be someone you could be proud of. I
started working to turn my life around." She takes a
shuddery breath. "I tried to undo the damage I'd done.
Tried to make it right. But it all caught up with me..."

I can feel her blood slugging out from between my fingers, and the knowledge that my pathetic attempt to save
her is hopeless floods me.

"It's okay," I choke out. "I love you."

"I had to give myself up," she gasps, talking faster now,
rushing to get it all out. "It was the right choice—the only
choice. We had it all planned. You and your father would

settle in a safe place, and I would turn myself in. I loved you both so much. More than anything—don't ever doubt that, baby. But they got to us—just before he was about to get you out."

"Got to him? You mean, Khartoum?"

"Yes." Her eyes fill with tears. She whispers, "I brought that to him. I killed him."

"No—"

"Yes," she says fiercely. "Don't flinch from it. He wouldn't have."

My heart feels like it's being crushed.

Dad.

Every wrong thought I've entertained about him these past months burns in my memory.

"He was going to bring me here?" I whisper. "To Madeline Island?"

She nods, gaze fierce on mine.

The only way you can get to it in the winter is by snowmobile. It's only for us to know about, though. A secret.

God, *Dad.*

She grasps my forearm with one hand, her grip suddenly, unexpectedly strong. "Listen, baby—you can't trust Archie. He's part of it. Part of…" Her lips move soundlessly, eyes closing as a wave of pain rolls over her.

I know what she was going to say, though.

The Nest.

A Russian, an American, and a Brit.

Polzin is Sirin.

My mother is Phoenix.

A chill comes over me. Archie is Griffin.

"Archie," I say, numbly, unable to believe it. For so long, Archie has been the only known in my life. The only constant. "How long have you known?"

"Not long," she breathes. "Since last year. I used the file— and Sergei—to draw him out."

I choke out a raw sob of a laugh. "Only you."

Right then, she smiles, and it's like when I was a boy. Her expression is loving and indulgent, eyes warm with affection. It's been so long since anyone looked at me like that. She lifts her hand to my face. "Christopher—"

Right then, there's a crash behind us. I whirl, jumping to my feet as Polzin storms into my periphery, Will in pursuit. Will's expression is grim, and for the first time since I've known Polzin, he looks terrified. My weapon's in my hand and I'm ready to fight, but I don't need to, because Will is on it. He tackles Polzin and hauls him up, slamming him into the nearby wall, his blade to the man's throat.

Polzin starts babbling pleas in Russian, but Will ignores him.

"You killed them," he grits out. "You'll hear their names before you die."

I turn back to my mother, only dimly aware of Will talking, reciting names.

Her eyes are closed, her face like chalk.

"Mom—" I tap her cheek, but her eyes stay closed. "*Mom!*"

Behind me, Will's still talking. Names interspersed with smacks and groans from Polzin.

"Will!" I cry. "She's dying. Help me!"

Will's voice stops. There's a gurgle and a thump, and the next moment, he's at my side. I know without looking that Polzin's dead, dispatched without further ceremony. Without hearing all those names Will wanted to tell him.

"I'll call 911," Will says, pulling out my phone.

Just then, my mother's eyelashes stir. She opens her eyes with obvious effort.

"The file..." she breathes. "It's in the old light-house...under the roof eaves. West side...you'll see. Protect it, Christopher. You mustn't let Archie..."

"I understand," I assure her, stroking sweat-damp strands of silvery-blonde hair back from her forehead.

Her breathing is thready. "Don't remember me like this, baby. Remember how we used to be."

"You and me and Dad on the beach in Brittany," I agree. "That stupid dolphin lilo."

I've long since let go of her hand in order to maintain the pressure on her chest. The pathetic lurch of her chest as she heaves a hoarse laugh makes my heart twist.

She curls a feeble hand around my wrist. "You and your father gave me back my life...I'm so sorry I messed everything up."

I glance helplessly at Will. He's talking to somebody on the phone, gaze dark. He's thinking what I can't think.

What I won't think.

I turn back to her. "Mom, I can't lose you again," I tell her. "Tell me what to do. There must be something—"

She clutches my arm. "Look at you," she breathes. "I've watched you. Your career. God, your beautiful paintings! I only wish you didn't isolate yourself so, but that's my fault. You shouldn't..." Her eyes are changing, growing cloudy, and I wonder whether she can even see me.

I press my forehead to her cheek. "I brought Polzin here," I whisper. "I'm so sorry."

"No," she gasps fiercely into my ear. "I brought him here. This was all my doing, baby. Mine—nobody else's. And now I get to be with your dad again."

"Mom, please, don't—"

"You saved me, you and your father. The mistakes were all mine." In a rush of breath, she adds, "You made my life worth living. I've loved you more than anything. Anyone. Never forget that."

"I love you too. Always. Just *please* hold on—help is coming." But even as I say the words, I know it's too late. Even as I hear the rattle sigh of her last breath and feel her grip slacken. As her arm shifts to a resting place.

"Mom!" I gather her up. Clutch her to me.

There's a hand on my back. Will's hand.

Will.

I can't let her go, and he doesn't make me. Just stays with me, his hand steady on my back as I clutch her to me.

We stay like that for a while. I have no idea how long. Maybe minutes, maybe an hour. Me holding my mother's body and Will, a calm steady presence at my back.

Time has ceased to exist. I feel like I'm lost in a deep, dark hole, and Will is the only thing anchoring me to the world.

It's a voice—a new voice—that drags me back.

"Well now, isn't this touching?"

Archie.

CHAPTER TWENTY-FIVE

Will

Reynolds is standing in the kitchen doorway, weapon trained on us. My hand's bleeding like a motherfucker, but that's the least of our problems now.

"All this time, she had us all fooled," he observes. "But she always was a clever girl." He smiles at Kit, genial. "The apple doesn't fall so very far from the tree either."

Gently, Kit lays his mother down, taking a moment to close her eyes before he gives Reynolds his attention.

"Hardly," he says at last. "I had no idea about you. I should have realized."

Reynolds shrugs. "You thought you had me all worked out. You thought I loved her."

"Yes," Kit admits. "I should have listened to you. You used to say, 'First look at the facts. Then look at the players and ask yourself—*why?*' I added two and two and got five—but that was what you intended, I suppose."

Reynolds's smile is wry. "A little misdirection goes a long way. Despite that, you were a good pupil, Kit. It's a shame it has to end like this, but the truth is, you're rather too much like dear Amanda. As promising as you first appeared, you have her rather bourgeois attachment to morals. It's your biggest weakness."

"Not yours, though," Kit observes.

"No," Reynolds agrees, his expression ruefully amused.

"You were responsible for the bombing, of course."

Reynolds inclines his head in acknowledgement, as though accepting a compliment.

"For God's sake, *why?*" Up to now, Kit's done a good job of keeping his emotions in check, but with that one hoarse word, they're exposed—grief and horror and disbelief.

Reynolds eyes him for a moment before he answers. "Amanda was one of us—the Nest, as the CIA dubbed us. Stupid name. It was the three of us. Me, Polzin, and her—Phoenix. Then she and Len got together, and she...changed. I tried to keep her in line, but it was a losing battle, especially after she gave up field work. Ultimately, I discovered she planned to expose us." He sighs. "There was nothing else to be done."

Kit's cry of inarticulate pain makes Reynolds wince—not with sympathy but with a sort of embarrassment, as if Kit's made some social gaffe. "You were lucky it was me that found out," he tells Kit tightly. "Khartoum was quick and clean. Len wouldn't have known what hit him. If it'd been Polzin, he'd have made Amanda suffer a hundred times more—probably through you, Kit. Can you imagine what a man like that would've done to a child? Instead, I brought you up as if you were my own son."

"You expect me to be grateful?" Kit cries. "You murdered my parents! And for what?"

Reynolds shrugs. "Power," he says, "and money. What else is there?" His gaze flicks to me and away again, just letting me know I'm in his sights. That he hasn't forgotten me. "Anyway, enough of this," he says. "You'll need to tell me where the file is. She told you, of course."

Kit says, "I won't be telling you anything, Archie." His tone says they both know the truth of this.

Reynolds has been calm till now, but the flash of temper in the old man's eyes at Kit's defiance frightens me.

I raise my arms slowly above my head and start to climb to my feet.

"Will—" Kit hisses.

"Stay down!" the old man barks at me. The knuckles of his hand gripping the gun are white.

I still, half-hunched over. "You want the file?" I say. "I know where it is. Maybe you play nice with me and I walk."

I feel Kit's gaze boring into my back. I'm fixed on Reynolds, though.

"I don't trust you," Reynolds says at last. "But fine, let's hear it. Where's the file?"

I straighten fully, keeping my movements slow, hands up. "I need assurances first." I jerk my head at Polzin's corpse. "My business is done. I got no gripe with you."

Reynolds sighs, annoyed. "Fine," he says. "You talk, you walk. You have my word."

"That's not going to be good enough," I say, stepping forward, closing the distance between us, moving diagonally so as to cover Kit.

"Stay back!" Reynolds barks.

"Will—" Behind me I hear Kit scrambling to his feet.

I keep my hands up, keep pacing forward. "She said it's in the roof space," I say, my gaze on Reynolds, calm and certain. "You wanna know where?"

"Not one more fucking step!"

I know from the look in Reynolds's eyes that this is it. I'm at the end of my rope and about to fall, and it's not one bit like I used to imagine because everything has changed. Polzin is dead, and Kit—Kit fucking *loves* me.

I have this endless moment to feel every particle of the great weight of regret that suddenly swamps me over what I'm about to do.

"*Will!*"

In this moment, I know with absolute, unwavering conviction that I want to live. I *desperately* want to live. But the truth is, I'd take any number of bullets for Kit.

I launch myself at Reynolds, and my arm hits his, sending the gun off target.

But not fast enough.

The bullet punches into my chest with the force of a locomotive. Everything slows. It seems to take forever just to hit the ground. There's commotion, and then Kit's face above me.

His eyes are wild. He's saying something, but there's just ringing in my ears.

I want to tell him not to worry, not to be sad, but I'm beyond that.

Blackness creeps in from the edges of my vision. I close my eyes and enjoy the feeling of Kit there with me. The feeling of him blows through me like sunshine.

CHAPTER TWENTY-SIX

Kit
Three months later
The Spark Gallery, London

"I'm so glad you finally finished this piece," Magda says.

The show is over, and the waiters are clearing the last of the glasses and canapé plates.

The guests are long gone.

We're standing in front of the completed Prometheus triptych. It's the best thing I've ever done and—Magda says—the centrepiece of this show. A few weeks ago, I heard she was putting together a collection of paintings by young British painters, and I contacted her on the off chance she still remembered me.

She remembered me rather well, it turned out.

"You must've finished this one, what, three years ago?" She points at the first painting, at the eagle with its claws buried in the titan's belly, beak poised to rip into him.

I nod, saying nothing. The man who painted that picture feels very far away now.

I used to think that painting was about me. I was the eagle, taking, devouring. When I got home from Madeline Island, though, I looked at it again and saw it with fresh eyes. Saw Will as Prometheus, bound to the rock by chains of guilt.

Doomed by his guilt.

I'd been thinking about the second painting, *Prometheus Unbound*—Hercules freeing Prometheus from his chains—since I'd finished the first. Over the years, I'd made hundreds of preliminary sketches for it, trying out dozens of possible compositions, but none of them had ever captured what I was looking for. But when I got back from the States, I sat down pretty much immediately and painted it straight off. A lean and troubled Hercules looking down at the slain eagle as Prometheus bursts free.

And finally, there was the third painting. *Prometheus the Fire Bringer.* Will, bending down to offer a tiny burning phoenix to a fair-headed boy, the boy staring at it in wonder and fear.

It's unmistakably Will in that third painting. I can't think of him as Prometheus at all.

"I got another offer for it tonight," Magda says, interrupting my thoughts.

"Not interested," I say. "It's not for sale."

She huffs her annoyance. "What was the earthly point in calling me if you had no intention of selling, Christopher? Do you think I put on these shows for the benefit of my health?"

"Fine, I'll withdraw it," I say mildly.

She huffs again, even more annoyed. "No. But I expect your first proper show in the next twelve months, and *everything* better be up for sale!"

I offer her a tiny smile. "Scout's honour."

"You're a reprobate," she informs me, striding away. "I don't believe a word you say."

I stand there for long minutes after she's gone, looking at Will.

I miss him.

I stayed in the States long enough to know for sure he'd be all right. Spent eight days sitting on hard plastic benches, several of them in the awkward company of Will's dad, a very pleasant, very normal bespectacled man who looked far too prosaic to have fathered a man as big and vital and extraordinary as Will.

I have no idea what Dean Ashford made of me. I was a basketcase at the time, barely eating, running on little more than coffee and smoothies. I remember very little of our conversations.

Will's CIA partner turned up after a couple of days. Agent Wagner. She made all the right concerned noises about Will, but she really wanted to talk about the Roc file and Polzin—did I know anything about the code in the file? Had I heard of this or that person? I just shrugged at her questions. After a while she got tired trying to get me to talk, I suppose. She pressed her card into my hand and left.

To her credit, she sent flowers the next day, a huge bouquet of sunburst yellow, creamy white, moody indigo. The blooms faded as the days wore on, while the machines around Will beeped and hummed. And through it all, he remained perfectly still and unaware. Eventually, the nurses cleared them away without him ever seeing them.

Will went through three rounds of surgery over those eight days. There were a couple of very bad nights before he finally stabilised. As soon as he did, I booked my flight home. Told myself it was time to let go. That I needed to come to terms with everything that had happened. With being in love with a man who would do anything for me... except live.

The truth is, though, I haven't come to terms with that.

I don't see how I ever can.

I decide to walk home, calling my goodbyes to Magda as I leave. It's a cold, clear night with a near full moon. Terrible for surveillance work, but perfect for an evening stroll. It's difficult to switch off the agent part of my brain, but I'm trying. After all, I'm just Christopher Sheridan, painter, now.

The house—the one I've lived in since I was a boy—is dark and quiet, a tall thin townhouse with high ceilings and plasterwork mouldings. It's on the market. I've put in an offer for another place in Clapham. Archie's stuff has been gone since before I got back from the States.

I didn't need to look through any of it—MI5 carted it all away.

The house feels different, somehow, from when I set out for the show this afternoon. I walk into the hallway, closing the door behind me. Something's off...so subtle, I can't quite say.

I check each room, systematic.

Then I enter Archie's study.

His back is to me, but I'd know that brown hair anywhere. Those broad shoulders. My heart turns over at
the sight of him.

He's looking at the painting of my mother over the fireplace.

I'm humiliated by the salty lump that forms in my throat.
I couldn't speak—even if I wanted to, even if I could find
words worth saying.

He turns—slowly, painfully. His jaw is set, black-coffee
eyes hard on mine. "I love you too, Kit."

My laugh is half sob. "*What?*"

He steps toward me, his expression wary. "You said I was
the only man you ever loved."

He moves stiffly. It hurts my heart to see him still so de-
bilitated, but my voice is ugly when I answer him. "It's a
bit late for that, don't you think?"

"Is it?" He keeps limping toward me.

"For Christ's sake, sit down," I snap. "You look like you're
about to fall over."

"I been sitting plenty," he says, though he does finally
stop, now that he's right in front of me. He doesn't try to
touch me, though.

At last he says, voice heavy with regret, "I should've said
something that night. I know that."

I shake my head, a tight, angry gesture. "Why would you?
All that was in your mind that night was your mission."

"Polzin was already dead when I took that bullet, Kit,"
Will replies grimly. "I didn't take that bullet for my mission, I took it for *you.*"

"No, you didn't!" I sneer, and now I'm rehearsing the words I've been through in my own mind a thousand times since I came back home and imagined what I'd say to him if I ever saw him again. "You *wanted* to die."

Will hauls me up against him, eyes burning into me. "That was the last thing I wanted." He gives a harsh laugh. "Well, the second-last."

My eyes sting, and my throat feels thick. "Don't lie to me. You think I don't know you wanted to die?"

His gaze is sorrowful. "I'm not lying. I did used to want that—or at least I didn't care whether I lived or died. But I changed, Kit. *You changed me.*"

We stare at each other for a long moment, then he groans and dips his head, kissing me hard.

He tastes of cinnamon.

I don't—*can't*—fight him. I kiss him back for long moments, desperate for him, only to tear my mouth away and demand, "How can I trust you? You nearly died— *deliberately!*"

He frames my face between his hands. "I get why you're angry. But hear me out. Maybe I don't deserve a second chance with you. Maybe I don't deserve a second chance at life at all, but I got one. And I'm telling you the truth when I say there's only one reason I stepped in front of that bullet, and it was nothing to do with my men. Nothing to do with my mission. In that moment, I'd never wanted to live more in my life."

I stare at him, desperate to believe him. Petrified to believe him.

"When they told me in the hospital you'd gone back to London, I thought maybe you—" He breaks off, seeming to steel himself to go on. "—Maybe you'd changed your mind. Maybe you never meant it after all, when you said you loved me."

"Jesus, Will, *no*—" The words tumble out of me unbidden, and Will meets my gaze with a wary look, as though he's scared to set too much store by those words.

"Eventually," he says, "I got to thinking about what you said to me in that alleyway. Accusing me of being on a suicide mission—"

"You were."

"Yeah," he admits. "But not at the end, Kit. I changed. People can change. Sometimes they change for the worse, but sometimes somebody comes into their life and inspires them to be different, better. For so long, vengeance was the only thing in my life—I couldn't see beyond it. But I do, now, because of you. And yeah, maybe I don't deserve you yet, but I'll spend my life trying to be worthy."

I search his eyes, disbelieving. *Will*, worried about being worthy of *me*? He's the one who's loyal, who's true. The idea of him feeling undeserving of a man like me is so very wrong.

And then I think about my mother. The power of her words. The hopeful way those words worked inside me in the days and weeks after Madeline Island. It was as if she reappeared in my life just to blaze a path for me, out of my shame for what I'd become. Showing me neither of us were corrupt in the end.

Like a fucking phoenix, rising up when I'd needed her most.

Maybe Will and I can deserve one another after all. Maybe we can have another chance.

"How can I trust that I won't lose you?" I whisper. "I don't think I can do it."

He raises a hand, brushes the side of my face with his fingertips. "You *will* lose me," he says. "But until then..." He strokes my cheekbone with his thumb. "Maybe I'll lose you first, I don't know." He kisses me again. "Maybe when we're eighty. In between me yelling at you to clean up your paints. Me finishing my crossword puzzle in my rocking chair..." He sighs. "I don't know, Kit. I can't know. Neither can you."

I stare at him, searching his face for any chink in his apparent sincerity.

"No more solo heroics," he promises. "We're in it together. Partners." Again he kisses me. It feels so good, it makes my brain foggy.

"You never know when to stop pushing, do you?" I whisper.

"I don't," he says. "I really don't."

I close my eyes in defeat.

"What do you say?" Will urges.

When I open my eyes again, he looks hopeful, a sparkle in his eyes that tells me he knows he has me. I suppose he always has.

A little part of me doesn't want to give way yet, though.

I slide my fingers into his dark hair. It's grown out a bit. It looks good. "Is this really how you're going to beg me?" I ask.

His brows knit.

I give him a look. A Kate look. Superciliously, I say, "This might play better on your knees."

It's a joke, but he goes to do it. Grunting as he lowers himself down, broken body straining with the effort of doing my bidding.

"Will, no! *Stop!*" I grab for him, taking his descending weight into my arms and hauling him back up.

When he looks at me, all raw and hopeful, my heart expands so wide it feels like it might break apart. "You're impossible," I say, overwhelmed by utter gratitude that he's here.

Alive.

With me.

"And I fucking love you," I add. My voice is all broken up, but I don't care.

He stares at me for a second, then, with an inarticulate noise, drags me in tight. Kisses my temple fiercely. "Okay," he says finally. "But please don't ever leave me like that again. I don't think I can take that twice."

"I won't," I whisper.

We stand there for a minute, just holding each other.

At last, Will says, "Can we go to bed now? I haven't slept for eighteen hours."

I laugh weakly. "Yeah."

I take his hand and lead him from the room, past the armchair where Archie sat as I did my homework as a boy, past the table where he laid his hands of Patience.

Above the fireplace, my mother spins, bright as a phoenix in her yellow sundress.

~ The End~

We hope you enjoyed your time with Will and Kit as much as we did!
Thank you for reading!!

Acknowledgements

We are so very grateful to our funny and talented author friend LB Gregg, who read this book in different states of roughness over time and always came back with encouragement as well as crucial ideas and insights that helped us see new things. We also owe a debt of gratitude to our author pal Susan Lee, who read over the project with care and passion, and came through with important insights and feedback that made things stronger. We're thankful to Sadye Scott-Hainchek, who did a beautiful proofreading job. And last but definitely not least, thanks to Letitia of RBA Designs, who brought creativity, talent, and enormous patience to the job of creating a pair of covers that two hugely opinionated authors could fall in love with.

About Joanna Chambers

Joanna Chambers always wanted to write. In between studying, finding a proper grown up job, getting married and having kids, she spent many hours staring at blank sheets of paper and chewing pens. That changed when she rediscovered her love of romance and found her muse. Joanna's muse likes red wine, coffee and won't let Joanna clean the house or watch television.

Twitter: @ChambersJoanna
Website: https://joannachambers.com
Email: Authorjoannachambers@gmail.com

About Annika Martin

Annika Martin is a NYT bestselling author who enjoys writing dirty stories about dangerous criminals and hot spies. She loves helping animals and kicking snow clumps off the bottom of cars around the streets of Minneapolis, and in her spare time she writes as the RITA award-winning author Carolyn Crane.

email: annika@annikamartinbooks.com

website: www.annikamartinbooks.com

Get fun stuff, freebies, exclusive content, the latest news and more! The Annika Martin newsletter: http://www.annikamartinbooks.com/newletter/

Also by Joanna Chambers

The Enlightenment Series
Provoked
Beguiled
Seasons Pass
Unnatural

Porthkennack Series (Riptide)
A Gathering Storm

Other novel length titles
The Dream Alchemist
Unforgivable
The Lady's Secret

Novellas & short stories
Humbug (A Christmas Tale)
Rest and Be Thankful (appeared in the Comfort and Joy anthology)
Introducing Mr. Winterbourne (appeared in the Another Place in Time anthology)
Mr. Perfect's Christmas (appeared in the Wish Come True anthology)

Also by Annika Martin

Edgy mafia romance
Dark Mafia Prince
Wicked Mafia Prince
Savage Mafia Prince

Hot, dangerous spies
(Annika Martin writing as Carolyn Crane)
Off the Edge
Into the Shadows
Behind the Mask

Taken Hostage by Kinky Bank Robbers
The Hostage Bargain (FREE series starter)
The Wrong Turn
The Deeper Game
The Most Wanted
The Hard Way

Criminals & Captives
Prisoner

CPSIA information can be obtained
at www.ICGtesting.com
Printed in the USA
LVOW13s1322290517
536143LV00009B/653/P